THE OTHER SIDE OF THE LOOKING-GLASS

DAKOTA JACKSON

OPRELLE PUBLICATIONS

Published by Oprelle Publications (USA) LLC

236 Twin Hills Road
Grindstone, PA 15442

FIRST EDITION

Printed in the United States of America

ISBN: 979-8-9857483-8-3

Content Warnings:

Grooming, manipulation, brief non-explicit mention of statutory rape, brief violence and self harm.

The Other Side of the Looking-Glass contains heavy topics. Please read with care.

For Jae, who read it first.
Thank you for everything.

SCENE I.

"Who in the world am I? Ah, that's the great puzzle."

— Lewis Carroll, *Alice in Wonderland*

1

Wren Blackwell liked it when I cried.

"It makes your eyes all bloodshot and really brings out the blue," he elaborated. "It's pretty."

I didn't know much about Wren Blackwell aside from the fact that he was Emmeline Blackwell's older brother and Emmeline Blackwell was in drama club with me. Wren had come into the auditorium early to pick her up and caught the tail end of our exercises, where I just so happened to be making myself cry. Matt loved to give me the dumbest exercises like that. He said I was born with a brilliant talent for acting and it was high time I showed it off.

First day in the drama club, first day with him in charge of it, and I'd already shown everyone what I looked like when I cried. Sometimes Matt made me want to pack a suitcase and hightail into the woods. That's parental guardians for you.

"Please don't listen to anything he says," Emmeline said from behind me, grinning. "He's a freak."

Matt and I had only moved to this little suburban town a few days earlier for his job as a drama teacher there at John Avery Yates High School, or Jay High for short. I'd yet to make any real friends within that little time, but Emmeline was coming close. We had multiple classes together, now drama club together, too, and honestly she was so friendly that it was a little hard not to drift her way and be her friend. She was tall, tan, and effortlessly pretty. Her long blonde hair was tied up into space buns with little strands falling forward over her eyes in that perfectly imperfect way. Her lips were coated in bright red lipstick and her eyelashes in dark black mascara. It really brought out the light hazel of her eyes. I suppose in the same way my crying brought out the blue of my own.

"It was a compliment," Wren said, shoving Emmeline the second she came down the stairs from the stage. It was a playful shove, the kind between siblings that I'd never gotten to experience for myself. "Not everyone is a pretty crier."

As an actress in the drama club, that *was* a compliment, I supposed. After all, I would hate to look terrible and ugly even in scenes where I was supposed to be upset.

Looking at the Blackwell siblings, I would guess they were pretty criers, too. It was hard to find anything about them that *wasn't* pretty. Wren was a few inches taller than Emmeline, which made him about a foot taller than me, and he had the same sculpted facial structure and sharp eyes. His hair wasn't blonde like hers, but rather a light brown, fluffy and untamed over his head. His eyes were dark brown and hooded in that mysterious but intriguing way, almost like a character pulled straight from a dark romance novel. A smirk played over his lips naturally, as if it were there all the time. What an unfair gene pool their family was given.

"Right," Emmeline said, "but Naomi's new and you're weird and it's gonna scare her off." Her voice was lower, but not low enough for me to not hear it.

"It's okay," I cut in, joining them where they stood in front of the first row of seats, trying to figure out which of them to look at. "Thank you."

"See?" Wren gestured around with his hands, arm muscles flexing beneath his shirt. "Not everyone is as sensitive as you are, Em. It's a pleasure to meet you, Naomi."

He put his hand out for me to shake and I took it carefully. His grip was feather-light, as if he was afraid to truly touch me, but his body was closer than strictly necessary and his eyes remained fiercely locked onto mine the entire time. Based on the feeling of his cold fingertips grazing my wrist as he finally pulled away, I was afraid for him to truly touch me, too. My heart was beating erratically. I wasn't used to attention like his, that dark gaze locked on mine, unwavering even with all the movement of people around us.

"You too," I replied quietly.

From the corners of my eyes, I could see Matt up on the stage, watching us carefully. He was inching away from the flock of students attempting to talk to him in order to come our way. They all wanted to make a good first impression on the new, young drama teacher. He's my guardian, so saying so makes me want to throw up, but I could understand why all those teenagers were curious about him; he was fairly attractive. He towered over everyone, his hair was dark and so long that he was always pulling it into messy buns, his eyes were a blue so unnaturally bright that he got asked weekly if they were contacts, and his ears held sparkly gold gauges that matched the septum ring in his nose. It didn't help that he was totally full of himself; wearing low cut collared shirts rolled up to expose his arms, smiling at anyone who'd look his way, sauntering around as if he was the jock in a teen movie. He acted as young as he looked. He attracted flocks of girls like moths to a flame.

Matt broke free of the crowd and quickly skipped down the stairs to come up beside me and placie a ring-clad hand over my shoulder. He stared down at Wren with the few inches he had on him.

"May I ask who you are and what you're doing in my auditorium?" he asked, smiling pleasantly. Technically it wasn't his auditorium, of course, but also technically, Wren shouldn't have been in there without a visitor's tag from the front office. Matt always was a little more adherent to the rules when things were new. Seeing as it was his first official day teaching, his reaction made at least a little sense.

"Wren Blackwell, sir," he answered, putting his hand out to Matt with a lot less fluidity than he had given it to me.

Matt took it stiffly. I could see his veins pulsing with the tight grip.

"Emmeline's brother, I presume?" Matt asked, smiling honestly at Emmeline. She was biting her bottom lip, looking two seconds away from bursting out laughing.

"Yes, sir," he confirmed. "I'm here to pick her up."

Matt only hummed in response. He wiped the hand Wren had shaken off on his pant leg rather dramatically. *Strange*, I thought. He was acting with no tact. He'd never been very protective over me, but I'd also never really been in a situation that required him to be. I should have known that having him as a teacher at the high school I attended would bring it out. I'd have to deal with this for every guy who even breathed in my direction for the rest of the year. Those poor souls.

"Matt," I hissed, shaking him off of me. He seemed to think nothing of it, burying his hands deep into his pockets and laughing airily. Most things weren't serious with him. "Can we go?"

It was nearing five o'clock by then. For the first drama club meeting, it had gone on much later than I'd expected.

Matt nodded and went to collect his things, eyes flickering back to me more than once.

"Go start the car or something," Emmeline said to Wren, pushing him away down the aisle. He chuckled, waved goodbye to me, and then he was gone.

"What sort of gross masculinity battle was that?" she asked me the second he was out of earshot, laughing through every word.

It surprised a laugh out of me, too. I was glad not to be the only one who found the interaction abnormal.

"It's sort of gross to think of Mr. Molina and my brother fighting over you, though," she said seriously, securing her neon pink backpack over her shoulders. "They're young, but not that young... And they're older, but not old enough to be DILF material either."

"Ew." I winced at the thought. "That is so not what was happening. Matt's my guardian. He's like my dad."

She tilted her head, reminiscent of a labrador puppy.

Quickly I tried to explain, as briefly and with as little detail as possible, by absolutely word vomiting with: "Well he's not actually my dad. My real dad lives a few towns over with his wife. Matt just has custody over me. Kinda always has. He raised me because, uhm, you know what? It's actually a long story."

Emmeline cut her eyes to me, apparently shocked by that. Most people *assumed* Matt was my father. Or at least my older brother. Apparently, though there were no blood ties between us, we looked a lot alike. We had the same pale complexion, the same big thick lips, the same curved button nose. I actually preferred it when people assumed he was my family, because then I didn't have to explain how he sort of was, sort of wasn't, had sort of never labeled it.

Her mouth formed an *O* but no sound actually came out. I watched as her gaze went back and forth from me to Matt, trying to draw connections, do the math, and figure us out. It was too soon here at Jay High for anyone to delve into my home life. I shouldn't have said anything at all. It felt a bit like being stabbed in the heart when she took a small step backwards, putting a few more inches between us.

"I gotta go," I mumbled, angry with myself for probably having ruined the friendship before it could even begin.

"Wait!" Her hand wrapped around my forearm, holding me in place. I jerked away from it on instinct.

"Sorry," she said. "Can we exchange numbers before you go?"

I was too shocked to do anything other than hand my phone over. I felt silly seeing her with it. My sparkly, sticker-covered phone case between her two soft hands, sharp, painted nails clicking over all the cracks in my screen.

"See you tomorrow in Chem, okay?" she said, handing my phone back and walking away without another glance.

Her contact name in my phone read *Emmy!!* with a bunch of hearts and smiley emojis. I couldn't help but grin down at it. She was not much like me at all, but I didn't mind. I was looking forward to getting to know her better, hopeful that someday we'd act alongside each other on this very stage.

It was unsettling to realize that I was also hopeful Wren would be in the crowd, watching me with that same attentiveness he had earlier; the kind I had never been given before, and the kind I was always desperate to have.

2

Most things had yet to be unpacked in the house. I'd gotten half of my clothing out of my suitcases and onto hangers before calling it quits. Matt had gotten maybe two shirts out before groaning like a toddler and putting it off for later. That was a week ago, back on the first day we moved in. So by the time we got home after the first drama club meeting Friday night, there were many things left to do.

We didn't do a single one of them.

Instead I set up the old Wii and games while Matt ordered pizza. He wanted to have a game night; just the two of us. He must've been feeling especially fond of me. From his mama-bearing around Wren to that then, he was clearly in a mood of some sort. Not that I was bothered by it, really. I kicked ass at Wii Bowling and Matt couldn't get a spare if his life depended on it, not that he'd ever admit such a thing. Besides, our typical game nights were rather tainted affairs, based on the company and the tangled web of emotions attached to them.

The thing was, Game Nights were normally something we did once a month with Jin and Julie Nakano, my birth father and his wife of a few years. Jin and Matt had been friends since elementary school, as they were next-door neighbors growing up. Jin and my mother, Elizabeth, had me as sophomores in high school. My mother died during complications giving birth, and after less than a year of parenting me alone, Jin didn't want to do it anymore. Matt didn't want me to go into the system, so he volunteered to take me in.

Jin stayed a part of our lives as a distant friend for a long time, like he was some long estranged relative and not the only blood family I knew. He went away to college, studied abroad, made new friends, and eventually found Julie. He came back as a constant in my life when I was around twelve. He came back to settle down with a wife and a steady job and a house, but not for me.

Matt never once lied to me about our story, never once kept any of that secret, and so I'd never known what to call any of them besides their first names. Matt raised me, but he made sure I knew he was not my father. He said it in plain words. But there was no way in hell I'd call Jin my father, either, especially after he came barreling back into my life without an apology or his side of the story to tell, but with a new wife and a house he didn't want to take me into.

He and I had never once spoken about the elephant in the room, which was that he was my birth father, my blood family, and he gave me to Matt and disappeared for half my life. We never acknowledged it. I didn't know how to talk to him and he didn't know how to talk to me. Our communication had always passed through Matt, if it ever happened at all.

So Game Nights may have been an effort of some kind that Jin made to be around me, to be a constant in my life after so long gone, but they were awkward. It wasn't the most fun for a fifteen year old girl to hang out with a bunch of thirty year olds who she didn't know how to explain her relationship with. I liked it much better when it was only Matt and me. I never had to wonder where we stood, if he cared about me, or why things were how they were. Matt wasn't sentimental, he never had been, but I knew well enough why he took me in and I knew he wasn't going to let me go. That was sufficient.

Matt stumbled over a few loose boxes and bags on his way from the kitchen to the living room. He had changed out of his work clothes and into a big baggy t-shirt and sweatpants. He was holding a bag of chips between his teeth, his phone under one armpit, plates under the other, and a can of soda in each hand. He looked ridiculous.

"Matt." I laughed and took one can of soda from him for my-self while watching him struggle with the rest. "You're such an idiot."

"Hey now. Respect your elders," he said, dropping everything unceremoniously onto the coffee table.

"If they give you a reason to respect them," I reminded him, grinning.

That was something Matt always said: *Only respect your elders if they give you a reason to respect them. They ain't special cause they're old.* The first time he said that to me, it was in response to a conversation we had about his blood family. I'd never met any of them and I always wanted to know why. He told me his parents didn't approve of his decision to watch over me, and they demanded he show them some respect by changing his mind. He didn't, of course, and he only grew to find respecting people out of obligation to be a stupid concept. He lost his real family for me and never once complained about it. As he always did, he made it into something comical, sucking the seriousness straight out.

Once the pizza delivery guy came and went, Matt and I set the pizza open on the table with our chips and sodas around the box. I fired up Wii Sports and we played in between bites. He had to wear the wristband so he wouldn't send the controller flying into the flat screen with his greasy hands and overly aggressive swings. It had happened before. More than once. More times than it should've.

Mere minutes in, it was already a million times better than any of our previous nights playing games and ordering take out. It was good to be in a different town than Jin and Julie. They weren't far, not much farther than a twenty minute drive, but it felt like the town's border was a wall between us. I could remind myself that they were somewhere else and put it out of my mind entirely.

I didn't hate them, not really, but it was easier to continue feeling that way when we were apart. Moving away helped.

"Whaddya think of Jay High?" Matt asked, flicking his wrist to throw the bowling bowl on the screen in a bout of laziness.

I recapped my first day in an amount of detail that was wholly unnecessary. From walking through the halls to my classes, to collecting and reading different syllabi, to the choice I made between lunch options in the cafeteria (a burger over the soggy-looking pizza), I tried to remember every tiny little detail to share. I just wanted him to know I was okay. That's clearly what he was looking for in my words. He hung onto every one of them as I spoke. It was clear he was jittery about the move. I never had many close friends in our old town, but I liked it there nonetheless. Even with Jin and Julie so close. Probably because it was all I really knew. I grew up there. Moving, while nice in many ways, was also a lot. Moving was a big stressor, and evidently my life had enough of those as it was.

When I got to the end of my day, to the point where we'd been in the drama club together, I trailed off ineloquently. Upon mentioning the Blackwells, he stiffened the slightest bit. It was just enough for me to notice in the way his fingers straightened around his slice of pizza. I thought it was too soon for him to have a reaction like that to someone he'd only met that day, but I never knew with him. He was the type to make snap judgements and stick to them.

I cleared my throat and his body relaxed at once, as if I'd caught him doing something wrong.

"So... Uh, what was that with the Blackwells today, anyway?" I asked Matt as I tore the crust off of my slice and handed it over to him. I hated the crust so he always ate it for me.

"I should be asking you the same," he said stiffly, cocking an eyebrow and taking a small bite of the crust.

I narrowed my eyes. He could never speak straight forward with me. Everything always had to be riddles and mind games and needless back and forth.

"Matt, seriously," I said, flicking my wrist to throw the bowling ball without looking the same way he had before.

"Oh come on," he complained, watching the screen as my *Mii* got a strike. "It's gotta be rigged."

"*Matt.* Why were you acting like that?"

"I wasn't aware you were into older men," he told me, not peeling his eyes from the screen. His voice was tight. Angry, perhaps.

"Wren's not that old," I said. His lips quirked, but I couldn't tell if it was in the beginning of a laugh or a grimace. Neither was good. "I mean, I'm not! It wasn't like that. He was just introducing himself."

In response, he hummed the same exact way he had towards Wren earlier. It was the type of sound that was condescending without a word needing to be said.

"What?" I asked, annoyed. "What is it? Say what you wanna say."

"You know I don't like rules and bossing you around like some overbearing parent," he began, separating himself from the term *parent* in that strange way he always did. He wiped some sauce from his cheek before finishing, "but I'd prefer if you stayed away from his type."

"His type? We don't even know him."

"I know he isn't a student at Jay High."

"So what?"

"As in, he graduated already. As in, that's a *man*, not a *boy*, and he shouldn't even be looking in your direction." Matt's voice raised, which I hardly ever heard it do. He looked ghostly pale.

I said nothing. He took his turn in the game, sending the ball right into the gutter before it even reached the pins. Both tries. His hands were trembling. When my turn came, I stayed frozen. I stayed frozen until Matt turned his attention to me. His face was back to its normal neutral expression, but his eyes remained unfocused.

"Okay," I told him at last, quiet and gentle. "I think Emmeline and I are friends now, though."

This brought a smile to his face, a soft one.

"I'm glad you're making friends." He nudged me with his shoulder. "Take your turn so we can switch to boxing. I'll destroy you then."

"You're on."

Game nights were never perfect, but that was still the best one I'd ever had.

<h1 style="text-align:center">3</h1>

The following week in drama club, Matt realized he'd introduced himself but never let the rest of us introduce ourselves. So we got into a big circle on the stage and went around sharing our names, ages, and 'fun facts.' There were only about twenty-three of us in total across all four grades. Well, across three grades, really. Not a single senior had signed up. I still couldn't be bothered to remember many of their names. I was hardly paying attention at all.

That was until the boy beside Emmeline introduced himself in a tiny, self-conscious voice as "George Washington."

There was a beat of silence before the first chuckle. It came from the girl beside me with the pin straight platinum blonde hair. Once she laughed, it set off everyone else, too.

"That's enough," Matt said, stern but calm. "You're not messing with us, are you, George?"

He shook his head vigorously. His hair was a dusty brown color down to his shoulders. It flopped over his face when he moved.

"Well then," Matt said, clearly wishing he could laugh himself, "your parents must be very patriotic."

This set everyone off in laughter again. Except this time, George smiled, too. Matt looked very proud of himself for it.

"Though I'm sure you must have a much more fun fact than that, Mr. President, sir," Matt went on, friendly and honest.

George smiled again, but buried it into his knees that were pulled to his chest. Once the auditorium fell silent again, he lifted his head and told everyone his fun fact: "My face is carved into Mount Rushmore, but they totally botched my nose."

Emmeline snorted. I met Matt's eyes from across the circle and he was laughing. He mouthed, *I like him*, and I nodded, deciding I did, too. Finding friends at Jay High was easier than I expected it to be. The drama club, which I joined against my will after far too much nagging on Matt's end, was shaping up to be a lot more interesting than I expected it to be.

After our introductions were over—an ordeal that took no longer than fifteen minutes and was no more entertaining after George had introduced himself—Matt had us do some insane acting exercises around the stage. It was still very early in the year so he wanted to spend most of our time getting to know each other and ourselves through the strange stuff he asked us to do—like these exercises.

To begin, the twenty or so of us spread across the stage, staggered in lines so there was someone within just about every square foot of it, and listened to him like a drill sergeant—that is, of course, if drill sergeants had messy buns, shiny piercings, and flowy patterned pants that made them look like displaced hippies (because, yes, Matt wore those).

Once we were all spread out and quiet, waiting for his command, he started to scream out random conditions. Our exercise was to act through whatever condition he gave. It began with walking around "like pedestrians in New York," then it was "swimmers in a pool of peanut butter," and finally, "dinosaurs on Mars."

Arms flailed, feet dragged, laughter spilled from lips (much to Matt's displeasure because *dinosaurs don't laugh, my children*) and time absolutely flew by.

Whether or not any of these exercises were helpful to us in terms of our growth as actors, I wasn't sure, but it was fun nonetheless. I wouldn't have expected it to be with how stupid I felt doing it, but it was. There was something strangely liberating about dumping all of my hesitancy to the side and letting my body move in absurd ways alongside a bunch of others doing the same. What I loved most about acting was pretending to be someone other than who I really was, somewhere other than where I was truly stuck, even if only for a little while. Nothing had succeeded in separating me from reality more than these exercises had.

By the time we wrapped up, a sheen of sweat had formed across my forehead and my cheeks were hot as stovetops, but I was smiling. I'd never been an athlete—if that much was not already obvious—so it felt extremely strange to be so tired out from a few hours of the drama club. Not only that, but it felt like I was part of a team for once. Everyone else also appeared to be tired but happy. They walked by me with wide grins and taps on the shoulder, murmurs of how much fun that was or laughs of how embarrassed they were once it was over. It was the sort of camaraderie I didn't think existed outside of sports or impenetrably tight-knit friend groups (of which I'd never known).

Emmeline was last to reach me where I stood at the edge of stage, panting, waiting for Matt to gather our things. She lit up at the sight of me and threw one of her arms around my shoulder. The other she threw around George, who was simply trying to get past us to go down the stairs. She tugged us together into an awkwardly close huddle as if we had all been friends for years and there was nothing at all strange about the sudden proximity.

"Man, this year is gonna rock," she said, completely out of breath.

George looked petrified, eyes fluttering between the two of us as if trying to remember if we'd ever spoken together before—which we had not. I'd only learned his name hours earlier, after all. Yet I felt as if this was okay, this could be normal, even, so I leaned into it and laughed.

"Matt is literally so much better than crusty old Mr. Pimbley," she went on, turning entirely to George for confirmation. "Like we couldn't even tell you, right?"

George just nodded, looking like a mouse caught in a trap. It was clear that he and Emmeline knew each other before then, but if my inclination was correct, they weren't exactly friends yet.

"Was he the drama teacher before?" I asked.

"Yep. He was like ninety and thought Shakespeare was the only thing worth performing. *Romeo and Juliet* can only be put on by the same cast so many times before it's tired out, though."

"He casted me as Juliet's nurse last year," George mumbled, grimacing with the thought.

"I thought her nurse was a woman," I said, meeting his deep green eyes. I was shocked to see long eyelashes and smooth skin. George was a looker beneath the beanies and protective sheet of hair he hid under.

"She is," he lamented.

Emmeline snorted again. I cracked a smile, even though George was clearly a bit distraught over the memory. Eventually he ended up laughing, too. It was comfortable. Being with the two of them was already comfortable. We stayed that way for a long while until George checked his watch and went dashing down the stairs, swearing and sweating.

At that point, I pulled myself from Emmeline's grip to get ready to leave myself. Matt would be out any second to take me home and he hated having to wait. He was a bit like a kid in that way.

I picked my bag up from the ground beside the stairs and zipped it shut. The stage held a layer of strange blackish dust that clung to absolutely everything, so the bottom of my bag was covered. I swiped at it aggressively in an attempt to get some of it off. It created a mini tornado as it sprung away from the fabric with each hit of my palm.

"Woah, what did that bag ever do to you?"

It was Wren's voice. I could already recognize him without looking.

I tried to find Matt, but he was still nowhere to be seen. I supposed that one conversation wouldn't be the end of the world. Anyhow, it wasn't like Wren was some kind of monster. Matt had simply judged Wren off of an assumption, off of his age and his friendliness towards me. There was no hard evidence that *his type* was of any concern. He seemed nice enough to me. A lot like Emmeline, actually, and Matt was glad I'd befriended her.

"How old are you?" I asked, then immediately threw a hand over my mouth... The hand I'd been slapping at the dust on my bag with. I pulled it away and gagged. How disgusting. I was a mess.

Wren's eyebrows, sharp and thin, raised halfway up his forehead. The smirk was still on his lips, but kinder this time.

"I'm twenty-five," he answered slowly, eyes following me as I rubbed my cardigan over my mouth and my hands down the sides of my jeans, trying to get all the stupid dust away. "Are you alright?"

"Yeah, yeah, yeah, I'm good." I felt the heat flying up my neck and into my cheeks.

For a split second, his smirk softened into a real smile. I willed it to come back once it was gone. I wanted it to stay there, to be directed at me again. He was so pretty. The flush in my skin felt like it was everywhere. *What was wrong with me?*

"Do you need a ride home?" he asked, as natural as a brother would ask their younger sister… Like how he'd ask Emmeline.

It sobered me up to reality very quickly. Perhaps Matt had to worry more about me than anyone else.

"No." My voice was too loud, my answer too quick. "Uhm, no, I'm okay. Thank you."

"Let me know if you ever do," he told me, taking a tiny step closer. "Emmeline has come to care about you very much already."

I was sure she had. Emmeline texted me nearly every hour of every day since we exchanged numbers. I tried to respond back with as much enthusiasm as I could muster each time. I wasn't like her with big demonstrative words or actions, or endless thoughts to share, but I liked her a lot. I wanted her to stick around. We'd become close quite quickly.

"That teacher isn't giving you trouble, is he?" Wren asked, voice low. He was looking around for other people, probably Emmeline, possibly Matt.

"Huh?"

"Molina," he clarified. His jaw was set.

"No. God no," I breathed out, confused as to when men suddenly started thinking I needed protection from other men. I hadn't even thought to be concerned before then. "Matt's my guardian. He was just being a bit protective last time."

"I see." Wren took a step back, rolled his shoulders, and un-clenched his jaw. It could've been a trick of the stage lights above our heads, but I swear he looked disappointed.

Thick, blood red curtains lined the backstage area in rows of three on either side. From the middle one on stage right, Matt finally came waltzing out with enough force to blow around those very curtains. He was always one for an entrance. His feet pounded and echoed along the floor as he walked.

"Goodnight, Naomi," Wren said with a nod. He was gone before Matt had even made his way across the stage to where I stood.

4

A few months into the school year, Emmeline added me to a groupchat with George. She named the group *Boo Shakespeare* and blew it up with all of her thoughts and ideas for the big performance drama club would be putting on at the end of the year. Matt announced the previous week that we'd be doing *Alice in Wonderland*. Auditions were set for the week before holiday break and the performance itself would be in late May. We had plenty of time for her extravagant plans, but not much before auditions.

Hence why Emmeline and George ended up over my house that weekend, scripts in hand, rehearsing endlessly. Emmeline was going for the lead, Alice, of course. She wanted me to go for the Queen of Hearts, which was basically the second lead, even though I would've rather been in a small featured role like a gardener or even Humpty Dumpty. George was dead set on the March Hare for whatever reason. With all of this in mind, we took turns reading the lines of our prospective roles until we'd memorized every last one of them. It was deep into the night before we got to that point.

Emmeline was sprawled across my bed, head hanging off the edge, legs resting on my pillows, crossed at the ankles. The floral bedspread was in shambles; thick comforter bunched up as far away from Emmeline as possible without being off the bed entirely, white silk pillowcases hanging on for dear life, fitted sheet untucked and inching off the mattress. If Emmeline hadn't looked so comfortable there, I would've shoved her off to fix it all immediately. She was lucky.

George, far more naturally, sat at my desk. He looked much less comfortable, though. The desktop was a little too short for the bright pink faux fur chair I paired with it. His knees kept knocking against the bottom of it, rattling the lamp and organizers full of pens, pencils, and note cards on top. Eventually he pulled his legs up to sit criss-cross on the chair, but it was a tight fit and he still looked horribly uneasy.

I sat between the two of them, right there on the butterfly-shaped rug centered in the middle of the floor. My room wasn't very big, and it was sparsely furnished, so there were not many other seating options. I didn't mind much. I was happy with them there, filling the space of my room with their presence and laughter. It was hardly inconspicuous when I snapped a picture of each of them, hoping to print them out and add them to the photographs lining the walls around my closet. Most of them were only of Matt and me. It would be nice to add some others.

"Naomi," Emmeline whined, slipping a little further off the foot of the bed. "What am I supposed to do if Carla auditions for Alice, too?"

"There's no if. Obviously she's going for Alice," George added unhelpfully.

I still had some trouble at that point connecting names to faces, but Carla was easy enough to remember. Rather, she was hard to forget. She was the girl with the long, platinum blonde hair who'd started the laughter after George introduced himself.

After Matt announced our big showcase the other day, he'd paired us off for exercises with the script. I was with Carla. We were meant to each take turns as Alice in the first scene, providing constructive criticism to one another as we went. I never took a turn. Instead I listened to Carla recite the lines flawlessly until time was up.

Before she left that night, she told me I'd be better off playing the Mock Turtle, as it was half calf, half turtle, and I'd know a thing or two about being half and half. It took me an embarrassingly long amount of time to realize what she had even meant, and when I did, I had half a mind to report her for it. But I was too confused on how she even knew I was half Japanese. It wasn't like I spoke of Jin to anyone. Nor was it like I grew up with his culture or influence. Oftentimes I forgot this was part of my identity myself.

Even Emmeline and George hardly knew anything beyond the fact that he was my biological father I still had contact with. Besides, it wasn't long after Carla said that when Wren came walking into the auditorium to get Emmeline, smiling directly at me. Until he saw my expression, that is. He followed my gaze to Carla and squinted, as if agreeing to be upset with her for whatever reason I was. That made me smile. I decided to let it go.

"You deserve it more than her," I told Emmeline fiercely, letting the delayed anger hit me.

George's head snapped to me and his lips tightened into a flat line, yet he said nothing. George interested me in that way. It was entirely too obvious when he had something to say, but he hardly ever said it. The difficult thing to parse was why. He was rather shy, of course, but we were friends. I wanted to understand what went on behind those guarded eyes. With all I kept hidden, though, I wasn't one to talk.

"Obviously I deserve it more," Emmeline was saying, apparently unperturbed by my sudden sharpness. "But she is a good actress. I mean she's totally fooled Mr. Molina into thinking she isn't a bitch. That's a feat."

"Well Matt's good at acting, too," I responded, smiling a bit.

This cheered Emmeline up thoroughly. She went off on a tangent about Carla and her bitchiness to which I could do nothing but nod along. George listened to her intently, sharing in the occasional chuckle as he marked up the pages of his script.

I suddenly felt that moving to this town was the best thing that had ever happened to me. Though George, Emmeline, and I had only been friends for a few months, they were the best friends I had ever had. We were hardly even what I'd call close—at least not yet—as none of us knew much more than the basics about each other, but even still, when I was around them I was happy. It made me want to strip back those hidden layers of myself, dig past the basics, and let them know it all.

It was truly amazing what a small change could do; what sorts of avalanches could from a decision as simple as Matt applying for a teaching job. As hours passed with the three of us holed up in my bedroom together, I couldn't help but wonder what else there could be.

5

Matt was lenient as a parental figure, but not so lenient that he'd let George stay the night. He liked George a lot, too, but he shot down the request quicker than I could finish asking it.

I had expected that, obviously, but that did nothing to quell the anxiety climbing in my chest at the thought of being alone with Emmeline for the rest of the night and the next morning. She was a commanding presence and I was nothing if not a quiet follower. I worried about what that meant for me. Would she one day realize I was below her and leave? Would she one day turn into someone rotten like Carla and use it against me? I could hardly take the thought of it. I'd been alone before her and I'd be alone again if there was an *after* her.

Most of all, I worried for my own self control. There was something about Emmeline that was so like Wren. There was something about those Blackwells that enraptured me. They gave me their undivided attention and I couldn't stop myself from sucking it up greedily. People like me weren't meant to be given so much notice by people like them. It created a monster I knew one day I wouldn't be able to tame.

Even so, I understood it was foolish to worry about it. Emmeline was good. She treated the rest of the night no differently than she had before George left. It was only me who felt the unnecessary nervousness. Even when we laid to sleep, I couldn't stop it. I held my breath when she moved and tensed when she got too close. It was a fitful night. I slept very little.

By morning, the feeling had mostly passed. I was back to being fine. Better than fine, actually, because I'd reverted to the previous night's headset of wanting to get closer to her, *needing* to be the best friends I'd only ever see other people be. The biggest issue was that I wasn't sure how to do this.

Matt made a large breakfast for the three of us and he and Emmeline chattered endlessly over it. I listened to them go back and forth with a warmth in my chest. I never had this much to go on about, especially so early in the morning, and I could tell Matt was thriving off of the change. He was a talker, much the same as Emmeline. It was unexpectedly sweet to witness.

Perhaps friends got closer through small intimacies like these—through meeting your parents and sharing your meals, by spending the night and making up for your shortcomings. I didn't know, but I definitely wanted to find out.

For as curious as I was to understand someone like George who never said very much, we were startlingly similar. There I sat doing the same exact thing, mind running rampant while I ate my food in silence.

"Naomi." Matt's voice drew my attention back up to them.

Emmeline was shoving a forkful of scrambled eggs into her mouth. Matt was holding his phone in one hand and his coffee mug in the other. His screen was lit up to his text messages with Jin. I could tell because Jin was the only person who texted Matt in large paragraphs like the one I could see there.

"What does he want?" I asked immediately.

I hadn't seen Jin since before we moved, so it was going on four months by then. I knew he checked in with Matt about us semi-regularly, but we never spoke directly. It was only a matter of time before he decided we needed to have another stupid bonding night.

"Jin and Julie were wondering if you'd like to get dinner with them on Sunday the 20th," he recited.

"Without you?"

"It appears that way, yes," he answered slowly, eyeing Emmeline out of the corners of his eyes.

He was clearly trying to be elusive since he was unaware of how much she knew. But by that point, I'd already told Emmeline all the key information: mom's dead, dad's alive but hardly around, and Matt's the one who took care of me. Always had been. Simple enough.

"Why?"

"Now I may be going out on a limb here," Matt said, lifting his mug to his lips, "but I assume it's for your birthday. Y'know, since that's the 21st? The big one six?"

"We never do things for my birthday without you." I never wanted to. Matt was our buffer. I wasn't sure I could take it alone.

"There's a first for everything, my little one," he answered facetiously. Then, more seriously—or as seriously as Matt could possibly get, at least—he added, "Besides, Jin suggested the new bistro in town. I hear it's expensive. Run him dry if you'd like. Just give them a chance."

Maybe it was the thought of running Jin dry, or maybe it was Emmeline's piercing stare, or maybe it was hearing Matt ask me to do something without a smile on his lips, but I gave in. I agreed to have dinner with Jin and Julie on December 20th, the day before my sixteenth birthday—which just so happened to be the day before auditions for *Alice in Wonderland*, as well.

Matt thanked me, though there was no reason for him to be thankful, and Emmeline smiled as if this was some huge moment of change I'd welcomed with open arms. It was neither a huge moment nor welcomed with open arms. It was some tiny effort made nearly sixteen years too late that I begrudgingly accepted in hopes of emptying his bank account. Whatever. I intended to make the best of it.

Wren came to pick up Emmeline while we were finishing up with washing the dishes after breakfast. Matt had retired upstairs to shower by then. Emmeline was washing, I was drying. When the doorbell rang, I set the damp rag down and opened the door to him standing there. He smiled when he saw me.

"Good morning, Naomi," he said softly, peering past me to where Emmeline was just barely visible in the kitchen. She hadn't stopped doing the dishes for even a second. Her attention was razor sharp on the spatula we'd used for the eggs. Some were caked onto it. "You look nice."

I was in pajamas that were covered in splashes of dish water. My hair was in a messy bun over my head, something I never wanted anyone to see outside of this house. From this, I assumed the comment was meant to be a joke, but his tone was very serious.

"I look terrible," I told him honestly, confused.

He laughed. I liked how it sounded, and I liked how it felt to make him laugh even more.

"You look comfortable," he corrected. "It's a good thing."

I swept the baby hairs away from my forehead, trying to hide my grin. He took this moment to step through the doorway. When he stopped, it was so close beside me that I could feel the cold air radiating off of him from standing outside. It was starting to snow, yet he was in no more than a thin sweatshirt.

"Em, get your things," Wren called to her. She startled at his voice and nearly threw the glass she'd moved onto washing. He looked far too entertained by this.

"I thought dad was getting me," Emmeline said once she'd set the glass down carefully. I wasn't sure what she sounded like when she was sad, but if I had to guess, this was it.

Emmeline told me about as much about her family as I had told her about mine. Turns out they were more similar than either of us would have liked. Her mom had also passed away, but it was when she was a kid so she had gotten to know her at least for a little while. Her dad was a busy lawyer so he traveled more often than not. He was a lot like mine in the sense that he was alive, but not quite there, not really around. Wren was to her what Matt was to me: the step-in parent, the guardian by all means.

Wren looked apologetic when he answered her. "Work. Something came up."

Emmeline scoffed and stormed up the stairs to my bedroom. I would not have been surprised if Matt heard and thought there was someone breaking into the house. She was dramatic, I thought, but there was no guarantee that I wouldn't react the same way if it came to something with Jin.

"Sorry," Wren whispered to me, shaking his head. "Our family is a bit of a mess."

"I know."

Once I processed what I'd said, Wren was already laughing. I could never seem to say the right thing in front of him. My filter fell to pieces when he looked at me. If talking to Emmeline and George could be anything like this, we'd be super close in no time.

"That's not what I meant," I rushed out, flailing my hands around nervously. "I'm so sorry. Wow, that was so rude—"

"No worries," he replied, saving me the embarrassment of any further rambling. I liked that even when he laughed, he was smirking. He almost always looked amused. "You meant you understand it, huh?"

"Yeah." My voice was suddenly small. *I* was small.

A light came into his eyes that wasn't there before. Quietly, like it was secret for just the two of us, he said, "That's too bad."

I could hardly register what happened next until it was already over. He had leaned into my space, and for a split second, I thought he'd kiss me. I sort of wanted him to. But he had only reached his hand into my pocket and took my phone out. Feeling the tips of his fingers against my leg, even through the fabric, left me reeling. I was stunned into silence. I couldn't move even as he turned the screen my way to unlock it with my face ID.

The shower upstairs squeaked to a stop. Emmeline's footsteps were getting louder above us.

"There." He handed my phone back to me, locked as if it hadn't been touched at all. "I put my number in there. If you ever need anything; a ride, to talk about your family, *anything*, I'll be here."

I stuttered but no real words came out. He smiled—no, *smirked*, the same way he always did—and I felt the floor swaying beneath me.

"You must be lonely," he added in a whisper, head bent down towards me, "I know how that feels. I can help you through it."

I couldn't peel my eyes away from him. His eyes were so dark brown that it was hard to decipher where his pupils started and where they ended. It was easy to get lost in that look.

Emmeline broke the spell when she came downstairs and tugged me into a hug to say goodbye. I returned it as well as I could with how dizzy I felt, and then they were leaving. I hardly had the words *thank you* out of my mouth before the door was clicking shut behind them.

6

In the following days, I spent plenty of time staring at Wren's contact on my phone. Half of me wanted to delete it and the other half of me wanted to call him and talk until I had no words left.

Evidently I ended up doing neither. I simply stared at his name on my screen and the numbers accompanying it for so long during so many inconvenient times that my eyes began to strain and I missed multiple announcements in my classes. It got worse the closer time got to my dinner with Jin and Julie, to my birthday, to drama club auditions.

On the Friday before all of these things, Emmeline called me out on my spaciness during Chemistry. We got to pick our own lab partners in that class so the two of us shared a space in the back left corner of the room. The lab was crowded with two rows of five two-person desks—wobbly stools against tall, dark gray countertops—and all sorts of cabinets full of materials surrounded them. Emmeline and I had the workspace mere inches away from the large, clear cabinet containing the beakers and test tubes. If I shifted my stool too far to the right, I'd ram right into it. I knew this from having done it before.

Our Chemistry class was maxed out at twenty students so even on a good day it was hard to get through an experiment without any mishaps. So many teenagers in the same small space was a recipe for disaster. Especially if one of those teenagers was me as I was then; stuck completely inside my head and worrying about Wren. He'd seen right through me: I truly was lonely. And if he understood, if he could *help me through it*, then I really wanted to press the call button on his number.

For that class period, we had a relatively simple experiment to complete. Because I had been so caught up in staring at my phone, pondering again what to do, I missed the part where Mrs. Dion explained the potential dangers. While a simple experiment, it was not one hundred percent free of safety hazards.

It could not have been more than five minutes into our time experimenting when I handed Emmeline the wrong vial after she asked for a very specific one. She nearly had a heart attack when what she was doing caught fire.

"Naomi!" Emmeline huffed, screeching her stool back a full foot—stopping only when it rammed into the countertops that held the science department's assortment of fancy scales. "What's wrong with you?"

The little fire had gone out almost immediately after it started, but that did not stop it from being enough to scare her and the entire rest of the classroom. Mrs. Dion rushed over and scolded us both thoroughly. She recapped the safety hazards, which I listened intently to a second time around, and eyed our burnt experiment with disappointment. She was so upset that her pupils were shaking behind her thick round lenses and her lips were pulled into a tight frown. Normally she was nothing but sunshine and rainbows—to the point that it was rather unnerving. I felt awful for bringing her down.

"I'm sorry," I told Emmeline, trying and failing to organize our station for us to restart. I had no idea what anything even was.

Emmeline softly nudged my hands out of the way so that she could nonchalantly fix everything for herself. As she swept the burnt mess of our previous project away, the air filled with the smell of it: burnt chemicals and pungent ash. Our classmates at the table beside ours pulled their shirts over their faces with disgust. Those at the table in front of us turned around with sharp, accusatory glares. Up in the front, as far from us as possible, Carla scoffed and murmured something lowly into her partner's ear. Emmeline didn't look back at any of them but I did, feeling as if I had to.

Nose scrunching, I apologized to Emmeline again and elaborated with, "I've been distracted recently."

"No way, really?" She huffed out a laugh. I frowned and she asked me, "Is this about your birthday? Are you nervous to go to dinner with Jin?"

"Yes," I answered. It wasn't even a lie. I *was* nervous. It was weighing on me more and more as the days passed by. It might not have been exactly why I destroyed our Chemistry experiment, but it was why I was so focused on Wren's contact, so in a way, indirectly, it sort of was why I destroyed our Chemistry experiment.

"Alright," she said, frowning. Her usual lipstick was smudged in the corners of her mouth. I nearly reached out to wipe it away. "George and I are gonna go to the mall that night so if you need an out, we'll be around."

"Thanks."

"Course." She smiled softly at me.

Our counter space was once again clean and organized, ready for us to try again. Emmeline tucked the loose strands of her hair behind her ears, then leaned over into my space to do the same to me. She was an awfully tactile person. She had no qualms about getting up in my personal space. Unlike me, the proximity didn't seem to set her skin on fire. I knew I could've easily asked her to back off a bit and she'd do it without question, but I never really wanted to. I didn't mind the feeling of her gentle hands.

The second time around, our experiment went smoothly. I read the instructions in earnest and followed Emmeline's lead without any further mishaps. We finished in the nick of time.

The bell rang and students swarmed out the door to the hallway. Emmeline and I moved slowly behind them and stood against the wall directly outside our classroom. We liked to meet up there with George, who came from the other end of the science wing, before walking to lunch together.

While we waited, Emmeline swung her backpack around so it was on backwards and unzipped the main pocket. She began to dig around inside, notebooks and loose papers falling out one after the other. I kept having to catch them so they wouldn't get lost or trampled on. She was cursing to herself repeatedly.

"What?" I asked at last, arms full of her disorganized things.

She took everything back from me and shoved it haphazardly into her backpack. The zipper hardly closed after it.

"I forgot my wallet and apparently my phone, too." She groaned, throwing her head back against the wall with a dull thud. Her space buns served as a minor cushion. "Can I use yours to call Wren?"

"*What?*"

Her eyes slanted. "Can I use your phone? To call Wren? To get some lunch?"

I felt like an idiot, sputtering at the thought of her calling him from my phone when that was all I'd been able to think about doing for days. If she did, he'd have my number, too. If she did, she'd notice his contact. I didn't want to deal with the consequences of either of those things. My pulse jumped.

"Naomi?" Emmeline dragged out my name, snapping her fingers in front of my eyes. "Hello?"

I jerked away from her as I took my phone from my pocket. She reached for it when it was in sight but I took another step away. I could feel her gaze getting sharper on me. My fingers trembled as I unlocked my phone, opened up my contacts, and quickly deleted Wren from them. The next time her hand came out for my phone, I let her have it. For a split second, I thought she'd figured it out as she stared at my open contacts without moving. Then she shook the look off her face and dialed his number.

I could hear Wren answering over the other end of the line. He never spoke very loudly but he was still impossible to ignore. The deep baritone of his voice demanded to be heard. I couldn't help but force my ears to pick up on it.

"Yeah this is her phone," Emmeline was saying to him.

My eyebrows shot up my forehead. She looked at me and rolled her eyes good-naturedly. I felt childish blushing so I turned away. Flyers for clubs and sports hung along the white cement walls, one on nearly every inch of open space. Some had tear-off phone numbers or websites attached to the bottom like old job flyers. Others had bright, nearly illegible fonts and obscure pictures stolen from Google. Where there weren't flyers, there were quotes teachers had placed strategically like *don't give up on your dreams* or whatever else they found inspirational. I read each one that I could over and over until Emmeline was rushing through the end of her conversation with Wren.

"Uh huh, yeah, uh huh, okay, hurry up, yeah, thanks, love you, bye."

She smiled broadly at me as she handed my phone back over, his number sitting there in my recents. I'd have to remake his contact later.

George came upon us at that moment. He had a gray beanie pulled down almost over his eyes and a matching sweatshirt zipped up over his mouth. He looked tired and miserable. He tended to look that way after his Chemistry class, which was far more advanced than the one that Emmeline and I took.

"Cheer up, Prez," Emmeline told him, unzipping his sweatshirt so we could see his frowning mouth. "Wren's bringing us pizza!"

7

If there was one thing I absolutely hated about Jin and Julie, it was the way they overcompensated for not wanting to be my parents by attempting to buy me expensive crap I couldn't care less about.

Matt drove me to the bistro to meet them shortly before seven on the night we'd agreed to go. When he parked, we both stared in dumbfounded silence at its entrance. Through the windows, chandeliers and lines of tablecloth-covered tables were visible. Each was set with pristine dinnerware and napkins folded into birds and hats and other origami shapes. We couldn't see many people inside, but from the ones we could see, they were all in formal attire. Suits and ties, dresses and heels, peacoats and satin scarves. I felt severely underdressed in my dark jeans and sweater.

"What kind of bistro is this?" Matt asked, bewildered.

I shook my head in disbelief, having no answer. The thought of walking in there alone made my skin crawl. If Matt wasn't dressed worse off than I was—torn up jeans, stained hoodie and fluffy slippers—then I would've forced him to suffer through and come with me anyway.

It was impossible to not notice when Jin and Julie showed up. They came walking down the sidewalk to the restaurant hand in

44

hand as I was snapping a picture of it to send Emmeline. Jin's short brown hair was slicked back heavily with gel. He wasn't much older than thirty-two, but this definitely made him look well past it. He had on a collared shirt, dress pants, and a long trench coat. Julie, on the other hand, looked far younger than her actual twenty-nine years of age. Her smooth orange hair fell in one swoop across her shoulders, no product or hair clips forcing it that way. She had on a tight black dress that hugged her petite form and made her look even smaller than she already was. She was shorter than me and I was significantly shorter than Jin.

Together they made a nice picture of a seemingly perfect young couple. Their wedding rings glinted under the street lights, huge diamonds on silver bands. They looked happy together with those unaware smiles plastered across their lips. Perhaps it was cruel, but it made me sick.

I leaned over the center console to give Matt a side hug before I left. He rested his head over mine and clasped a hand over my shoulder.

"Run him dry," he told me, sounding much more serious about the idea than he had when suggesting it.

Jin and Matt's friendship had been rocky for quite some time. They didn't talk nearly as much as they supposedly used to, and neither of them seemed willing to change that. I wasn't privy to why that was, exactly, but I could assume enough. My existence definitely played a part in that strain.

I told Matt, "Will do."

I climbed out of the car and waved to Jin and Julie, who waited for me at the doorway. With our reservation, we were seated within seconds. I unfolded my bird napkin and laid it across my lap, determined to keep myself busy this whole night. I hated looking directly at Jin. I looked so much like him.

"Feel free to order anything, sweetie," Julie told me, skimming the wine menu herself.

I smiled with tight lips back at her. I had no real reason to dislike Julie, but it was hard to find reasons to like her nonetheless. She wasn't my mother, seeing as Jin was hellbent on not being my father, but she sure liked to play the doting step-mom role, anyway. I didn't like to play roles in real life. I had the drama club for that.

I stuck true to my word and ordered the most expensive meal on the menu. Then I ordered an expensive mocktail for the fun of it. Jin and Julie hardly seemed to notice as they ordered drinks and meals for themselves, absorbed in each other and how they would share everything. I found myself turning to the left, looking for Matt to make faces at. When I remembered he wasn't there, I felt a rush of sadness. I didn't know how to do any of this without him.

We didn't talk much. We exchanged pleasantries and tiny bits of information about our lives, but not much more. The conversation was awkward and stilted. Julie filled in most of the blanks, chittering away about anything and everything. I appreciated her attempts, but in all honesty, they didn't help much.

I was glad to have food to distract myself with when it showed up. The plates were huge, but not very full. Exactly as I'd expect from a place so expensive and high-end. I ate my meal slowly, hardly knowing what any of it was. I could barely remember the names and ingredients of any of the menu items, only the prices. Forkfuls of my dish later and I still couldn't say what it was that I ordered. Something slathered in sauce but lacking in flavor. Maybe a meat dish? Then again, maybe not. *Ugh.* I fought to suppress a groan. Nice restaurants were the worst.

"So Naomi," Jin started, lightly dabbing the corner of his mouth (which had nothing on it, mind you) with a folded napkin. The movement was so pretentious that I wanted to throw my mocktail at him. "Matt tells me you have a big day planned tomorrow."

That was news to me. I suppose auditions and my birthday all in one go *could* make for a big day, but I still wouldn't call it that. Perhaps this was his way of hinting at it? I never knew with him.

"Mhm, I guess." I took a large gulp of my mocktail, even if that was only to keep myself from tossing it. Surprisingly, it was good. It tasted like seltzer water and basil. "It's really only auditions, though. I didn't make plans."

"Well why would you?" Julie asked sweetly. "That's already quite the big deal, isn't it?"

Why would I? Normally people do things for their birthdays, don't they? Especially young girls for their sixteenth? *The big one six*, as Matt had said. Most would plan something huge aside from school activities and stressful auditions, I would think.

"I mean I'm not going for a lead role or anything," I ended up saying, narrowing my eyes.

"I'm sure you could get it if you did," Jin answered, though he'd never seen me act. I'd never done a big school show before. When I was younger, I took some small classes at the community center, but of course it was only ever Matt who brought me. We had a few performances there for family, where Matt would sit as close as possible and record videos from an old handheld camera, but Jin was never in attendance beside him. Whether Jin knew about those at all was beyond me.

"Right." My patience was thinning. The more I thought, the worse it got. I liked it better when Julie was going on about the upcoming snow storms. "I'm not, though."

"Any plans for your birthday? That's coming up isn't it?" Julie asked, hoping to ease the tension.

"I just told you." I set my fork down so it would stop clacking against my plate with my shaking hand. Were they really so stupid?

"Ah, well I'd hope you aren't counting tomorrow's auditions as your birthday celebration," Jin chimed in.

"My birthday *is* tomorrow," I snapped.

Jin's face paled and Julie momentarily lost her perfect mask of happiness. So they really had forgotten then. What was I doing there with them if they'd forgotten?

For a minute, no one said anything. Even when the waitress, who was decked out in a collared shirt and black bowtie, arm held in front of her body with a folded napkin over it, came by to ask how everything was, no one spoke. The waitress's smile faltered. Her fake work persona slipped from her posture, making her arm wilt and the napkin shift. Clearing her throat, she asked once more. I aggressively stuck up two thumbs, forcing my nose to crinkle up as well in a fake sign of happiness. She scurried off after that. Jin chuckled awkwardly, wringing his hands together above his half-eaten plate.

Finally he said, "It seems I lost track of the days."

The table shook as I let my hands fall back onto it, thumbs still up. This dinner was draining me.

"It's fine," I told him, but it wasn't. It really and truly wasn't okay.

None of us knew what to say after that, so we said nothing. Yet again, silence prevailed. The minutes dragged on in that tense silence broken only by our silverware knocking against our plates. I didn't want to be upset, but I was. I didn't want to care that they'd forgotten, but I did. If someone else, *anyone else*, could tell me that these feelings were okay, then I'd be able to handle them. But since no one was around who could, I wasn't able to.

My mouth tasted like ash. No matter how much fancy food I shoveled into it, the taste stuck to my gums. I emptied both my plate and my mocktail glass, and still, I felt sick. I felt faint. It was as if everything was going straight through me. Not only my food, but my breaths. They passed right through me like I wasn't real at all.

Stumbling to my feet, I decided to leave on my own. It was the only choice I felt I'd truly been able to make for myself all night.

"Will we see you on Christmas this year, Jin?" I asked, halfway hoping the answer would be no. He'd only started coming a few years back. It was always awkward when he watched me open a bunch of presents from Matt and none from him.

He nodded slowly. *Great*, I thought. Without another word, I turned on my heels and left.

8

I knew if I called Matt, he could've been there to get me within twenty minutes. I knew if I called Emmeline, I could've met up with her and George wherever they currently were, exactly as she had offered to me days before. And yet it wasn't either of them that I called when I stepped outside the bistro, my entire body vibrating with anger and hurt.

"Hello?"

It was nice to hear his voice but I couldn't find mine. My stomach was lurching and my heart was pounding in my throat. What was I even supposed to say? Did I even have the right to be so upset? Jin and Julie were in there spending heaps of money on me. They'd attempted to engage with me about my hobbies. What did it matter if they didn't know the exact day I would turn sixteen? They knew my birthday was coming soon. It could be a sincere mistake that they'd forgotten the exact day. That should have been enough.

"Hello?" His voice again, more urgent. "Naomi, is that you?"

"It's me."

"What's up? Are you okay?"

I felt burning around my eyes and squeezed them shut.

"About that ride," I prompted, trying to keep my voice level.

There was a brief silence over the other end of the line before he said, "Send your location. I'll be right there."

I shared my location, sat on the snow-covered curb, and waited for Wren to get me. I didn't want to go inside and say a proper goodbye. Jin would figure out I wasn't coming back soon, if he hadn't already. Then he'd call Matt, and Matt would wonder what happened, where I went, who took me there. There would be a huge deal about it then. It could come later.

I watched as cars passed by, their tires plowing through slush and salt. The street lights were far too bright and I could still hear the lively music and conversation from within the bistro behind me. Wind blew slowly, but ever present. It was getting hard to feel my fingers and toes. There was so much going on both in and out of my body that I felt like I'd explode. Holding myself together while I waited was overwhelming.

When I caught sight of Wren's scratched-up black sports car, I stood and jumped into the passenger side before he even fully stopped. He'd clearly rolled out of bed to come for me. His hair was all over the place, his eyes were crusted, and he was wearing plaid pajama bottoms. His eyes were wide and searching, no signature smirk in sight. Before I could think it over, I threw myself over to hug him. Slowly, his hands came up to hug me back. One rested on my lower back and the other wrapped around my head, holding me against him. I felt the tears beginning.

"Let's get you home," he said gently. "You're freezing."

"Take me with you," I told him. I couldn't go home just yet.

"Emmeline isn't home," he began, cutting his eyes to me. "I thought you knew."

"I do."

He stared for another second in silence before putting the car in drive and pulling out into the street. I rested my head on his shoulder the entire drive. We said nothing more.

The Blackwell's house was a mansion in comparison to the place Matt and I lived in. It was three stories tall with a two car garage, a balcony for each of the three bedrooms, and a plethora of massive arched windows. It was sleek with black rooftops and dark gray painting. It looked as if it was pulled from one of those upscale architecture magazines. In this town, surrounded by single family homes with cracked shingles and unpaved driveways, it didn't belong.

Wren pulled right into the garage and helped me out of my seat. I leaned against him as we walked. I felt so heavy. The garage led directly into the kitchen where marble countertops and a gas stove with six burners sat. I then felt as small and out of place as I did heavy.

I wasn't aware I'd started crying until Wren's thumb swiped under my right eye, wiping one of the tears away. It may have been my imagination, but I swear he murmured, *"Pretty."*

I leaned into the touch and let myself cry openly. The house was dark and still around us. It smelled of firewood and vanilla. It was homey. It felt safe.

Wren took my hand gently and led me up the wide staircase. His bedroom was the last door on the right. It was nothing like the rest of the house. It was cluttered, messy, and full of inexpensive decorations and furniture. It looked lived in, unlike the rest of the spaces. Even Emmeline had her room in a better shape.

He urged me to change out of my snow-soaked clothing while he disappeared down the hall to draw a bath. He'd left a dark gray robe over his bed for me. Everything felt surreal. He was so calm and collected about all of this. I felt absolutely anything but. I had no idea what I would be doing if he hadn't answered my call.

When I came out of his room again, the fluffy robe wrapped tightly around my body, falling all the way to my ankles, Wren was waiting against the wall for me. His eyes flashed as they ran over the length of my body. I tugged the robe tighter, feeling self-conscious. He only smiled and motioned his head down the hallway to where the bathroom door was wide open and I could hear the water running. I followed him there. He sat on the ledge of the large porcelain tub and tested the water with the tips of his long fingers as it filled.

I didn't know what to feel. Wren was kind, so kind that he went out of his way to help me and be there for me, but I was still scared. Matt would probably murder him if he knew we were in his house alone together. I didn't want to lie to Matt, or hide anything from him even, but I didn't want Wren in trouble for this. He was nothing but good to me. I was so worried it would fall apart somehow. That on top of the disaster of a dinner I had with Jin and Julie left me trembling where I stood in front of the sink.

"Naomi." Wren flicked the water off of his hand and approached me. I had to crane my head up to look him in the eyes. "Are you okay?"

I sighed heavily and collapsed onto the lid of the toilet seat. Even this was pristine. I put my head in my hands and rubbed at my eyelids. I felt the shift in the air around me as Wren came closer. He knelt down on the floor in front of me. If I shifted my legs, he could move up in between them. That's how close we were.

"No," I answered truthfully.

"Let me help," he said quietly, though there was no need to lower his voice between the two of us.

"You already are," I told him, as if it were obvious, because it should've been. What else did he think he was doing?

His soft laugh echoed around the tiled floors and painted walls. The bathroom was quite small in comparison to every other room of the house, so it made it feel like he was everywhere. I needed to get out of that stupid robe and bury myself under the bathwater. Maybe if I made it cold enough, I could escape the burning feeling building inside of me.

"*Naomi*," he said again. He said my name a lot.

I lifted my gaze and he was right there. We were face to face, no more than a breath apart. His hands came up from where they'd been resting on his knees and cupped my cheeks. I couldn't breathe.

"Relax," he said, words washing over me like a command I had to follow, and then my next words were swallowed by his lips on mine.

He was warm and overpowering. I chased him as he pulled away. His fingers trailed over my cheeks and tucked my hair behind my ears. It made me feel secure. I pushed forward until my body was fully against his and kissed him again. He groaned into the kiss, clearly taken aback. I could've done it all night if he didn't pull away. He was flushed and panting.

He couldn't look at me as he got back to his feet and tugged me to mine, as well. I was worried I'd upset him until his hair curled into my hair and pulled me back. He placed a kiss on my neck, then my jaw, then my cheek. He was holding me so tightly that I was losing circulation. It was hard to think of anything other than him. My breath was ragged, unable to come naturally as his fingers tightened in my hair and his lips kept pressing at any bit of me he could reach.

"Jesus," he gasped, teeth scraping at my ear lobe. "You're gorgeous, Naomi. So gorgeous."

I let his words envelope me, biting back the gasps trying to leave my mouth as he kept going. One of his hands came up and tugged the string of my robe to untie it. It fell open at once and cold air swept at my bare skin. His palms melted it away, hot hands roaming freely underneath the fabric. I didn't want that to stop, but I didn't necessarily want to keep going either. I'd never even kissed someone before. It felt like we were moving too fast.

When his hands found their way down to grip my hip bones, thumbs pressing into the soft space of my upper thighs, I couldn't contain the sharp hitch in my breath. The sound was like a sledge-hammer dropped between us.

He tore himself away from me with wild eyes, breathing heavily. The robe hung open, my naked body entirely on display in the space between the fabric. Wren, on the other hand, remained fully clothed. It felt wrong to be the only one so exposed. But I had no idea how to verbalize that thought. Nor did I know how to make him believe that I was both excited and nervous at the same time and my gasp was nothing more than an effect of that.

"Wren," I mumbled, attempting to find the words anyway.

"We shouldn't have done that," he said, but the look in his eyes as he stared at my body said quite the opposite.

"I liked it," I assured him, but I stumbled on the words.

He sighed heavily, dropping his head onto my shoulder. His breaths puffed against my skin. Slowly, carefully, I reached a hand up to thread my fingers through the hair at the back of his head. It was done with much more caution than he'd held mine before. His body slumped into mine as if the casual touch had drained all the energy from him.

"Wren, I liked it," I said again, not knowing how to correct any of this, but feeling like I absolutely had to. "I did. I like *you*. I've just... Never done that sorta stuff before."

"Really?" He snapped his gaze up to mine, something sparkling in his irises that hadn't been there before. "You like me?"

"Yes," I answered, swallowing thickly. "A lot."

"Good," he breathed, his hands beginning to wander again; one up and down my side over the robe, the other wrapped around the back of my bare neck.

Pinned in place again, I asked quietly, "Does this mean we're... Uhm, well, are we together now?"

"It means whatever you want it to," he whispered into my collarbone. "This was your decision, Naomi. You take the lead."

Never for a second had I felt like I was in the lead, or anywhere near a place where I *could* take the lead. Wren was the one with experience, the one who knew where to put his hands and how to position my head. Even so, he'd handed the choice to me. It felt like a huge dose of power and control. One I'd never been given before.

As an answer, I kissed him again. Our lips didn't line up as well as they had when he'd initiated, so he corrected my movements to make it so. With a shift of his body and a lift of my chin, it was a real kiss again. It was me who began the kiss, but Wren who finished it.

He thumbed at my bottom lip as he pulled away. "No one can know of this," he murmured.

Once again, the reins were back in his hands. He'd made the call, though I had to agree with him on it. No one could know of this.

By the time Emmeline came home that night, my hair had dried and Wren was holed up in his own bedroom. He told me he would handle calling Matt from the old landline to let him know I was there with Emmeline. Matt came to pick me up so shortly after that I hardly had time to tell Emmeline why I was there and not with Jin in the first place.

In the end, Wren was the only one who knew the whole story. He and I shared more than one secret.

SCENE II.

"In another moment down went Alice after it, never once considering how in the world she was to get out again."

— Lewis Carroll, *Alice's Adventures in Wonderland*

9

Despite the fact that Matt wasn't angry with me for walking out on Jin and Julie at dinner—like I was so worried he would be—I still felt awful about it.

I could hardly stop thinking about it long enough to enjoy the birthday pancakes Matt made me the next morning. It didn't help at all that I had Wren to start thinking about, too; with that kiss and his quiet words telling me it had to be a secret. I liked having him to myself in that way, but I didn't like how many things I had to juggle in my head at once alongside it. I didn't like how it seemed as if overnight I'd grown up, yet I'd also become someone who kept secrets from Matt like a rebellious teen. Not only that, but I'd turned into someone who simultaneously loved and hated Jin at the same time, wanted him to feel bad, but felt bad for him, too.

The only thing that made sense was Wren. He liked me even when I cried—he thought I was beautiful, even—and I needed that. I could silence everything else if he was there with me telling me things like that and kissing me like I wasn't so immature for how I'd acted.

But because my birthday was on a Monday, I had school and drama club auditions so he couldn't be there with me to do any of that. I felt jittery and off kilter all day.

Even Emmeline's balloons and George's rare full smile and clap on the shoulder couldn't pull me out of the mood I was in. They took it in stride, acting as if everything was completely normal even though I was clearly a mess. I knew Emmeline assumed it had to do with Jin, and George could probably deduce the same thing, so I let it be. As per usual, assuming my irritation had to do with him was never entirely incorrect, anyway.

The biggest issue of the day was auditions. At Emmeline's incessant begging, I decided to go for the role of Queen of Hearts. As our instructor, Matt was one of the judges. To keep things *fair*, Principal Odinson was also a judge. I had no problem with acting in front of either of them, or the crowd of other drama club members watching, even, but I did have a problem remembering my lines. I was so stirred up from the past few days that I couldn't recall any of those nights I spent beside Emmeline and George reciting each line for hours on end. I got up on stage and completely blanked. I botched it like I'd never botched anything else before in my entire life.

It was probably for the best that Matt wasn't the only judge. If he was, he would've let this horrible performance slide. He'd most definitely give me a second chance. I had since filled him in on my dinner with Jin and Julie and he seemed more upset about it than I was. My feelings and behavior were better understood by him than they were by me myself. Because of that, he seemed ready to play favorites and let me try the audition again. That was until Principal Odinson cleared her throat, jotted down a few notes, and gave me a look of pity as I took the hint to stalk off the stage.

To make matters worse, auditions went alphabetically by last name. So right after me, Naomi Nakano, came Carla Newton. Carla, who maybe was a bitch, but a bitch who could out act me on even my best days. My blood boiled underneath my skin as I watched her up on the stage. She enunciated every single line with perfection and performed them with a flair entirely her own. It was clear to anyone with eyes that the role was hers. With the sort of person she was, I wish I could've denied it. I wanted nothing more than to say she was awful and wholeheartedly believe it. But she wasn't and I couldn't. It made me want to tear my hair out.

I stood no chance. At that point, I knew I'd be lucky to get even Humpty Dumpty.

Watching George audition for the March Hare made me feel marginally better. He was the last person to go up and he definitely made it count. George had an air about him that was a bit contradictory, but fully effective. He was shy, and many believed he was self-conscious because of that, but he was rather cocky when it came to performing. His aptitude for becoming a character while on stage was incredible. He morphed entirely, in ways I could only dream of, and let the lines guide him. There was no one more entertaining to watch. He radiated confidence up there. For a split second, it allowed me to forget how poorly I'd done myself.

The entire auditorium of people applauded him when he finished. Principal Odinson stood up from her seat, saying out loud to Matt without a care in the world that his performance was the best they'd seen all day. Matt looked startled by the blunt admission, but he didn't disagree. Carla, who stood as far away from Emmeline and me as she could possibly get, looked downright murderous at that. This was yet another thing that lifted my mood the slightest bit.

Of course, no amount of small moments lifting my spirit could take away the fact that I'd bombed the audition. The results wouldn't come out for a long while, not until after the holiday break at least, but I didn't need them to know I wasn't getting anything good. The way things were looking, it would be Carla up there beside Emmeline and George on stage while I sat in the wings watching.

"Hey, perk up," Emmeline whispered to me as we walked out of the building together. "It wasn't that bad, I promise."

It most certainly was that bad, but Emmeline was a nice liar, at least. She always sugar coated things for the sake of my feelings, which, despite my embarrassment, did not upset me as much as I thought it would. It was mildly irritating, but not enough to make my mood any lower than it already was.

Thankfully, I was saved from answering her by George jogging up to join us. His beanie was pushed well past his eyebrows, hair spewing out of it as if he'd shoved it on with one hand without looking. His backpack was half-zipped and thrown carelessly over his right shoulder, which was already struggling to hold onto the sleeve of his sweatshirt. For someone so collected, his belongings were never put together the way one would expect. He looked a bit of a mess.

"Don't worry about it," George said, tapping me on the shoulder in that aggressively friendly way that boys who play on the same sports teams always do. It felt strange coming from him. He seemed to think about saying something more, but couldn't seem to find the words. That made me laugh under my breath. There was no way for him to make me feel better without outright lying, and George was not like Emmeline; he couldn't sugar coat to save his life.

"Whatever. I'm fine," I told them both, with a little more force than necessary. "I hardly wanted to be the Queen of Hearts anyway."

A month earlier, that might have been true. But by then, after countless nights rehearsing with Emmeline and George—who'd both become extremely invested in the three of us playing these particular roles on stage together—I wanted the role. I wanted the role *so badly*. That way, the two of them would look at me and know I was worth their time, that I could keep up with them and be what they wanted. Otherwise, I'd have nothing to offer besides my usual self, and I knew by that point in my life that she wasn't enough to make people stick around.

"Naomi—"

"Forget it," I cut George off, feeling my temper rising. I tried to squash it, but it wasn't working. It's not like I could explain everything I was feeling to them, either, because that would take far longer than we had before Matt came out with his keys and drove me home, but I needed to get it off my chest somehow. Right then, only Wren knew enough to help me do that.

"Happy birthday," they both said in farewell as they took a hint and left me alone.

I didn't feel happy, nor did I want to acknowledge that it was my birthday. What was the merit in celebrating another year of this life—the one my own birth father didn't even deem important enough to keep tabs on?

Biting my tongue hard enough to draw blood, I buried my face into my hands and pretended my eyes were completely bone dry.

10

Two short days later, the Washingtons hosted a holiday party at their house. Apparently Edgar and Martha Washington were huge on spreading 'Christmas cheer' and after excessive begging, they'd convinced George to invite some friends to their annual gathering.

For whatever reason, he chose Emmeline, me, and no one else. That made me smile against my will. We may have parted on tense, awkward terms in the school parking lot on my birthday, but those feelings were long gone by the time we arrived then. Emmeline tackled us both into a group hug and all was well again. Our friendship was blooming so naturally that I was ready to tell them things I'd never told anyone else before. And with my awful mood from days earlier and that botched audition still clear in my mind, I had a lot to say and not a lot of patience left to hold it in.

Edgar and Martha Washington were a kind, older couple with a well-maintained house and a love so strong for their son that it was a bit off-putting. They welcomed Emmeline and me inside their home with huge, straight white grins and firm handshakes with their calloused, wrinkled hands. Their house was small like mine, but far nicer. The outside was entirely reclaimed brick with brightly lit arch entrances and windows so spotless they looked nonexistent.

Inside it only got better. Much like the Blackwell household, their furniture was spotless and clearly all from the same matching set: smooth, deep brown wood tables and accompanying black leather couches. It was nothing like the mismatched Ikea furniture across the living room Matt and I threw together as a place to play video games and eat pizza. This was the type of living room that got put together on the sets for television shows to make everyone think the families were perfect and clean all the time. Perhaps the Washingtons were. Nothing was amiss yet.

Across every flat surface in sight—from tabletops to the ledge of the fireplace to the end of the railing against the staircase—candles flickered, their scents battling across the connected rooms. From what my nostrils could pick up right away, there was pine, cinnamon, artificial sugar cookies, and fresh linen. It was overwhelming, but not exactly unpleasant. It felt like the chaos of an honest home.

Edgar and Martha spoke fast and energetically, but somehow soft and gently at the same time. To me, it was a lot like what I assumed traditional grandparents hopped up on sugar might be like. Half of me wanted to laugh and the other half wanted to shush them. Half of me wanted to throw my arms around their shoulders and the other half wanted to run away.

George maneuvered himself between us and them, smiling tensely. His posture was rigid as a board. He clearly wanted some space. I wondered what it was like to have parents so lovely and involved that you ever wished for them to just go away. I mean, I loved Matt and he was fantastic, of course, but he never felt like a parent in the way I was forced to believe parents should be. For all intents and purposes, he was my father, but it wasn't the same.

I wanted to know what it was like for someone who didn't have confusing separations in their mind like that. Someone like George with his picture perfect, happily married parents and his tidy, cozy home.

As he tried to pry us away from them, they started speaking faster as if to get every thought out before we were gone. The two of them went on and on about how beautiful they thought we were, about how excited they were to see *Alice in Wonderland* (which was months out and still a sore subject for me), and about how happy they were to finally meet some of George's friends. Martha gushed on and on, telling Emmeline that she had lips like Katharine Hepburn and me that I had eyes like Meg Foster. Though I had no clue who that was, I thanked her all the same. George got exasperated with them so quickly he ended up taking Emmeline and me by our wrists and dragging us off. His parents' soft laughter followed us out.

"Sorry about them," George said, heaving out a breath and dropping our wrists.

The three of us huddled together in the hallway off the kitchen, surrounded by framed family photos and Christmas lights tacked to the walls around them. Edgar and Martha were already distracted then by other guests in the kitchen. I watched them for a beat longer, their large smiles and their genuine laughter. George's report cards were hanging off the fridge beside Edgar. His jacket was folded over the chair in front of Martha.

His parents looked alike in that strange way old white couples sometimes did. Matt and I used to play a game called *married or siblings* sometimes when we went out and saw people like them. I felt awful thinking about it then since they were so sweet, but it was true. Honestly, I would've guessed siblings for them: with their matching light brown hair parted at the right, their wide, deep green eyes, their thin light pink lips. It was hard to tell who George took his looks from since there was very little to set them apart aside from about six inches in height.

"I love them," Emmeline declared emphatically, stuffing a large frosted cookie into her mouth. I had noticed the tray of them sitting on the smooth kitchen counter earlier, but I hadn't noticed Martha giving Emmeline one.

George smiled at that, soft and self-conscious. It hit me at once that he was sincerely worried about what we would think of them. It was a strange thing to worry about other people's impressions of your parents. Though they're not your responsibility, quite the opposite, really, it always feels personal to hear what others think of them. It always feels like being judged yourself, but with absolutely no control of it. It's possible to act your way through a different version of yourself, but not your parents. They are who they are and you simply live with it, taking the brunt of what impression that gives others of you. It's nerve racking. I knew that all too well.

"Yeah, don't apologize," I told him, because that's what I would want to hear. "They're great. They must love you a lot."

George's brows ticked down. "I should hope so. They're my parents."

Emmeline choked on a bit of her cookie, eyes large. She was looking between George and me as if I was a short fuse ready to burst and George had just thrown fire at me. I realized that I sort of felt that way, too. His words weren't meant as a dig, but they dug out a piece of me all the same.

"Well, y'know, still... Love isn't guaranteed," I replied, trying to sound comical, but after the words were out, I knew that I'd only sounded pathetic.

Emmeline swallowed thickly. I could practically see the glob of cookie making its way down her throat. George only frowned, looking at me in that way of his that made me think he saw too much. We were treading dangerous waters with this conversation, though none of us had intended for it to.

Very slowly, George asked me, "Was dinner with your birth father that bad?"

He'd never brought Jin up before. I would be shocked if he actually remembered his name. It was a bit of an unspoken rule between the three of us that Jin didn't exist unless I mentioned him first.

Averting my eyes back through the doorway to the kitchen where Edgar and Martha were chatting amicably with their guests, I shook my head. The movement was so small it was hard to tell whether it was a nod of agreement or a shake of disagreement.

"What happened?" Emmeline asked. I could tell by the urgency in her words that she'd been dying to ask me for that question days.

This was what I wanted, wasn't it? The opportunity to explain myself to them; to spill my feelings and see if they'd understand me, validate me, help me through it? In which case, it should not have been so difficult to force my next words out, but it was like I'd forgotten how to speak. Each word came out of my mouth as a foreign sound to my ears. Painstakingly slowly, I told them everything about the dinner. Or at least I hoped I did.

"He *forgot* your *birthday*?" Emmeline screeched. Her reaction set me at ease, and heartbeat slowed in my chest. It *was* ridiculous, wasn't it?

George frowned deeper, his jaw clenching. As opposed to Emmeline, who showed every emotion across her face as she felt them, George held his cards close to his chest. I never knew what to expect when he opened his mouth to speak—whether it would be a childish, but well-timed joke or a wise, philosophical piece of advice. He swung both ways wildly.

"That could have been true?" he offered at last, quite weakly. When my lips parted open in confusion, he added, "That he lost track of the days, I mean."

"Sure." I barked out a laugh. It was so unlike me that I turned to Emmeline, half expecting the sound to have come from her. But I knew that it hadn't because she wasn't smiling. She was mirroring George's frown.

"No," I added forcefully, angrily. "There's no way that's true. Jin had to have known the date to come to dinner in the first place. It was his stupid idea."

George and Emmeline shared a look. It felt like being lacerated out of the conversation; a conversation about *my* birth father, *my* life, and *my* feelings that I was waiting for their validation or rejection from.

"What?" I asked, knowing venom was slipping into my tone.

"Nothing," Emmeline squeaked. "But... Maybe George is right, you know? Why don't you give Jin the benefit of the doubt this one time?"

I felt all my shackles rise as if her words had hit a button and sent them flying. I felt them like I felt the blood pulsing through the veins underneath my skin. *Benefit of the doubt?* Was Jin someone deserving of that? Of blind, unearned trust? That didn't seem fair to me.

"Right," I mumbled, feeling rejected. Wren would understand. He *had* understood. I suppose this was my proof that Emmeline and George wouldn't be able to. "Forget it."

"Wait," George said, and then trailed off awkwardly.

He was good at sensing when something was wrong, but he seemed to be at a loss on how to fix it this time. I stared into his eyes, refusing to break the contact, and wished I could read his mind. His mouth opened and closed, opened, paused in a perfect oval shape, and then closed again.

"Forget it," I said again. "You're probably right. It was stupid of me to care."

Emmeline began to say something more, but Christmas music started blaring from the kitchen, cutting her off. Martha had plugged her phone into the speakers, but, being a technologically-challenged older person, she failed to properly adjust the volume first. George ran through the doorway with both hands over his ears to help her.

I watched him go, feeling strangely alone even with Emmeline still right there beside me. We were too different for them to understand me. The two of them had optimistic outlooks on life and they handed out trust like it was a right rather than something hard-earned. They weren't like me. They weren't like Wren.

While I was glad to have learned this sooner rather than later, it still felt like falling from a cliff I hadn't meant to climb.

Wren was all that I had. He was really all that I would ever have when it came to this. So I needed him to be closer to me, and I needed him to stay there indefinitely.

11

After the disaster that was auditions, and those equally disastrous days following, winter vacation started on the wrong foot.

Even Matt couldn't find the words to make me feel better about it all; he knew just as well as I did that Jin had screwed with my head by forgetting my birthday, that my audition was ruined because of it, that something had happened to make both of these things worse at the Washingtons holiday party, and that there was nothing either of us could do to mend any of it.

What he didn't know was that something had bloomed between Wren and me recently, but it had to be a secret, I hadn't heard from him since my birthday, and it was starting to make me crazy. Wren was easily the closest person to me since Emmeline and George wouldn't understand, *couldn't* understand, what I needed them to. Wren was the only one. And so I needed him to answer my stupid messages.

On Christmas morning, I woke to the sound of voices conversing formally in the kitchen. Jin and Julie were early.

With a loud groan, I dragged myself out of bed. The sun seemed to already have risen while I was asleep; the bright sunlight filtering through my curtains and leaving little patterns across the rug. The baseboard heater ticked along the walls in that way older unused heaters always did when suddenly sprung to life again. It smelled like burning metal. Even so, it wasn't very warm. Matt warned me of this when we first moved, saying that the rooms upstairs were rather poorly insulated. It would probably be ten degrees warmer and a hundred times more comfortable down-stairs. Still, it took all of my willpower to slide into my slippers and leave my bedroom. I even debated going back the second my feet touched the stairs and Jin and Julie's voices got clearer without a full floor between us.

Not that I had to hear them for long. Once I was within eyesight, or earshot, or whatever it was that warned them I'd come down the stairs, a hush instantly fell over the room. Their voices sucked out of the air like I was a sponge for sound.

Jin and Julie were sitting side by side on stools at the kitchen bar, sipping mugs of coffee in an attempt to act normal, as if they hadn't fallen mute in my presence. Matt had undoubtedly made those mugs of coffee while they sat there and did absolutely nothing to help. Sure, they were the guests here so I suppose nothing was necessarily expected of them, but that meant nothing to me. They were lazy guests. Moochers, even. Maybe I had a bit of pent-up frustration blurring my viewpoint at the moment, but they'd al-ways been this way. I swore it.

Behind the counter, I could see their bodies adorned in soft matching Christmas pajamas—green and red flannel bottoms and long sleeve shirts covered in graphics of reindeer, candy canes, and stockings. Their hair and their faces, on the other hand, were done up as well as they had been when we went to the pub. Slicked back hair for Jin, straightened for Julie. As usual, they appeared to be trying too hard. For what, I wasn't sure. Surely it couldn't be for *me*.

Conversely, Matt looked natural and effortless in his black sweatpants, stained white v-neck, and moccasins (which he'd stuck red and white pom poms on the tops of for Christmas). He moved rather sluggishly around the kitchen while cooking breakfast on the stove. His hair was in a state of catastrophe like I'd never seen; it appeared to be an attempt at an updo with half of it falling out and down his neck, and the other half hardly holding onto the clip he'd stuck at the crown of his head. There was dried drool on his cheeks and his eyes were hanging low, the way they always did for the first few hours after he woke from a fitful sleep. I figured I looked much the same, with minimal Christmas spirit and eyes crusted over upon unfortunately waking to this reality.

If not for Jin and Julie, it would be a perfectly normal morning, a perfectly *welcome* morning. Alas.

"Morning, 'omi," Matt said to me, yawning, slicing through the silence easily. "Merry Christmas."

He motioned me over with one hand and flipped a pancake with the other. The sound of it sizzling against the pan was music to my ears. It smelled delicious, too, but the kitchen around him had seen better days. That was the thing with Matt; he was a fantastic, yet horribly messy, cook. There were chocolate chips scattered everywhere, used measuring cups and silverware laid out across the countertops, and batter all over the place, even on Matt. He had some smudged into his eyebrow.

I shuffled across the cold tiles and dropped my head onto his shoulder, hoping there wasn't any batter or flour there.

"Merry Christmas," I said back belatedly, not feeling merry in the slightest. He patted me on the head with a deep chuckle, already seeming to know that.

Jin and Julie took this as their cue to greet me as well, chiming in with half-hearted *hellos* and *happy holidays*. I repeated them back like a broken record. I was unable to find any false cheer to feed back to them. Not even to lighten the tension between us all, and that tension was *bad*.

Jin could hardly look Matt or me in the eyes, Julie looked as if she was going to pass out from stress, and I had absolutely no intention of helping either of them. In fact, I was feeling like making it worse. I'd become spiteful. Matt may have raised me to be kind, but he did not raise me to be kind at the expense of my own feelings. In instances like that—instances like Jin and Julie forgetting my birthday—I had learned to be rather callous and unforgiving. Giving the *benefit of the doubt* was hardly part of my prerogative.

Breakfast was more than awkward because of this. Julie singlehandedly attempted to carry the conversation while Matt and Jin shot daggers at each other and I stared at my phone, awaiting a message. I was hoping that I'd hear from Wren at last. He still hadn't messaged me since my birthday when he sent me wishes and a tiny heart emoji. I knew that it had to be kept quiet between us, but our messages were private. There was no reason for him to ignore me this way, was there?

I was lonely without him to talk to. I was lonely because there was no one else with the extent of knowledge on my family situation as him. So much as I wanted to tell Emmeline and George, that plan had severely crashed and burned. It was probably better this way, anyway; better that they didn't know how messed up I was. They wouldn't get it—*me*—like Wren did.

Jin clearing his throat broke me out of my reverie.

"Are you ready for presents?" he asked me hesitantly.

What a colossal joke it was that he decided to start giving me presents on the year I decided I never wanted anything from him again. Our relationship felt like it was always one step forward, one hundred steps back, as if we were simply incapable of finding a way to walk the same pace, the same level ground. There was a divide between us too large to breach.

"From *you*?" I asked in disbelief.

He swallowed audibly and nodded. My eyebrows cocked up as I huffed through a frown.

"If we're all finished, presents would be great," Matt cut in, hardly concealing how strained his voice had gotten.

He motioned them away from the table while I cleared our plates. They escaped to the living room and sat on the floor around the tree I'd picked with Matt, cut down with Matt, decorated with Matt. The tree covered in ornaments I made as a child with Matt, bought at stores with Matt, tied strings to with Matt. My laughter at the sight was sardonic. *How dare they act so casually?*

If Jin wanted a happy family with Christmas mornings and shared gifts, how come he dropped me with Matt the second parenting got too hard? How come we didn't have that this whole time? How come none of them would admit that Matt was my real father? He raised me, hadn't he? Sometimes the word *dad* was so close to slipping off my tongue that I almost let it, but then I'd remember how many times they asserted he wasn't and I'd bite it back. I didn't want to anymore.

Matt sorted through the presents under the tree and handed them out to each of us. He must've gotten things for Jin and Julie because even they ended up with small piles. A cruel part of me wished he hadn't.

"That one is a late birthday present," Julie told me, pointing at the big black gift bag Matt was attempting to find a name on.

His head snapped up at that, looking from Julie to me with bated breath. He either thought I was going to start screaming or start crying. Regardless of how much I wanted to, I did neither. I simply took the bag with a sharp laugh and a forced *thank you*.

Opening presents together was even worse than eating breakfast together. Jin commented on absolutely everything and asserted on holding the trash bag for our wrapping paper as if taking the traditional fatherly role would make me see him as a good one or something. Julie had her phone glued to me, snapping picture after picture as I opened each present. Matt was oddly quiet, watching all of us with a frown instead of opening any of his own presents. I tried to smile at everything I received, tried to muster up acknowledgements that it was Jin who'd given it to me, tried to keep my annoyance at bay. It was exhausting.

It was hardly eleven by the time we finished, and yet I was already ready to crawl back into bed and sleep for the rest of my life.

As I organized my gifts into piles to carry up the stairs, Julie came up by my side and apologized, trying to make excuses for Jin. I wanted none of it. I cut her off before she could even finish her sentence starting with, "Naomi, it's just that…"

It's just nothing, I wanted to yell at her. Nothing was a good enough reason for this. And even if something was, I wouldn't accept it. My feelings were hurt. An explanation wouldn't take that hurt away. An explanation would only make me feel like my hurt was unreasonable. And I was sick and tired of feeling like my hurt was unreasonable.

If Emmeline and George were around to see me stomping away from her, they would be so disappointed in me. They'd probably stop wanting me around entirely. I wasn't kind hearted like they wanted me to be. If feeling what I felt—regardless of what excuses other people had for making me feel that way—meant that I was being irrational or cruel, then that was fine by me. I'd be irrational and cruel for the rest of my godforsaken life.

Buried under the covers of my bed, presents lined up by my feet where I'd been too worked up to put them away, I waited for Wren's message. It never came.

12

I only felt like I could breathe again when I got a call from the Blackwells landline on New Year's Eve, Emmeline's voice demanding I come over there for a party. Wren's voice was audible in the background, as well, listing off tidbits of information to use to convince me, as if I needed convincing at all. Either one of them could have asked me at 11:50 that night and I still would have figured out a way to be there for midnight. Emmeline may not have been able to understand me the way that Wren did, but I still loved her. She was still my best friend.

Luckily, Matt had some friends who were dying to see him so it worked out well. He dropped me off at the Blackwell household with a warning to behave myself before taking off for his own festivities. It made me feel good to see him race out of their driveway, a look of pure excitement on his face for once. He hardly saw his own friends. Not since he took me in, apparently. That on top of the fact that Jin—who was once his very best friend—had become someone he was arguing with daily, meant he was probably lonely. I could see stress lining his face those days, could hear resentment lacing his voice in the early mornings when he took calls from Jin.

He needed a break as much as I did. Maybe even more. He didn't have someone like Wren, at least not as far as I knew. This was good for both of us.

The Blackwell house that I once thought was dark and far too pristine was already a complete mess by the time I entered. It was thriving with life; people all over the place and music blaring from multiple different places at once. I hardly recognized it as the place where Wren had once wiped my silent tears.

Assorted lights hung from the ceiling in tangled masses, red solo cups and cans balanced on every surface they'd fit—from the ledge of the fireplace to the kitchen countertops to unoccupied armchairs in the living room—and the furniture had been rearranged to create a giant open space where people were dancing.

Off in the corner, at the couch and coffee table that had been squished against the wall, I found Emmeline and George playing cards with a few other people. I recognized one of them from the drama club. I weaved through the throngs of people I didn't know, people I presumed to be Wren's college buddies or coworkers, and joined them.

Emmeline hopped over the arm of the couch to tackle me with a hug the second she laid eyes on me. She had on a sparkly black dress accented with layered silver necklaces and her signature deep red lipstick. She looked beyond beautiful. It made my heart stop. Suddenly my plain light pink jumpsuit felt boring. Even George seemed to have put more effort in with his hair tucked carefully behind his ears and a silk tie around his neck.

"You look amazing," I said to Emmeline, dumbfounded.

"So do you," she replied quickly. I hoped she was right. I hadn't seen Wren yet, but it was only a matter of time.

They were playing a card game called *Bullshit* with the Hughes siblings. TJ Hughes was a junior who did drama club with us. He was also known as the best baseball player Jay High had. He was extremely popular at school so no one really understood why he was such good friends with George, who hardly spoke unless spoken to, but he was anyway. He had dark skin and short dreadlocks dyed bright red at the tips. He'd dressed up in a loose, mesh crop top that exposed his muscular body underneath. It was a miracle he was able to hide out in the corner with us shy underclassmen.

His sister, Maya Hughes, was in our grade. She wasn't in the drama club, but she shared many classes with George, Emmeline and me. Before I came along, I think she was Emmeline's closest friend. She looked a lot like her brother, but smaller and with a lot less hair. Her curls were shaved nearly all the way off. If she were anyone else, the look wouldn't work. The Hughes were as blessed with genes as the Blackwells.

I didn't know either of them very well, but playing cards together was fun nonetheless. TJ had so much energy that it was hard to keep up with him, and Maya may have been quiet, but she was ruthless. I lost to her nearly every round we played. We lost ourselves in it for hours, completely unbothered by the party full of other people around us. It was dangerously close to midnight by the time we stopped, and the only reason we did was because Wren appeared.

"Planning to play cards right through the new year?" he asked. The question was clearly directed at Emmeline, but his eyes kept coming to me. I simultaneously wanted to hop the couch to tackle him as Emmeline had to me, and sink into the cushions out of his heavy-gazed sight entirely.

Emmeline looked at the clock and nearly kicked the table over. TJ scrambled to catch the deck of cards as it toppled over.

Wren only laughed. The sound became muffled as he brought his cup to his lips, downing the rest of whatever it was in there.

"It's about time to set up the champagne," he continued. "You can each have some, if you'd like. It's only a small amount after all."

"Of course we're having some," Emmeline answered before anyone could chime in with thoughts of their own.

Wren's gaze lingered on mine. I stood at once. It shook the table yet again. TJ sighed in exasperation, picking up the scattered cards for the second time in a minute.

"Naomi?" George asked, squinting.

"I'll help," I told Wren. I had no idea what I was doing. I just missed him. I wanted to spend more time together. I wanted to slap him for not reaching out to me sooner.

"That's kind of you." He put his hand out for me to grab so I could climb over the barricade of furniture and people between us. He squeezed once before letting go.

"You don't have to do that," Emmeline cut in, glaring at her brother.

"It's the least I can do," I insisted.

Emmeline said nothing else so I followed Wren away. Instead of going to the kitchen where I assumed we would for glasses and champagne, he opened the sliding glass door and stepped outside. The chill of the night air nipped at my exposed skin instantly and I shivered. His palms on my arms were like little fires. He maneuvered us across the patio to where the lights were dull and the windows were made of tinted glass that we couldn't be seen through.

"I know I've been distant," he whispered, looking down at me, "I'm sorry."

"Why?" I asked.

His hands rubbed up and down my arms, attempting to warm them. We were close enough that I didn't need him to do that, though. His body radiated enough heat on its own.

"We need to be careful," he told me, eyes cutting to the door we'd come out from. "I can't risk being caught."

"We can't?"

"Right, *we* can't," he amended. "I had to give it a few days to make sure things were safe for us, but that doesn't mean I haven't been thinking about you."

Though I had no idea what he'd meant by the first half of that sentence, the second half made me feel warm all over. I ducked my head, hoping to hide the furious blush climbing my neck.

"Naomi," he whispered, close to my ear, "how are things at home?"

Startled, I snapped my head right back up again. He looked so worried. His teeth were digging into his bottom lip and his eyes were huge. I hadn't thought even for a second that he would be worried about my home life like that. I thought we'd get together and immediately start kissing, making up for lost time. He was better than I thought. He was practically unreal.

"Okay," I replied honestly. Matt was unhappy recently, I knew that, but there wasn't much I could do about it. Jin had messed up and upset me, and that had upset him. Everything was messy like that.

On second thought, I told Wren, "Unsteady."

One of his hands climbed up my neck and wrapped around the back of my head. He pulled me to him at once and kissed me so hard my vision spotted. He tasted sweet like citrus.

"It's gonna be alright," he said against my mouth. "I get it. I'm here for you."

I'd been waiting to hear those words for so long that they felt like an answered prayer out of his lips. I was never all that religious, but the moment still felt holy. He was everything I needed.

We kept kissing until I could hardly catch my breath. He had me up against the cold railing covered in melting snow. Explaining that away would be difficult, but I didn't care. He was caging me in, making all my other thoughts disappear in that way I knew they would. I loved that about him.

It felt like the hardest thing I'd ever done pulling away from him. We needed to pour champagne out for dozens of people, though, and only ten minutes remained. We managed it somehow, even with my shaking hands and his heavy breathing.

When the ball dropped, he was with his friends and I was with mine. Emmeline, George, TJ, Maya and I clinked our glasses together after the countdown, smiling about new beginnings. As we tipped our glasses back to drink, Emmeline and I met each other's eyes over the rims. She smiled at me so wide that some champagne fell out and down her cheeks. She let me wipe it off. At my other side, TJ whooped and tugged George into his side, placing a wet kiss on the corner of his mouth. Maya rolled her eyes good-naturedly.

When we began to settle down, I looked at Wren across the room and he winked at me. It was a good start to a new year.

13

Wren stopped distancing himself from me so much after New Year's. We texted nearly every day, he called me late at night when I couldn't sleep, and he promised to always come early when picking up Emmeline after drama club just so we'd see each other for a bit. I felt closer to him than I had to anyone else in a long while—maybe even my whole life.

Emmeline knew many things about me by then, but not everything. I hadn't told her much since the last time I'd tried to open up and her and George had shot me down. Wren, though, I told him everything. He got to know the things about me that even I was having trouble deciphering for myself. Things like Matt's mood swings and Jin's increased, unannounced visits.

Ever since my birthday, Matt and Jin's relationship was at its worst. They talked all the time, but it never sounded pleasant. Matt, who I was used to seeing shrug everything off with sarcasm and jokes, had taken to yelling and lecturing. Jin, who normally took everything Matt said with a grain of salt, seemed to be fighting back. Every time I came around, they'd cut themselves short. Matt was unwilling to tell me what exactly was going on. There was no way he was still pissed about my birthday fiasco. *I* was no longer pissed about it. But if not that, then what? I had no idea what could possibly be going on between them. Somehow it felt like my fault anyway.

Seeing Matt upset was hard. Frown lines creasing his forehead and bags tugging at his eyes were unnatural. A frown was out of place on his lips, but that didn't stop it from being there those days. He looked sad, angry, tired, guilty, and anxious all at once. I couldn't help but mirror each of these emotions back at him, unable to figure out where they were coming from or where they would go.

Moving was supposed to make our dynamic easier. And at first it had. Being physically apart from Jin and Julie was a relief, but a very short-lived one. I desperately wanted to bring that back, push them away, make everything okay again. As okay as it ever was, at least.

Wren was a lifesaver during all of this. Each time I'd start to feel like I couldn't take it any more, he'd be there to calm me down. He'd call me and talk me through it, his voice low and soothing. He never told me to give Jin the benefit of the doubt. He never made my feelings feel insignificant. He even started to share his own experiences, showing me that I wasn't entirely alone.

"Jin should've stayed away with Julie. If he had never come back to us, this wouldn't be happening," I said to him late one night.

I had my head squished underneath my pillows in an attempt to drown out Matt's voice hissing over the phone at Jin through the walls. I couldn't make out the full conversation, but I could hear the curses thrown around. Matt was angrier than usual that night, throwing around words I'd never heard him throw at any-one before.

"No, it wouldn't," Wren replied steadily, quietly, "but you would never have known him, either."

"Good," I snapped, but I knew I didn't mean it. Wren knew I didn't mean it, too.

"Can I tell you something, Naomi?"

I grunted in agreement, staring at his contact flashing underneath the pillow beside my head. It was 10:47 on a school night.

"My dad left us for a while, too," he admitted.

My breath caught in my throat. Emmeline had told me that their father was gone often on business trips, making Wren the main guardian in her life, but she never said he'd *left*.

"When I was around your age, my mom died. Dad didn't handle it well. He threw himself into his work, taking every possible case he could just to stay away from home. It was too hard to be there, I guess. Sometimes he'd be on trips for days, even weeks, on end. Emmeline and I were left on our own. We were just kids."

"Wren—"

"But," he cut me off before I could babble on with apologies and attempted comfort, "he came back. Sure, he still travels and works far too much, but he came back. If he hadn't, I never would've become who I am today. He taught me a lot, whether he meant to or not. I wouldn't trade that for anything, no matter how much it sucked as it happened."

After a long pause, I mumbled, "That doesn't seem fair."

"It isn't." His empty chuckle vibrated through me. "That's life, Naomi. You'll understand that when you get older."

The room was suddenly silent all around me. Matt must have finished his nightly argument with Jin. I quickly thanked Wren for being there and hung up just in time for Matt to knock on my door.

I took my head out from under my pillows and laid on them correctly. I said nothing in response, but I watched the doorway. I could see Matt's shadow shifting back and forth on the other side.

"I know you're awake," Matt's voice filtered through the cracks. It was weak and low.

"I'll go to sleep now," I responded, just loud enough for him to hear.

His head thudded against the door with a sigh. The hinges creaked from his weight pressing against it. After a couple beats of silence, he spoke once more, even quieter than before.

"I'm sorry, peanut."

I listened to his footsteps as he padded down the hallway into his own bedroom. Once I was certain his door was shut and I was alone, I let the tears fall.

It had been ages since he'd called me that nickname. He used to call me that a lot when I was younger because I was always so short and skinny. Since my growth spurt in middle school, he stopped using it so much. Hearing it then made me feel torn apart, as if I was abruptly young, small, and vulnerable again.

My tears came calm, but steady. They fell until I was fast asleep.

14

Matt was awkward with me the following day. He kept on apologizing, but he refused to elaborate on what was actually going on. He asserted that it was nothing I should worry about. That obviously couldn't stop me from worrying anyway. How could I not when he was sleeping so little and yelling so much? Something was seriously off. I wouldn't accept his apologies without some sort of clarification, but he still wouldn't budge.

"Our arguments aren't your fault or concern," he told me on the drive to school that morning. His fingers were ghostly white around the steering wheel.

"But what are you even arguing about?" I was raising my voice by then, too. It was infuriating to feel so purposefully left out.

"I said it's not your concern," he snapped, then instantly looked remorseful about it.

For the remaining ten minutes of the drive, neither of us said a thing. I slammed the door when I got out and stormed off to my classes without a goodbye. We didn't see each other again for the rest of the school day.

For the cherry on top, the cast list for *Alice in Wonderland* got posted. It was the very end of the school day when Matt came out of his office with the paper. He taped it to the wall with a grimace, then went right back into his office again, the door firmly shut behind him.

Exactly as expected, I didn't get the Queen of Hearts. Carla did. I didn't even get the role as her understudy. I got the featured role of the Cheshire Cat instead. I haven't the slightest idea why that's what I ended up with. I dare say I would have preferred nothing. The only thing that role was better than was the Mock Turtle.

Emmeline and George were both ecstatic, though, because they got the roles they wanted: Alice and the March Hare. I tried to be happy for them, but I was upset that I couldn't have gotten something better. I was upset that we would hardly be able to act together at all. My lines were so scarce.

"It's okay," Emmeline whispered to me, tugging on my sleeve to pry me away from the cast list taped to the wall.

We huddled up against the lockers nearby that no one ever used because they were rusted, oddly shaped, and too small for the average backpack. The three of us always huddled. It was as if we were always sharing secrets that no one else was in on. It was ironic since I'd only ever shared one secret with them, and it had explosively backfired.

"You wanted me to be the Queen of Hearts," I told her, ashamed that I couldn't deliver.

"Cheshire Cat is cooler anyway." George shrugged. I cracked a tiny smile. I knew this comment wasn't him just trying to make me feel better; he loved wacky roles, so he sincerely believed that to be true.

"Yeah!" Emmeline agreed eagerly. *She* was just trying to make me feel better. For some reason, I didn't really mind.

The rest of the drama club members were slowly filtering out of classrooms and coming down the hallway to read the cast list, as well. TJ reached it first with a bunch of his baseball buddies. When he read it, he jumped up and down with joy, overly pleased at his role as King of Hearts even though he and Carla could hardly be in the same room together for five minutes without bickering. His friends patted him on the back and offered confused congratulations as they sauntered off again.

Carla came next. I jerked backwards into the lockers behind me, hiding like a coward. I didn't want to see her smug look when she noted my role versus her own. Emmeline and George seemed to know exactly what was happening as they both repositioned themselves to block her from my view. I hoped this would block me from her view, as well. As luck would have it, it did not.

"Better luck next time." The words she said were nice, but the way she said them was not.

She'd shoved her way between George and Emmeline to stand in front of me. She legitimately looked down on me. As always, Carla looked beautiful in the most cruel way. Her long hair was pinned back and her angled eyes were layered with makeup. Her lips were curled into a patronizing smirk and her hands were placed over her hips.

"Congratulations, Carla," I said, because what else was I supposed to say when she was right there in front of me like that?

"I don't need congratulations from the likes of you," she retorted.

I don't know what I ever did to make her hate me so much.

"Why are you even over here then?" Emmeline asked sharply. She took a step closer to me protectively.

A small crowd of people was gathered around the cast list still, but we were rapidly gaining their attention. We were causing a scene in the most ridiculously cliche way ever.

"Emmeline," Carla drawled, "you got the lead role, didn't you? You have the honors of playing Alice herself?"

Emmeline nodded slowly. People inched closer to us, watching the exchange like passersby watch the aftermath of car accidents.

"That's nepotism at its finest." Her eyes rolled back so far that all I could see was the whites of them.

"Excuse me?" Emmeline asked.

George shifted on his feet uncomfortably. I wasn't sure what was going on, but he seemed to have an idea. I tried to catch his eyes, but he'd let his hair fall in front of them again. My heart hammered in my chest when Carla took another small step closer to Emmeline and me.

"Come on." She bent over so that her eyes were level with mine. Her smile was cruel. "We all know Emmeline here only got cast as the lead because of Mr. Molina."

I couldn't help the gasp that came out of my mouth. A satisfied look crossed over Carla's face in response.

"That doesn't even make sense," Emmeline answered plainly. "Mr. Molina isn't *my* dad."

Carla laughed outright and stood up straight again. Some of her friends had shown up to take place on either side of her. Their relationships always unsettled me; it seemed like she was the domineering leader and they were nothing but her mindless minions.

"Well he isn't really Naomi's dad either, but that doesn't stop the favoritism, now does it?"

I felt rooted to the spot, frozen from the middle of my gut outward. Not only because she had said something so harsh, but because I couldn't get my mouth to move to argue against it. Worse than that, while I floundered pathetically, I noticed Matt's office door was open and he was right there in the hallway, eyes glued to the crowd we'd attracted. He looked sick with how pale his skin had gone.

One by one, everyone around me followed my line of sight to him. One by one, their voices quieted until the entire area was eerily still.

What was Matt thinking right then? What were any of them thinking? Was I the only one who felt like my world had been tipped on its axis? Was I the only one who disagreed with what Carla had claimed?

Matt *was* my father! I'd fought it for long enough. He was my father and pretending like he wasn't was draining me.

"Break it up," Matt ordered, strict but clearly upset.

His office door slammed shut behind him, shaking the ground beneath us. People dispersed immediately after. Even Carla had nothing left to say before she was racing off.

I waited there for him for half an hour before giving up and going home with Emmeline.

15

Wren was more than shocked to see me in his kitchen that night when he came home from work. He was in a deep red collared shirt and black slacks, as effortlessly attractive as always. He froze in the doorway the second he noticed he wasn't alone. Emmeline and I were there, attempting to cook dinner, but not faring very well.

"Welcome home my dearest big brother," Emmeline called out, grinning.

She was standing in the corner of their kitchen with vegetables all around her on the countertop. She couldn't find the exact cutting board that she wanted so she'd been aimlessly waving around a knife for about fifteen minutes by then. I was standing on a stool, digging around in the cabinets above the stove in hopes of finding that cutting board so she'd stop. Luck was not on my side yet, as I'd found nothing more than travel mugs and mismatched tupperware.

"Should I even ask?" Wren's eyes flickered from me to Emmeline repeatedly.

I said, "No" at the same time that Emmeline delved into explaining the entire situation in depth, starting with why I was on a stool to why I was there at all.

Wren smiled at his sister's antics, but frowned a bit at me. He now knew about Carla causing me problems on top of whatever was happening between Matt and Jin, Matt and me, Jin and me, and all three of us together. I must've seemed like such a train wreck to him.

He ambled further into the kitchen, kicking off his shoes between steps. He took the knife from Emmeline and slid it back into the block it came from. Then when he reached me, he wrapped his arms around my waist and brought me down off the stool. I yelped the second he touched me, shocked that he'd even think of doing that in front of Emmeline. Though she didn't seem to think anything of it. She was too busy pouting at her knife-less hands.

"Does he know you're here?" Wren asked me rather pointedly.

"I texted him," I mumbled.

I had texted Matt once when we left school, saying I was going to Emmeline's since he didn't feel like coming out to bring me home himself. I was angry and anxious so the message wasn't my kindest. Since then, my phone had buzzed with roughly a thousand responses from Matt, but I hadn't checked a single one of them.

He had the worst timing deciding to call me right then after I said that to Wren. I stared at his contact while it rang, not sure what to do.

"Take the call," Wren said. His gaze burned into mine. "Tell him you're staying the night."

So I did. Matt couldn't even utter a greeting before I was telling him I was going to stay at the Blackwell's.

Emmeline was cheering about slumber parties while I did. Somehow she'd gotten the knife back between her hands. Wren wrestled it away, telling her to shut up and go away so he could cook dinner instead. I decided to excuse myself to another room.

They were loud and Matt still hadn't said a thing. I could hear him breathing, though, so I knew he was there.

"If that's what you want," he answered at last.

"It is."

"Alright." His voice was rough around the edges. "I'll pick you up tomorrow morning."

I pictured Matt's face in the hallway earlier, how he was as white as a sheet with his eyebrows low and pulled together and his lips parted. I pictured the way it all twitched when he looked at me, how he slammed his door shut at the silence of the hallway.

"Uhm, about earlier," I began, not entirely sure what I even wanted to say. "At school…"

"Don't. Please. It's fine." He sounded exhausted. "Is Carla always that way towards you?"

"Yeah."

"I'll do something about it," he decided. "I'm sorry, Naomi. For everything going on recently. I've been a real shit old man. I'll make it up to you."

My throat was itchy and red-hot. The skin around my eyes felt too tight. I put my hand over my throat and lightly squeezed, trying to force the feeling away. When that didn't work, I rubbed the pads of my fingers under my eyes, trying to loosen the skin up. That failed too.

"I just want to know what's going on," I whispered to him.

"I know." He truly did sound like he regretted whatever it was he was hiding. "Your father and I have had some disagreements lately, that's all. None of it has to do with you. Don't worry."

I let that hang in the air for a while. I hated when he referred to Jin as my father. He knew I didn't call him that, or even think of him as that.

"Carla was wrong, y'know," I told him, because I was tired of not telling him. If he could say he was my old man, then I could tell him that I didn't think the same way as those kids at school: that I didn't think *he wasn't really my dad.*

I hung up right after, unable to listen to anything that came after the sharp intake of his breath. He didn't call or text again. Giving space was a strong suit of his, though I think that came from a place of uncertainty rather than a place of respect. Whatever it was, I appreciated it then.

Wren made chili for dinner. We ate it together around their giant dining room table. I sat beside Emmeline and across from Wren. He wrapped his ankles around mine beneath the table. It sent a thrill throughout my entire body. His signature smirk was there even while he ate. It made me feel giddy. I focused on it so that my thoughts wouldn't go drifting anywhere else again.

Wren kissed me goodnight in the hallway upstairs. To our left, Emmeline was behind the closed door of the bathroom. He held onto me and didn't stop until we heard the door knob moving. Wren slinked back into his bedroom at the same time Emmeline came out of the bathroom. I had the sudden urge to laugh, or to heave out the breath that Wren had stolen from me, but either of those things would have raised flags with Emmeline. So I bit down on my tongue so hard I tasted blood.

Before we fell asleep side by side in her queen bed covered in mismatching blankets and pillows, Emmeline linked her fingers through mine and held. Hardly aloud, she whispered that she was there for me. I refused to think about how this made my chest ache, how it made me want to cry again, because I was too confused about why that was.

Gripping her hand tighter, I fell asleep feeling warm.

16

Jin and Julie came over early in February for our first official Game Night since Matt and I moved. Matt put it off for as long as possible using the excuse of *"The house is still a mess, we haven't finished unpacking."* It finally stopped working, so then they came over.

Jin and Matt seemed to be at some sort of understanding by then. To my knowledge, they hadn't argued for days. And if they were willing to spend the night in the same building playing games together, something must have changed. Based on the awkward greetings they gave each other at the door, and the intense stare Matt gave Julie as she took off her coat to hang on our rack, it was more of a stand still than it was a reconciliation. They must've tired themselves of fighting so much.

Jin and Julie both seemed different from the last time I'd seen them. Julie wasn't all dolled up in a dress and a full face of make-up, but rather relaxed in a loose sweater and jeans. She was even wearing sneakers instead of her usual fancy boots or heels. Jin had changed his look some, too. Instead of having his hair gelled back in that horrible way he tended to do it, it was down naturally. There was a slight wave to it as it fell around his ears, much the same as my own.

They'd brought with them a bag of drinks and snacks; soda and iced tea in cans, a variety of flavored chips, a bunch of candy, and a container of store-bought cookies. Normally they brought nothing. They had a bad habit of simply taking from Matt whenever they came around. I couldn't tell whether this now was an attempt to mend whatever issue Matt had with Jin or if it was an attempt to yet again buy my affection. Either way, I found I didn't care. I wasn't upset at all because for once, they were acting like normal people.

They even picked the games to play instead of requiring me to choose every single time. In the past, it was my job to decide which games to play and for how long because they were obsessively focused on making sure I had fun. Realistically, it just made me overtly aware that they were trying to force something that wasn't there between us. This time was different. This time was actually kind of nice.

I chose to play Wii Sports first, as I usually did, and absolutely destroyed them at bowling. From there, Matt decided we should play Mario Kart. Jin won six rounds in a row, leaving all of us absolutely floored. Matt declared war and they bickered like a bunch of teenagers over whether cheating in the game was possible or not. They were laughing so much. It was as if the past month and a half hadn't happened at all. I got a glimpse of the best friends that they once were, the ones Matt had told me about, but I'd never fully believed. I could see it then; the way they'd gotten along before I was in the picture.

From there on, I let myself pretend that nothing had happened, as well. This was the sort of family game night I could get used to.

We finished the night with the board game *Life*, as per Julie's request. Matt hoarded all of his money, Jin got the worst house and job possible—which I found especially funny, even if he and I were on good terms at the moment—I didn't move more than three spaces every turn, and Julie was on her fourth child. Each time she landed on the space, she'd grab her stomach as if it was real life with a tiny smile. Jin would then kiss the top of her head. I'd look away politely and Matt would clench his jaw, as if annoyed by it.

All in all, it was a pleasant night.

So pleasant, in fact, that when Jin proposed I spend the night over at their place the following weekend, I didn't hesitate before replying, "Sure."

Matt could have died from shock. His filter disappeared entirely after that while he sputtered about with *what* and *why* and *are you really, really sure?* Each time I'd just nod, mumbling nonsense about how it might be good and how I'd be fine. What I always wanted for my life was something a little less dysfunctional than what I was given. I loved Matt, and the life he gave me had been a good one thus far, but it was still complicated. I wanted something simple, something like my birth father either caring about me all the way or not at all. So if Jin was finally willing to be there as my guardian, if even for just a night, who was I to turn that down?

"It's about time anyway," I said to them, watching as Matt's expression turned sour and Jin's turned sad.

Julie was suspiciously quiet throughout the whole exchange. She held onto Jin's hand in her lap, clearly showing support for the idea, but she never said a thing. Her lips remained firmly shut in a line so tight they were losing their natural pink color. Rather than focusing her attention on Jin or me as we continued to speak slowly about the details, she locked her gaze onto Matt, eyes pleading for something I couldn't comprehend. If she wanted his blessing or something, I'm afraid she'd never get it. Matt and Julie got along decently, but I could see in the way that he looked at her that he wished she were someone else... That he wished she were my birth mother. Perhaps that wasn't fair to her, but such was life.

"Naomi," Matt lowered his head towards me and whispered, though I'm sure Jin and Julie could hear our every word anyway, "Are you positive about this?"

He asked in a way that implied I *shouldn't* have been positive about it. He asked as if begging me to say no. I could understand his confusion, but not his persistence in getting me to change my mind.

"Yeah," I affirmed. "It's fine. I'd like to go."

Matt opened his mouth, most likely to ask a variation of the same question yet again, then seemed to think better of it. He nodded once at me, then once at Jin. He wouldn't meet any of our eyes. His protective mode seemed to have kicked in again.

"It's fine," I assured him again, begging the twitch in his lips not to form into a frown. It did anyway.

Jin and Julie left on that note. We parted with plans to see each other again in a week.

When I called Wren that night to tell him the news, he seemed about as happy about it as Matt did. I wondered what either of them would do if they knew this similarity. I wondered what it was that made it so hard for them to just be happy for me. I knew trusting Jin and Julie so easily was fairly dumb, but wanting to build a real relationship wasn't, right? I wished I knew why the two most important men in my life couldn't see that.

17

Carla kept to herself during our drama club meeting the following week. No snarky comments, no taunts, no side eyes or scoffs, even. She kept away from George, Emmeline and me in complete and utter silence. Even her interactions with Matt and the other drama club members were short-lived. She was suddenly a new person.

I knew Matt had yet to "do something about" the way she acted towards me, so it was off putting to see her so docile. It was almost as if she felt bad about the other day. Thinking so made me angry. She should've felt bad, yes, but I didn't want her acting like she was the one hurt by it. She had no right to seem so changed, so affected, by Matt overhearing everything said around that stupid cast list. She was the problem. I wasn't going to fall for her calm before the storm. *I wasn't.*

Most of our time then was spent rehearsing for the big play. We were taking it scene by scene, going over lines and movements until they became second nature. Matt took it easy on no one. He taught with vigor, not afraid to throw in criticism whenever something felt off—which was more often than not. I was afraid he'd lose his voice from how often he shouted out "Cut!" and then proceeded to ramble loudly about the *lackluster performances* we were giving. It didn't help that he was back to being anxious and moody all the time like he had been when he and Jin were fighting daily.

He might have been especially harsh on Carla that afternoon, too, but no one came to her defense. She wasn't at her best, of course. Not with the guilt laced beneath her perfect facial features. It had made her thin eyebrows, which normally arched perfectly above her bright eyes, go low and bunchy. Her lips were pursed, but washed out within her skin without their normal lipstick. Her hair was tied back into a loose, low pony, blonde wisps flowing out every which way like she hadn't tried at all. Not only was she acting like a different person, she practically looked like one, too.

Matt called rehearsal early due to the course it was taking. No one had their heads or hearts in it—not even him. It was getting us nowhere to run lines or talk stage directions in such conditions.

"Mr. Molina." Carla sounded unsure of herself as she followed Matt across the dusty stage to where he'd dropped his bag and jacket earlier. "I wanted to apologize."

Matt dropped into a crouching position with a heavy sigh. Doing that always made his long limbs look ridiculous, but he found it comfortable for whatever reason. He scrubbed his hands over his face and pushed back the loose bits of his hair from his forehead. His bun was coming undone.

"What could I possibly need an apology from you for?" he asked, exasperated but not unkind.

I tried to take a step closer to them so I could hear better, but someone's hand on my shoulder kept me in place. I turned to see TJ. He was watching them with a frown as well. His eyes met mine for half a second and it spoke all the words he didn't say out loud: *don't, it's too risky, it's not worth it, everything will be fine, just stay out of it.* I felt my shoulders fall and listened to those unspoken commands. His hand remained on my shoulder anyway.

"Uh, well, the other day—" Carla had never stuttered like that before. She was tugging at her ponytail, running the pads of her thumbs over the hairs in a calming manner. "I didn't know you were there... I'm so sorry, Mr. Molina."

Matt sat back on his bottom, a laugh slipping past his lips. It was not his usual, pleasant laugh. It was the laugh he'd sometimes allow to burst out when Jin called and said something on the other side of the line that I could never make out. It meant that nothing was funny at all.

"Whether I was there or not has nothing to do with what you said," Matt said coldly.

"Right, of course," she rushed to agree. "It's just that... I feel so awful you heard such cruel things from me."

Matt softened for a split second. I almost thought he was going to let her go without another word. But then he steeled himself and said, "You should. You should feel awful for being cruel, no matter who hears it or not."

Carla jolted away from him like she'd been slapped. I felt that way, too. I'm sure Matt could be at risk of losing his job for speaking to her like that. TJ's hand pressed harder into my shoulder, sensing my internal panic.

Carla muttered out another apology, sounding close to tears. Matt jumped to his feet and stopped her before she could run away. He looked terribly guilty himself.

"That was wrong of me to say," he told her sincerely, "I apologize for allowing my personal feelings to get the better of me."

Carla's eyes shook with unshed tears. "It's okay."

"It's not." He laced his fingers together in front of his chest. They moved with him as he took a deep breath. "I appreciate you apologizing to me, Carla. Thank you. I recommend you do the same to everyone else involved."

"Yes, sir," Carla replied, sounding the slightest bit more like herself.

"Ew, don't call me sir," Matt responded at once, drawing a laugh from Carla. His seriousness disappeared just like that. "That makes me sound so old. Do I look that old to you?"

She went on laughing, suddenly at ease again. Matt joined in, looking somewhat normal himself. I yanked TJ's hand off of my shoulder and stomped down the steps to where Emmeline was sitting in the front row beside Wren. They had waited for me.

Wren offered me a lazy smile, eyes low and intense. It took all of my will power not to jump into his lap and kiss him right there. I had him drive me home even though I was perfectly capable of getting there with Matt like usual. Neither one of them questioned me on it.

18

"Things still unsteady?" Wren asked me quietly.

Instead of dropping me off and driving away, he had insisted on walking me inside. Since Emmeline desperately needed to use the bathroom anyway, I let them both in for a while. Wren and I then stood a foot or so inside the doorway, feet split between the tiles of the kitchen and the carpet of the living room. He took my hands between his the second we were alone. They weren't soft or small like Emmeline's had been. They didn't fit snugly in the same way either. They were giant and calloused, tight and all-encompassing.

"That's one way of putting it," I responded, shutting my eyes.

His hands were tough but if I shut my eyes, he smelled the same as Emmeline; clean and earthy like pine and sandalwood soaps. It helped me bring myself back to the way I'd felt so safe in their house that night, beside her in her bedroom while we slept everything away for a while.

"Are you sure staying with Jin and Julie this weekend is a good idea?"

I sucked in a deep breath through my nose and slowly blew it out of my mouth. I was getting sick of this same conversation over and over. If it wasn't Matt asking, it was Wren. If it wasn't Wren asking, it was Matt. Neither of them would let it go. It was like they *wanted* my relationship with Jin to remain bad.

"It's fine," I snapped, tearing my hands from his.

"Naomi." He reached for me again, but stopped as soon as we heard the water pipes trill all around us. When the bathroom on the bottom floor of the house was used, the pipes would sound everywhere beneath the walls. It was a perfect warning to us both that Emmeline was still there, about to join us again.

Quickly, he whispered, "Don't be upset. I just don't want you getting hurt if it isn't what you expect. I'm looking out for you, you know I am. I know you best."

"I know," I assured him. "I won't."

I pressed onto my toes and kissed his cheek. He turned to catch my lips once before pulling away. Emmeline skipped into the room and joined us moments later.

She smiled brightly at me before they left. Her lipstick had faded throughout the day, leaving her lips a muted pink rather than the usual deep red. It was always nice to see her face without the makeup, just the same as it was nice to see her hair without the space buns. I liked seeing her without all the effort she put in. None of it was necessary. She was a Blackwell; a person blessed with innate beauty and charm, a person I felt drawn to no matter what else was happening.

Miserably, I wished I could tell her everything. I wanted to lock us in her bedroom together, buried underneath the covers with our hands clasped, and tell her absolutely everything about myself—including the thing I had going with Wren, the confusion I had about Jin and Julie, and the person I thought of as my only true parent, Matt. I wanted to delve into the good and the bad, the rotten and the clean, the wrong and the right.

I needed someone to see me, every part of me, and be okay with having it out there. I knew that Emmeline was the closest person I had to do that with. She was the best option I'd ever get for sharing everything without fear. And yet I couldn't. Because it had failed once before, I'd already come to terms with Wren being my person instead.

It's just that Wren *was* one of my secrets. And it felt so bad to keep him one. I wanted him to take me on dates, meet my family as my boyfriend, and introduce me to all of his friends. I wanted him to hold my hand on the street, hug me when he said goodbye, and kiss me in public. I wanted to scream about us off the rooftops to let everyone know. I didn't want to hide forever. I didn't want to hide it *now*.

Wren scolded me for even entertaining such a desire. He said it was foolish.

"We don't need anyone to know about us," he'd whispered to me, hands around my waist. "It's no one else's business what we do."

"But hiding feels wrong," I had answered, dodging his lips to keep talking. Sometimes it was really hard just to talk to him. "It feels like I'm lying to Matt and my friends."

"Naomi." His hands came up, one under my chin and the other around the back of my neck, holding me in place to look at him. "*It's no one else's business.* You like what we have, don't you?"

"I do," I whispered, because I liked him and I liked how he made me feel, even if I didn't always like everything else. "Sorry."

"It's fine," he told me dismissively, his entire body relaxing, "but promise this is our secret. It won't be good if it isn't."

"Promise."

I never brought it up to him again. I kept my promise. No matter how much I wanted to break it just for Emmeline. I kept my promise.

SCENE III.

"Who am I then? Tell me that first, and then, if I like being that person, I'll come up; if not, I'll stay down here till I'm someone else."

— Lewis Carroll, *Alice's Adventures in Wonderland / Through the Looking-Glass*

19

As Matt drove me to Jin and Julie's place that weekend, he held onto the steering wheel so tightly that his knuckles were past the stage of being white and had turned red instead. He clearly wanted to ask me if I was sure about it for the one millionth time, but thankfully he kept his mouth shut. I couldn't handle hearing the question even one more time.

"If you're worried I'll get my feelings hurt," I said to him, thinking of Wren telling me, *I just don't want you to get hurt if it isn't what you expect,* "then don't. I'll be fine."

Matt's response was nothing like what I expected. He wouldn't look at me, wouldn't say a word out loud, wouldn't even grunt an affirmative to let me know he'd heard me at all. Instead his teeth ground in the back of his mouth loudly and his jaw clenched so hard that I saw the veins pop out in his neck. My words were meant to soothe his worries, not worsen them, and yet they did just that.

I continued talking, wanting to get through to him more than anything that this was fine, it was good even, "I know not to get used to this, alright? I know how Jin is. I won't get upset when nothing major changes. I know what I'm getting myself into."

Matt whispered something to himself that sounded suspiciously like, "No you don't."

The rest of the car ride was uncomfortably quiet after that. In an attempt to keep my mind busy, I sent a couple text messages to Wren. I was hoping for some reassurance, but he didn't respond. The messages were not even read. He must've been working. I then sent one to Emmeline, brief and vague, and she replied within seconds. She sent me pictures of her bedroom which she was apparently attempting to clean after I told her it was a disaster last sleepover. I smiled at the screen.

I wanted to tell her everything so badly. I even got myself to type out a long message admitting everything I'd been hiding, but I couldn't bring myself to hit send in the end.

Promise, I'd told Wren. *Promise.*

Besides, she wouldn't understand. I knew that. I *knew* that.

Matt didn't come in to say hello to Jin or Julie. He pulled into their driveway and gave me an awkward goodbye before speeding off again. Once it was set in stone that I'd be staying with Jin for the weekend, Matt took his friends up on an offer to go on a mini vacation, so he was then on his way there. They were staying at a casino, but not to gamble. They planned on playing virtual reality sports games and drinking overpriced beer all night. I expected Matt to look much happier as he left to do that. Instead he looked more like he was on his way to a funeral.

Julie opened the door shortly after I knocked. She was wrapped up in a giant fuzzy blanket with a jar of peanut butter and a spoon. She looked like she was getting sick.

"No Matt?" she asked, shifting her weight from foot to foot to look around behind me.

"No, he's in a rush," I lied, stepping through the doorway. "He says hello though."

Julie didn't seem to believe me, but that was fine. It's not like the truth was any better of an answer seeing as I didn't know the reasoning for why Matt was acting the way he was.

Behind Julie, Jin was waiting for me with a big smile. He looked so small standing in the center of their living room, which was large and spacious like the Blackwell's. It had a big L-shaped leather couch and a plasma screen television mounted on the wall in front of it. Two large windows sat on either side of the television, thick dark curtains hanging open around them. The glass was so clean it hardly looked like it was there at all, just like the ones at the Washington's house. The floors were light hardwood with rectangular accent carpets scattered across them. It was open and beautifully decorated with minimal knick knacks on the few tables.

I had never spent much more than a few minutes inside of their house before so I had never gotten the time to look around at everything and take it in. It was so different from the messy, lively place I shared with Matt. It was quiet and homey in that stereotypical way. It felt a bit unreal because of that. There was hardly any sign of life; no picture frames on the walls, only strange paintings, no mail on the counters, only jars of flour and sugar, no shoes or jackets out of place, only organized coat racks and pristine welcome mats.

It was warm, too, a bit uncomfortably so. I couldn't fathom how Julie was wrapped up in a blanket. I wanted to change into shorts and drink a glass of ice water. It smelled nice, though. Lavender and tea tree oil and the remnants of a recent meal. It was relaxing. The air felt so clear.

"Let me show you to your room," Jin piped up, fiddling with the wedding band on his thick finger.

I followed him across the house and up the spiraling staircase to the spare bedroom that would be mine for a night. When he opened the door, I was hit at once with blinding light and bright colors. The windows were situated in the perfect place along the wall to receive the sharp beams of sunlight as the sun set. On top of that, the walls themselves were painted a ridiculously hot pink.

This room wasn't furnished and decorated like the others in the house. There was a haphazardly placed twin bed for me and that was about it. The rest of the space was occupied with large boxes, paint cans, and loose tools from the open toolbox in the corner.

"Sorry for the mess," he told me, throwing a spare blanket over one of the larger boxes. "We're in the process of renovating this one."

"This is quite the renovation for a guest room," I pondered, stepping over tools to plop myself on the unkempt bed.

Jin's laugh in response to that was airy and awkward. I looked at him through the hair falling over my eyes. He was leaning against that box he'd thrown a blanket over. He was looking at me, but his eyes were glazed over as if he wasn't really seeing me at all. The air quickly grew uncomfortable around us.

My phone pinged multiple times in a row, snapping us both up. I sheepishly reached out to silence it, but stopped when I saw that it was Wren's contact name. I hovered my hand over the screen, trying to quell my anticipation while Jin watched so he wouldn't ask who it was. I made no further move.

He knew how to take a hint, at least. He cleared his throat and backed out of the room to leave me be. As he did, he said, "Make yourself comfortable and come down when you're ready."

I swiped open my messages with Wren instantly.

Wren
5:48 p.m.
Hey baby girl
sorry I missed your messages earlier. I was with my dad... He's home for once.
Are you alright? Is Matt still upset?

The tension released from my shoulders and I blew out a shaky breath. I wished Wren could be there with me to get through this weekend together. Even his presence over the phone through little text bubbles was calming.

Me
5:50 p.m.
Yeah, Matt was acting weird
Jin's acting sort of weird too
I'm alright, though. I miss you.

Wren
5:55 p.m.
Call me if you need anything
I've been missing you too ;)

Feeling significantly better after that tiny bit of interaction with Wren, I changed into my pajamas and joined Jin and Julie down-stairs.

They were waiting patiently in the living room for me. There was a movie pulled up on the plasma screen and snacks all over the coffee table. It felt a bit like they were impersonating Matt, seeing as movies and junk food were his thing, but I couldn't blame them. It's not like I would've enjoyed their protein shakes and classical music. At least they were trying. They were trying for *me*.

I wiggled myself into the space between them on the couch and let myself think—just for a moment—of what it would be like to have this all the time. So much as I told myself I wouldn't get the wrong idea, wouldn't get attached, wouldn't get my feelings hurt, I was already well on my way all of those things.

20

Not even halfway through the movie, we paused it to have some real dinner. All the snacks—including the full jar of peanut butter with a spoon—weren't cutting it for Julie apparently. So she dragged both Jin and me out to the kitchen and had us sit at the table while she whipped up some fried rice and tofu.

We didn't say much to each other as we waited for her, but the silence wasn't uncomfortable any longer. It was a lot like the silence between Matt and me in the mornings before we've fully woken up—calm and familiar. I watched Jin as he watched Julie. He had a fond smile over his lips, half-covered by the glass of water held between his hands. Seeing him in a natural space like this brought him down from someone faraway, someone I couldn't identify with no matter how hard I tried, to someone I could recognize, someone I could admit was family. It was all too easy to forget everything in the past and just be there. I was briefly at ease.

But feeling that way was quickly followed by guilt. Guilt for giving into them so easily, guilt for not giving into them sooner, guilt for relating Jin to Matt for even a second, guilt for thinking about what life could be like if Jin had kept me in the first place, guilt for wondering if he'd change his mind now. I had to face the fact that it was impossible for anything to be easy now. No matter what Jin and Julie did. No matter what Matt did. No matter what *I* did.

Things were *uneasy*, I'd told Wren. Even as Julie served us steaming plates and we ate together amicably, it was uneasy. I was a fool for pretending otherwise, even if it had only been for a minute.

"How is it?" Julie asked me, squinting at the scowl across my lips.

I shoved a huge forkful of the food into my mouth. It was surprisingly good. The flavors were strong and the ratio of vegetables to rice was perfect. She'd even cooked the tofu in my favorite way, where the inside was soft but the outside was golden and crispy. I chewed it quickly, despite the heat burning my tongue and throat.

"Good," I replied, blowing air through my lips to cool my mouth off. "Very good."

She smiled in relief and resumed eating her own serving, which was twice the size of mine. She scarfed it down like it was all going to grow legs and walk away or something. Jin rubbed her shoulder affectionately, drawing her attention to him so she'd slow down.

She noticed me watching her and laughed in that same airy way Jin had upstairs a few hours earlier. Tense, forced, and nervous.

"I guess I was hungrier than I thought." The words sounded like they were being dragged out of her.

"I can see that," I mumbled, eyes cutting to Jin and his plate half the size of hers. "You do have double the servings."

Based on their reactions, something was wrong with that statement. I suppose it was rather rude of me to so bluntly comment on her eating habits like that, but I didn't think it was bad enough to get the entire pitcher of water knocked over into my lap. Julie had jolted, her knees knocking underneath the table, and everything on top was jostled. The pitcher tipped onto its side and emptied all over me in seconds. The water was room temperature, at least, so it was only uncomfortable because it startled me, not because it was freezing.

"My goodness." Julie hopped to her feet, rushing to me with loose tablecloths. "I am so sorry!"

I stood as well, watching as a puddle of water formed beneath my feet. Jin and Julie both attempted to sop it up off the table and floor. The tablecloths Julie had given me did nothing for the way my pants were soaked through. I felt waterlogged and must have looked like I'd peed myself.

"I'm just gonna go change," I announced, slipping past the two of them to the staircase.

There was water in my socks, too. It squelched against the floorboards as I walked to the guest room. I tore them off of my feet in disgust and tossed them at my bag the second I stepped through the doorway. I could hear Jin and Julie talking downstairs, voices clearly distraught but hushed in an attempt not to reach me.

How had things gone from so peaceful to so awkward in the span of thirty seconds? Could I truly not control my mouth for one night? Julie was probably mortified and I hadn't even thought before speaking. I had a horrid habit of doing that. Most times it was a response to feeling upset, though, and I wasn't upset. I was confused, and *uneasy*, perhaps, but not upset. So why had I gone out of my way to be so disrespectful?

I took a few steps further into the room, trying to tear the wet pajama pants off as I did. But I seemed to have forgotten how hard it is to undress while maneuvering around a messy room mid-renovation, so I ended up stumbling. With one leg halfway out of the pant leg, I toppled over like the water pitcher beside those stacks of cardboard boxes. In a last minute attempt to catch myself, I reached out towards the large box with the blanket over it. My hands caught the blanket, but not the box underneath it, and I ended up in a heap on the floor anyway. Thankfully I didn't make much of a sound in doing so. Jin and Julie's voices below never faltered for a second.

Cursing under my breath, I shrugged the blanket off and pulled myself to my feet again. I used the large box for support in doing this, and then in keeping my balance as I finally got out of the wet pants successfully.

Standing in the middle of Jin and Julie's guest room in a baggy, worn-out t-shirt and my underwear, numerous things clicked into place. First and foremost, this wasn't a guest room. At least it seemed that it wouldn't be for much longer.

The big box in front of me, unlike the others, was not plain. All across the right side of it, right where the blanket had laid before I'd accidentally tugged it off, was a picture. A picture which was a rough outline of a *crib*. I tore at the box, hoping to find that it was unsealed, and therefore storing something completely different, but it wasn't. It was brand new and it was a crib.

I should've figured it out sooner. What with Julie's recent baggy outfits, tired feet, and eating habits... The eating habits I'd called out and gotten water all over myself for. Oh my god, it was so obvious.

Before I could stop it, I was laughing. Out loud and hysterically. Julie was pregnant. That's why I was there. Julie and Jin were having a baby and they needed to break the news to me.

"Oh my god," I said aloud to myself, still laughing at the absurdity of it all.

"Naomi?"

I swung around at the sound of his voice. Jin stood in the doorway, eyes glued to the box on display before me. Of course.

"I was coming to check on you," he explained helplessly.

"As you can see, Jin." I motioned at my lack of pants and the box with the crib inside of it. "I'm doing quite well."

His mouth opened and closed repeatedly. He was clearly at a loss. Meanwhile, I couldn't stop laughing. It was so bad that my eyes were welling up with tears and my chest was getting heavy.

Jin said nothing for a long time. He didn't even look at me, just stared at the box like it would give him the answers he needed.

He backed away from the doorway with shaking legs and said, his voice unnaturally low, "Get dressed so we can talk."

21

The last thing I wanted to do was listen to Jin by getting dressed and rejoining them downstairs to *talk*. Yet that's exactly what I did, because what other choice did I have?

The dining room table was cleared by the time I came down, having momentarily halted my laughter at last. There was no sign of the spilled water, no sign of the soaked tablecloths, no sign of the meal itself, even. It was as if none of it had ever happened. If it were possible to rewind time and make that so, I'd do it in a heartbeat. But this was real life and real life wasn't that kind. So there the three of us stood, between the kitchen and the living room, unable to find a place to go to make this conversation any easier.

"I'm sorry this is how you found out, dear. We intended for this to go much smoother," Julie told me, doing her best impersonation of a doting mother—that way I always hated her for.

"So it's true then; you're having a baby?" I asked, knowing the answer, knowing there was no reason to drive the knife further into my abdomen by asking to hear them say it in plain words.

"Yes." It was Jin who answered. There was no hesitation in his voice. No remorse either.

I tripped a foot or so to the side, feeling physically wounded. I had to grip the back of the couch for support, not trusting my own two legs to hold me anymore. It felt like he'd torn something straight out of me with that one word, that simple admission. There was no more denying it; this was real.

The laughter was threatening to come back up. It was trying so hard to escape me that I felt a pit deep in my chest and a red hot tightening around my throat. It took everything in me to stay silent, to keep my eyes on them both without shaking.

"We invited you here this weekend to tell you," Julie went on.

She must have thought that her words were helping, but they were not. In fact, they were making everything worse. It had made no difference to me whether they intended for this to go better or not, but it made all the difference in the world that they had invited me here for that sole reason. That changed everything I'd been thinking for the past few hours. None of this effort had been for me. Their efforts had *never* been for me.

Was it unfair of me to hate someone who didn't exist yet? Was it unfair of me to feel jealous of their unborn baby?

I wanted two loving parents who made the effort for me and me alone, *I* wanted the simplicity of a family that never left me behind, even when things got hard, *I* wanted to be raised in someplace steady, *I* wanted Jin to be the father everyone told me he was. *I* wanted it. It wasn't fair that I had to sit back and see it happen for someone else... It didn't feel fair.

"Naomi," Jin's voice was soft and hesitant again, "We want to make up for lost time and be a part of your life... We want *you* to be a part of this baby's life."

I felt rooted to the spot. Hot streaks burned a path down the skin of my cheeks, pooling together underneath my chin and falling to the ground beneath my feet. Things were blurry all around me. Jin and Julie's faces were distant and distorted. Even so, I could see the look of hope in their eyes—hope that I'd accept this major life change and be happy for them. And my god, do I wish I could've just been happy for them.

"I don't know what to say," I admitted, voice scratchy.

"That's okay," Julie reassured me, all bubbly and fake, "We know this is a bit of a shock."

"It's more than that," I snapped. I thought the words had stayed locked within my thoughts until I saw Jin's jaw drop open.

"Naomi," he tried.

I didn't like hearing my name from his mouth. It was nothing like hearing it from Wren, who emphasized it with passion and his undivided attention. I needed to hear it, I needed to hear Wren. I needed to see him before I came apart at the seams.

I took a few steps forward, keeping my hands on the couch in case my body went weak again. My movements were jerky, but successful. If I tried hard enough, I could get away.

"Please wait." Julie's hand circled my wrist, holding me still. Her fingers were trembling. Or maybe I was trembling. I didn't care either way. I needed to get out of that stupid house.

"I can't," I whispered, choking on the words.

"This child will be your sibling," Jin said, as if I didn't already know that.

"And we'd like for you to be the godmother, as well," Julie added.

"*What?*"

"Please," Jin mumbled, sounding close to tears himself. *What the hell did he have to be crying over?* "We'd be honored if you said yes. We're all family, aren't we?"

"Are we?" I asked sardonically. "Because last I checked, families aren't supposed to abandon each other."

"Let's all take a moment to breathe," Julie suggested, holding her stomach. It was a simple, thoughtless action, but alongside her words, it made me seethe with anger.

"Matt's the only family I have," I declared. "He stayed by me when you didn't want to, he changed my diapers as a toddler, he brought me to school and hung my report cards on the fridge, he cooks me dinner every night, he was *there*. Matt raised me, Jin, he—"

I cut off with a gasp, realizing the tears were coming full force. What good was any of this doing? What purpose was there to this lecture? Jin couldn't change the past that he'd made and I couldn't change the past that I'd been forced to live. There was nothing to do but move on. I lowered my head, sucking in a heavy breath. Jin and Julie were silent before me, probably as stunned by the turn of events this night took as I was.

"I'll be the baby's godmother," I said at last, attempting to make some sort of amends.

"Thank you," Julie answered quietly.

I waved it off, feeling exhausted. Her thanks meant nothing.

Neither of them said a thing as I turned tail and stomped back up the stairs. Neither of them said a thing when I came back down with my shoes on my feet and my bag over my shoulders. And still neither of them said a thing as I stepped through the front door and left without another word.

My fingers dialed Wren's number as I paced down the dark street, wanting to be as far away from them as possible.

It rang one singular time before he answered, saying my name and asking me, "Where are you?"

I bursted into tears again. Hearing him was a relief, but it was also my safe place to break down. I sat down right there in the middle of the street to wait for him to pick me up. A sick sense of deja vu fell over me.

22

The drive home was a blur. Through the smudged glass of the car window, the trees and houses we passed by were all one giant smear of gray. Through my swollen, tear-filled eyes, everything was gray. Wren was the tiniest bit of light within it all. His hand on mine was the tether keeping me in place, keeping me in the present. Without it, I would've sunk under. We both knew he had every right to rub it in my face, to tell me *I told you so*, but he said nothing. He never asked me to say anything either.

I expected to end up inside the warmth of the Blackwell household by the end of the drive, but he took us to my own house instead. Something akin to disappoint must have shown on my face because Wren's hands quickly found my cheeks.

"My dad came home," he reminded me, "and it's best you don't meet him right now."

"How come?"

"Haven't you had enough of shitty fathers for one night?"

I swallowed, averting my gaze from his inky eyes to the center console between us. Everything was dark gray. The rough pads of his fingertips brushed over my cheeks, smudging the tears aside.

He murmured compliments into my ear, and yet everything re-mained dark gray.

"You were right," I told him, because he was. He'd warned me of this outcome and I'd ignored him. Even though he was the only one who knew this feeling, the only one who could help me through it, the only one...

"I knew I would be," he answered quietly. It felt worse than if he was to just say *I told you so.* "Let's get you inside."

Like a marionette on strings attached to his hands, I let him guide me without any resistance. He led me out of the car, along the short paved driveway, and into the house where all the lights were off. No one was supposed to be back home before tomorrow afternoon.

Wren didn't bother flicking on any of the light switches. He simply kept guiding me through the dim halls and up the creaky stairs until we were in my bedroom. My legs gave out as soon as we stepped up to my bed. I felt the weakest I ever had before, as if Jin had torn something out of me that I needed, but wasn't aware of having in the first place.

Wren sat beside me, the mattress dipping with his weight. I could see his eyes flickering around the room, taking it all in. This was the first time he'd been here. If I'd known this would happen, I would've cleaned up. Maybe redecorated entirely. Heat rushed into my cheeks with embarrassment seeing him in all his glory on top of my floral bedspread, gazing around at my pink desk chair, fairy-light covered walls, and butterfly rug on the floor. I may as well have put a flashing light on my forehead telling him how juvenile I was.

"Naomi," he called to me. There it was; there was my name in the voice that I loved so much. I felt my body sink further into the bed, easing up. One of his hands began to stroke through my hair. "Should we talk about it?"

Should we? Of course. *Would we?* Absolutely not. I didn't want to talk about it. It would probably do me good to get all of these jumbled thoughts out of my system, but talking it over was the very last way I wished to accomplish that. I wanted everything to disappear. If I could clear my thoughts for a few hours, I'd feel better, I knew it. And no one was better at helping me do that than Wren.

So I answered him, "No," and tugged his body down beside mine. He came easily, fitting up against me effortlessly.

He didn't push the issue again. Even when my tears came so heavy and consistent that our kisses were salty with them. He just murmured compliments to me between each one, his words soft over my skin like a blanket. I sunk into my bed, letting it all wash over me. My heart pounded powerfully beneath my ribcage. It wanted to burst straight out of me, take all the pain with it. I squeezed my eyes shut and let Wren do that for me.

We had never kissed this way before. Our interactions up to then had always been hurried and wild, frantic but secretive. These were slow and languid, timid but rough. His entire body hovered over mine, caging me in, and I could see nothing else. Only his eyes lit ablaze with desire and his hands as they wiped tears from my cheeks. When his lips worked their way down my neck, I nearly blacked out. Everything in me was racing; my heart, my blood, my mind. I needed him to make it stop so the tears would dry for good. I couldn't figure out how to do it on my own.

One of his hands cupped my cheek, continuing to wipe away the tears, and the other trailed down, carefully undressing me in pieces. I held my breath, letting him lead as he always did.

"It's okay," he reassured me, right before there was no going back from what we did next. "It's okay that you want this. You're okay."

I wasn't confident that this was the way I *did* want this, but Wren's words were absolute. Even if it wasn't perfect, it would be with him, and that was what I truly cared about.

It hurt. I thought there would be some point in which it got easier and I could stop crying, but that time never came. I kept crying the entire time, but Wren didn't mind. He told me over and over again how beautiful I was anyway. He took the tears off my skin with his fingers, with his lips, with his tongue. I could focus on nothing other than him and the pressure within me, the physical pain of it overpowering any other thoughts.

I don't know how long it lasted. I don't even know what Wren looked like beneath all of his clothing. I couldn't pry open my eyes as it happened. I couldn't open my mouth either. My jaw ached from how hard I'd clenched my teeth together, and my neck hurt from the angle I held my head at. There was pain everywhere, but the world was still around us at the end. There was pain everywhere, but no longer the intangible kind in my head. I had no space for such things anymore.

Wren collapsed beside me again, breathing heavily. His body was hot and sweaty. Mine must've been, too, but there were so many sensations that I couldn't pinpoint each for sure. Besides, it didn't deter him from drawing me near, my head against his beating heart. His lips pressed over the crown of my head and he spoke to me again.

"So beautiful, Naomi." His chest vibrated with the words. "You're so beautiful. I only need you. We only need each other."

A sob tore its way up my throat, but I bit my tongue to keep it inside. I could taste blood, smell blood, feel blood on my skin.

"I love you," I told him, feeling the words reverberate in my aching chest.

He peeled himself away from me and smiled, pleased.I wanted him to stay with me for the night, but he couldn't. He redressed himself in minutes afterwards and kissed me goodbye before rushing out. Leaving was safest, he said, because who knew when Matt would come home. The risk was too high. I knew he was right, but that didn't make it any easier when I was left all alone.

Following the few orders he'd given me, I dragged my weak body up, remade my bed, went pee, and hopped into the shower. I sat with my knees drawn into my chest in the corner of the bathtub, allowing hot water to pelt against my bare skin. I let everything wash straight off of me and down the drain. I let heat rise until my vision was blurry through the steam.

Despite all of this, everything still hurt.

I only need you, Wren had said, *We only need each other.*

I felt the truth in that statement more than anything. I wished he'd have stayed, consequences be damned, if only to ease my thoughts and pain for a little while longer. There was no other way I knew how to.

23

When I was much younger, probably only six years old, there was one night when Jin came by out of the blue to stay over at Matt's place. My first memories of him are from then. He'd shown up while we were eating dinner—my favorite meal of dinosaur chicken nuggets and curly fries—and begged for a place to stay. Matt was reluctant, even I could tell that much as a child, but he agreed in the end. The reason for either of those things is as unclear to me now as they were then.

The first words my birth father ever spoke to me were, "Hello there, Naomi. I'm Jin."

The first words I ever spoke to him were, "Woah, Matt says my dad's name is Jin too!"

I'll never forget the silence that fell over the room after that. I'll never forget the look on Jin's face, either: a strange mix of guilt and pride at the same time. Apparently the agreements between them about me were not clear back then. I suppose Jin had expected Matt to lie to me, to erase him from the picture entirely. In many ways, that would have been the better option. But Matt was not a liar. He was many things—many, many things—but never a liar.

So I got the whole story right then and there when I was six years old. The story of my parents, of their friendship with Matt, of how I ended up with him and not them. They sat me down and explained it as well as they could to a child, as well as they could without breaking my fragile little heart. But of course it broke anyway. Especially after I begged Jin to stay, to be my father alongside Matt, and he proceeded to never sleep over again.

I understood nothing of the situation then. Now, a decade later, I'm afraid to say that I still don't.

Why those memories have filtered back into my mind now, I'm not sure. Wren left hours ago, my skin is finally dry after the shower I took, and I'm now here alone in the dark, curled into the same couch we had ten years ago when Jin and Matt explained why I had no real person to call *dad*.

I suppose that's all there is to it. Objects hold memories in the strangest of ways like that. The fabric beneath my skin was woven out of polyester and years worth of my life. It's held onto those memories for me like a safe in which I bury my least desirables. Occasionally the past will slip through and there's nothing to be done against it; nothing can be done against the pieces of oneself that bubble up unbidden through those cracks. There's nothing to do but face it head on.

So I did what I must. I let it out, I let it hurt me. I wondered how much longer it would feel this way. I wondered if the wounds would ever scab and scar over, or if they'd bleed forever.

I missed Wren. The feeling was all-encompassing, as if I was drowning in it. I wanted him to come back and pull me out of it. I *needed* him to come back and pull me out of it. I was going to be crushed to death if he didn't. The pressure on me was excruciating and no one else but him could alleviate it.

It must have been well past one in the morning when two piercing headlights bled through the curtains over the windows and landed on me. The distant rumbling of a car engine reached my ears just before it cut out altogether. It was followed by rapid, pounding footsteps, a key turning in the lock of the door, and heavy breathing. Matt had come home.

His figure loomed in the doorway, frozen in place. His long hair was a bird's nest. Dark strands went every which way from out of the tie wrapped around them at the crown of his head. What was normally silky soft looked frizzy and damp with sweat. The golden septum ring in his nose was sideways, his shirt was buttoned up incorrectly, and neither of his shoes had been tied. It had been ages since I'd seen Matt look so rumpled, so out of place, so utterly human.

Whether to feel relief or guilt at the sight of him was unclear. My thoughts were in shambles. So much had happened since the last time I saw Matt that I felt like a new person, a different person—a person he wouldn't know if he knew all that had changed. I couldn't piece together enough words to explain what was happening to me. I could only cry. The second his eyes met mine across the room, I could only cry.

He dropped everything and rushed over. His body sank into the cushion beside me and I instantly folded myself into him. He smelled like smoke and rich, musky cologne. It was far more comforting than it should have been. My breaths left me in broken outbursts that I struggled not to choke on.

Matt hushed me quietly as his fingers began to run through the hair on top of my head. His hands were huge and his fingers long and cold with rings all over them that made the touch bumpy. Even so, it was cautious and calming. Being wrapped up protectively by him made me feel so young. Feeling the violent beating of his heart underneath my ears made me remember that he was young, too.

"Jin told me what happened." His voice was a gentle whisper. It hardly sounded like him at all. "Do you want to talk about it?"

Should we talk about it?

"No," I sobbed vehemently, burying my face further into his chest. The haphazardly done-up buttons of his shirt pushed back against my skin. One lodged right into the corner of my eye.

"Okay," Matt answered, shifting so those buttons weren't in my face anymore. "That's okay."

I wanted to talk about nothing, think about nothing. But I felt like I *needed* to say something. I felt obligated to tell him something to explain my breaking down. So I did. I told him what I'd done.

"I had sex tonight."

His breath hitched. For half a second, his fingers stopped moving. His heart missed an entire beat before it carried on. I felt it all happen, but I wouldn't mention any of it. This obviously wasn't what he had been expecting to hear, and I would assume it's the very last thing he'd ever want to hear right now from the child he raised.

"Okay," he said quietly, clearly grappling for words. He kept repeating it, *okay, okay, okay.* It took a long while before he could form anything else. When he did, he asked, voice trembling, "With who?"

Telling the truth was out of the question. But bringing myself to lie to him was out of the question, too, so I worked around it entirely by simply telling him, "He's a friend."

Matt seemed to think this over. I wished I could take everything back. I wished I could run to Wren and let him do it again. I wanted him to kiss the tears from my cheeks and tell me how beautiful I

was while he did. I wanted him to make my mind blissfully unaware again so I wouldn't think of Jin and Julie and the baby and
everything else wrong. I wanted so much. *Too much.* It scared me.

"It hurt." The words tore themselves out of my throat with a cry.
It was raw and scratchy. I hadn't intended to share that with him,
but after the words were out, they wouldn't stop. "It hurt so much."

Matt's grip tightened and I felt his chest heave. His breathing
was nearly as uneven as mine. The realization that I'd made him
cry felt like a punch to the gut.

"It shouldn't hurt this much," he murmured, sniffling.

We said nothing else for the rest of the night. Matt held me until
I could cry no longer and I passed out right there on the couch.
I woke up beside him in his bed the same way I used to when I
had nightmares as a kid, the same way I had the day Jin left after
our one and only sleepover, telling me he couldn't be the father I
wanted him to be.

Peering around the room shrouded in darkness, Matt's body still
but snoring beside me, I cried all over again. It hurt so much.

24

Moving forward from that weekend was cumbersome. Ever since then, Matt had been on edge with me. It was obvious that he wanted me to confide in him but I couldn't. There were a million reasons why I couldn't. Even worse than that, he and Jin were back to fighting. I was once again the central point of a never-ending battle between two grown men who were my fathers—in two different, but undeniable ways, but wouldn't accept it—again; in two different, but entirely undeniable ways.

With all the grace of a toddler learning to walk, I evaded any part in those arguments. I stayed completely away from Jin, kept as much distance as I could from Matt, and refused to comment on anything that had happened that night to anyone. Even when Emmeline and George pushed me to explain why I was suddenly so different in the following days, I kept my mouth shut. They knew as well as I did that I'd undergone a change so drastic it was practically metamorphosis, but explaining why was simply impossible. I hardly knew myself why I'd been led to where I was, why I could never go back to where I'd been before. It would do no one any good to try finding sense in something without any.

That left me with only one option: seclusion. I purposefully isolated myself, allowing the mind-numbing loneliness to eat me from the inside out. In the small moments when I got to speak to Wren, he'd fill those spaces and make me feel whole again. The cycle was exhausting, but, naturally, as with any circle, there was no end to it. I looped around and around in this emotional stalemate, having no one to blame but myself. If I'd done one thing differently before, even one tiny, little thing like saying *no* to that sleepover at Jin's, then nothing would've turned out this way. I'd have never lost my temper, I'd have never slept with Wren, I'd have never forced this barrier between Matt and I, never restarted those arguments between Matt and Jin.

It surely didn't help anyone that Thomas Blackwell, Wren and Emmeline's father, was supposedly sticking around for a while. A while as in indefinitely. Wren told me it had been years since he'd lived home for so long. His timing was impeccable.

With him back, Wren was tense and unhappy, and Emmeline was nervous but ecstatic. I hadn't seen Wren since Thomas began picking Emmeline up from practice and Wren began working longer hours. I heard from him less and less, too. The stress levels in their household were rising unnaturally and I could do nothing for them, nothing about it, because things were much the same in my own household.

It was well over a week before Wren came to pick up Emmeline again. That made it well over a week before I saw him in the flesh again. Finding the time and excuses to be together was hard, impossibly so, with everything else going on. My house was off limits because of Matt, his because of Thomas, and everywhere else because of some other reason. We talked constantly, text messages and hushed phone calls that kept me as sane as possible, but nothing compared to seeing that signature smirk of his with my own eyes. Nothing compared to hearing the way his voice formed my name, his eyes held my gaze, his hands brushed against my shoulders and neck and waist, innocent but burning, casual but pointed.

It took all of my self control not to tackle him to the ground the second he was in my line of sight. As effortlessly as always, he was breathtaking. In slacks and a button down, with his hair swept over his forehead like the wind had undone all his hard work with the hair gel, he stood in the aisle between the auditorium chairs. He watched the last minutes of our acting exercises with patience, one eyebrow cocked up in amusement.

There wasn't a single thing off about him, like I knew there was about me. I knew my hair was a mess, my clothing was rumpled and my outfit mismatched, my eyes low and bruised with bags. I knew I looked like I'd been hit with a freight train. I knew even before George had so kindly told me so earlier.

Matt didn't officially announce we were finished for the day. He simply called the end of our exercises and then disappeared backstage. People trickled out slowly after that, confusion written all over their faces. Ever since the cast list got posted and Carla caused that scene in the hallway, whispers about Matt had been endless.

"Do you think Mr. Molina's okay?" Lucy, a freshman who got the role of the Duchess, if I'm remembering correctly, asked TJ, who had taken it upon himself to be the big brother to everyone in the drama club.

TJ's eyes flitted over to me. They went wide after noticing I was already staring back. Guilt creased his brows. Lucy didn't seem to catch any of this, too focused on staring through the blood red curtains to where Matt was silently packing his things.

"Yeah," TJ answered her after a pause, "I'm sure he's fine."

Lucy frowned, clearly not believing him. It appeared as if TJ hardly believed himself.

"He hasn't been right since that day," the short, pale boy beside Lucy added. His name was lost on me.

"What day?" Lucy asked.

His gaze shifted towards me much the same as TJ's had before. Again, like deja vu, his pupils blew out wide and he looked sorry for me.

"In the hallway," he whispered back, apparently assuming I wouldn't be able to hear him anymore. "When Carla went at Emmeline and Naomi?"

"Oh," Lucy sighed, frowning hard. She was a sweet girl, taking it upon herself to worry about others so much. "Yeah that was awful."

"But he isn't really her dad, right?" Another girl, another name I didn't know. "So what's the big deal?"

"I honestly don't know," the pale boy responded.

The comments kept going on and on, different theories and opinions about Matt and me filling the air. Nausea rose in my throat. As much as I wanted to cut in and set the record straight, I couldn't. My relationship with Matt was currently as confusing to me as it was to them. There was nothing I could say that would simplify any of it. In fact, I'd probably only make it worse. I was avoiding Matt like the plague in hopes that the awkwardness and secrets of that night would wash away with enough time.

"Hey," Emmeline whispered close to my ear. Shivers ran down my spine. The last time someone whispered so closely to my ear, it was Wren, we were naked, and I was crying. "Ignore them."

I couldn't look her in the eyes as I mumbled an agreement and allowed myself to be led away. She took my hand and brought me off the stage to where Wren was waiting.

It may have been the most thoughtless mistake of my life, but I didn't care. I threw myself at him and buried my face in his chest. Having him so close was intoxicating. There was no self control left in me anymore. His arms wrapped back around me, slowly at first, then tight and harsh all at once. It was only a split second, like a momentary lapse in judgment, before he was releasing me again.

"Naomi," he whispered into my hair, "let go. Not here."

I sprung away like he was on fire. I'd made a promise to him that this thing, *our thing*, was a secret.

"I'm sorry," I mumbled, hanging my head.

"Rough week, hmm?" Wren asked casually. Lifting my gaze to his, I saw fire beneath those steady brown eyes. A smile remained on his lips. Deciphering what this expression meant was beyond me. It made blood rush through my ears.

"I guess," I whispered, feeling like I should have been begging for his forgiveness.

"Worse than rough," Emmeline cut in, looking between the two of us with furrowed brows. "That's the most emotion I've seen out of her in days. What the hell have you done, Wren?"

The floor had been torn out from underneath me, but Wren laughed easily. I looked from him to Emmeline, who was starting to laugh as well. Before that moment, I hadn't realized that she didn't look suspicious at all. Confused, and perhaps a bit offended, but not at all suspicious. They laughed together like it was the funniest thing in the world and I stood, completely dumbstruck, willing my heart to stop thundering in my ears.

The three of us left together shortly after, no further discussion about it. We often used to leave together like this before that one weekend. Doing it again felt like setting things back to normal, like a step in the right direction for once.

Even if I felt eyes burning holes into our backs the entire way.

25

It was hours before Wren and I got some alone time. Sleeping over at the Blackwell house that night hadn't been my original intention when I left the drama club with Emmeline, but once I was there, leaving again felt ridiculous. One short, clipped text message to Matt later and I was settling in for the weekend.

Which meant I had to get through meeting their father Thomas and joining their family night before I could have Wren to myself. After hugging him in public, where any number of people could have seen and figured us out, I was terrified. I needed to speak to him, to know what was going through his mind and what that look in his eyes had meant.

"Naomi Nakano," Thomas Blackwell greeted me, his hand outstretched towards me and a smirk far too similar to Wren's across his lips. "It's nice to finally meet you. I've heard so much."

Stupidly, I turned to Wren—as if anything their father had heard about me had come from his lips. The line of his jaw popped out, sharp and tight. I dropped my gaze again.

"Same to you," I answered, shaking Thomas's hand.

His head cocked a bit to the side with a small, genuine smile. For the first time, I allowed myself to truly look at him. Thomas was about Wren's height, maybe an inch or two taller, with broad shoulders and a large, muscular chest. His black suit was well-worn, but also well-ironed and fitting. His hair was brown like Wren's, too, but a bit darker and not as fluffy. It was parted down the middle and slicked with gel against his scalp. Wide, deep blue eyes stared without judgment, and thin, angled eyebrows sat without creases. His smile was small and honest. Not large like Emmeline's or intimidating like Wren's, but somehow similar to both all the same.

Everything I knew about Thomas Blackwell up to that point had come directly from stories Wren and Emmeline told me. Based on all of those, I expected someone entirely different. I expected a rigid, cruel old man. Thomas was neither of these things. He was young and friendly. He was handsome—of course he was, he was a Blackwell—and unexpectedly mellow. I had no idea what to do with these conflicting images I had for the man before me.

Things only got more confusing as time wore on. Thomas cooked us all dinner and we sat around the table together eating it through lively conversation. Not only was the food delicious, but the conversation was pleasant and smooth. Thomas inquired about our lives and listened attentively to each answer. Emmeline spoke to him in earnest, happiness lighting up her facial features. Wren replied in short, even tones, but his answers were honest. I, not knowing what to make of any of it, kept my words as limited as possible. None of them seemed to mind. Thomas least of all.

Wren had told me Thomas left them for a long while when they were still just kids. Emmeline told me that she sometimes missed him so much it was like he wasn't alive somewhere else at all. Seeing the three of them there, circled around me and interacting as any other family would, I found it hard to believe. *Who was the real Thomas? How could Wren have learned anything from this man the way he assured me that he did when talking me out of hating Jin?* He must be faking it. He had to be.

One thing I've found to come out of a life like mine—complicated, confusing, *uneasy*, whatever you want to call it—is self-regard where it doesn't belong. To me that means I find a way for everything to circle back to my own life somehow. I find correlations everywhere I possibly can so that I'll feel a little less alone, even if that's at the expense of others. With the Blackwells, that meant I found myself questioning everything about a man I had only just met so that he would fit the mold I wanted him to.

If Thomas Blackwell was the bad guy I pictured in my head before meeting him, then Wren and Emmeline were that much closer to being the same as me. If Thomas Blackwell was this perfectly earnest man who cooked, cleaned, and actually knew his children, then they were not. If he was somehow both, I didn't know where that left them. I didn't know where that left me.

Even after spending hours around them, learning first hand how hospitable and responsible Thomas could be, I asserted to myself that he was a bad father. The same way I asserted to myself that Jin was a bad father, even if both *bad* and *father* weren't wholly accurate terms for me to assign to him.

Long after dinner, and well into watching movies together in their living room, I allowed myself to shift the slightest bit closer to Wren. Ever since I'd walked through the door, I had maintained my distance from him. It was torture, but I couldn't risk another slip-up. With Emmeline beside me, half-asleep against Thomas who was beside her, also half-asleep, it finally felt safe enough. Wren was the one who chose to sit on my other side, after all.

There was still plenty of space separating Wren and me, but my tiny movement drew his eyes my way. I felt him watching as I inched my hand across the cushion between us. Right before my fingertips hit his thigh, his hand shot up and slapped down over mine. It effectively froze my movements as well as my heart. I watched him, light from the television flashing color against his face, and felt like my lungs had been torn from my chest. He truly was angry with me.

Making as little noise as possible, I slid off the couch and excused myself from the room. All I'd wanted for hours by then was his attention, even if he was upset with me, but after I'd gotten it, I felt like dying. When Wren told me we only had each other, I believed him. If he was upset, then what did I have? *Who* did I have?

Breathing grew increasingly difficult as I rushed up the staircase. Blood rushed in my ears. I wasn't even aware I'd been followed until he spoke.

"Naomi," Wren said, quiet but desperate. He was only a foot or so behind me, holding onto the railing of the staircase like a cane holding his body upright. "What's wrong?"

"You—" My throat tightened around the words, making it nearly impossible to force out the rest. "You're upset with me."

"Baby, I'm not upset," he exhaled, walking into my space and slowly gripping my shoulders.

"But you... I hugged you at school."

"You did," he agreed, thumbs rubbing small circles over my skin.

"I shouldn't have."

"No, you shouldn't have," he agreed again, leaning down so his face was closer to mine.

He smelled like the spice from dinner and the liquor Thomas had cracked open for the two of them. Neither scent should have been appealing, but it was Wren they came from, so they were.

"I just missed you so much," I told him, still worried, still shaking with fear. "I feel like I have no one else but you."

"Aw," he cooed, kissing me once lightly. "How can I be upset when you say something like that?"

I chased after his mouth, longing for the feeling only he could give me. He complied, kissing me again and again and again. I began to feel light headed by the time we pulled apart.

"You're not angry?"

"No. I only missed you too," he replied, nipping at my bottom lip. "So much it's hard to control."

"Oh," I breathed, feeling his hands snake around my body and drag me closer.

We went no further than kissing against the wall in the hallway, but it was obvious that Wren wanted more. He murmured how much he needed me, how much I needed him, and I would've caved to his desires if Emmeline and Thomas weren't right below us. Even so, separating myself from him was beginning to feel like cutting my own skin off.

26

I stayed with the Blackwells for the entire weekend. Thomas and Wren ended up going out together for a long while so I got plenty of alone time with Emmeline. We FaceTimed George late Sunday afternoon and talked for hours—or more like Emmeline talked for hours. My mind was mush after all the kissing Wren and I did so I could hardly form a coherent sentence, and George was even quieter than usual—which meant he said damn near nothing. He only grunted and sighed and sometimes, if we were lucky, let out a laugh.

"You should've been here, Prez," Emmeline was saying, (she had recounted the events of our past two days in excruciating detail to him. They did not sound nearly as fun as she thought they did). She tapped her fingernails on the phone screen aggressively when he didn't immediately respond.

"Next time," George answered slowly, adjusting his beanie. Most of his hair was buried beneath it, as were his eyebrows.

Even through the screen, where his face was no more than a few pixels, I could feel his gaze sliding to me. Something was seriously off with him. Had I any energy left for more people's problems, I would've pressed the issue, but—as awful as it may sound—I didn't have it in me. With Jin and Julie and the baby, and Wren and Thomas and Emmeline, and me and me and *me*, I had no space left in my mind. George deserved better. I knew very well that he deserved better.

Only when I was packing my things to go home did I stop and think Emmeline deserved better, too. I realized it in those final moments before I stepped out the door that I'd hardly been present with her recently. I felt like an awful friend, an awful person.

Right before the door clicked shut behind me, I stopped it with my hand and threw myself back inside, right at Emmeline. She was in the same fuzzy gray pajamas she'd worn to sleep the night before, hair down and in a tangled mess over her shoulders. Her eyes were sleepy but clear. She was in my view for a split second before there was nothing in my view at all, my eyes squeezed shut as I hugged her tightly. Even with the startled yelp that came out of her mouth, and the way her heart skipped a beat before slowing, she supported my weight.

"Naomi?" Her hands twitched against my back.

I pulled back enough to see her again. Beautiful, even as startled and confused as she clearly was.

"I'm sorry," I told her, my voice shaking. "I'm so sorry."

"Huh?" She pulled back an inch as well, hands sliding down my back but not letting go entirely. Silently, I was grateful for that. "For what? What's there to be sorry for?"

Putting it into words was harder than expected. Was it too blunt to say *because I've been a terrible, terrible friend, thinking only of your brother and myself but never you, even though every-thing sucks right now, but never you?*

"Because I..." I stopped myself. Yes, of course that would be too blunt. Admitting that to her out loud would be admitting to far too much at once.

"Hey," she said softly, so, so softly, the same way that everyone had been lowering their voices around me recently, as if I'd break at the sound of something louder. "It's okay. Whatever it is, it's okay."

Her smile was gentle. It tugged at the corners of her mouth as if her body knew a small smile wasn't suited to her face. She was meant to have huge, sunshine smiles that lit up entire rooms. I dropped my head forward onto her collarbone, being a bit too short for resting on her shoulder.

"I don't deserve you," I whispered quietly into her shirt, knowing she'd never be able to hear it.

It must've sounded to her like a choked back sob because she murmured back to me, "Please don't cry."

We stayed that way for what felt like forever. Her hold on me never let up. My heart was racing inside of me, something unnameable, and completely intangible, gripping it tight. My chest, my head, my limbs; they all felt heavy. I wanted to stay there with her like that forever.

"Bye, Emmy," I said at last, forcing myself away from her.

Something flashed in her eyes. Her hands fell from my back and one of them came up, hovering in the space between our faces, almost as if she was going to grab mine. But then it fell, her face went neutral, and she said goodbye back.

The entire way home—a walk since I needed the air—I couldn't help but feel like somehow my apology had ended up all wrong.

For a split second back there, there had been a look in her eyes that I knew I recognized. Only I'm not certain *why* I recognized it. She looked sad and desperate in a way I'd never seen her look before, a way I wasn't aware someone as charming as Emmeline Blackwell *could* look. It made me feel even worse. Attempting to apologize had backfired. Once again, I was reminded that Wren was the only one I had. At least that apology worked in my favor and he went on loving me the same as before, no clouds in his eyes when we pulled apart from each other.

The thought of losing Emmeline was nauseating. I fought to keep my body from pitching forward into the cement of the sidewalk under my feet. Stumbling along, I blinked back tears and forced myself to think of something else, *anything* else.

The trip from their house to mine was not exactly suitable for walking. It was long, annoyingly windy, and required waiting at far too many crosswalks. It didn't help that it was not yet spring, so snow remained piled against the sidewalk and salt was scattered uselessly on top of it. I could feel chunks of it getting caught in the crevices on the bottom of my shoes. I stomped along, swerving around as much as possible while remaining on the sidewalk. The closer I got to my house, the less sidewalks there really were, so I wanted to use them while I could.

By the time I saw my road up ahead of me, my nose and ears were practically frostbitten. Hardly any feeling was left in them. My toes and fingers, on the other hand, I *could* feel because they were painfully cold, but not yet numb. It was nearing the end of March, so it was infuriating to me that there was no sunlight or warmth at all. I wished I had simply called Matt to come pick me up. Being cold made me miserable and his car was in the driveway, anyway, so I knew he was around.

Except his car wasn't the only car in the driveway. Beside his, there was a much nicer, cleaner, and newer car—Jin's car.

I walked up the driveway slowly and came to a stop between the two. Blinking back and forth between them, I peered through the passenger side window of Matt's, where I normally sat, and the driver's side of Jin's, where there was only ever him. There was dirt and scattered trash across the floor of Matt's, both having come from my own feet and backpack respectively. The seat was tugged far forward but laid all the way back, unmoved from the last time I was in the car and wanted to take a nap. All these little things were signs of life—my life—that Jin and his perfectly vacuumed, spotless car lacked.

For a fleeting moment, I contemplated smashing his window. I thought about picking up a rock from the yard and hurling it through so that shattered glass would pile all over his seat. I thought about leaving my mark. But before I could, the moment had passed.

Matt and I lived on the lesser side of town; the one with smaller houses and thinner walls. I'd never thought about it much before, as it was never a concern, but it was all I could think about then as I stood in the driveway, clearly able to hear Matt and Jin's voices drifting to me from where they stood inside, presumably in the living room, *talking about me.*

"–mad for nothing! She agreed to be the godmother." That was Jin.

"Because you cornered her!" Matt then, loud and furious. "She's just a kid, Jin, what did you expect?"

My heart hammered in my chest. I crept up the rest of the driveway and crouched underneath the windows beside the front door. I could hear everything perfectly clear from there, even the shifts of their feet on the floor or the heavy sigh before Jin spoke again.

"*My* kid," Jin replied. All the air shot out of my lungs. Never in my entire life had I heard him refer to me that way before. "Naomi is *my* daughter. Need I remind you of that, Matthew?"

My body collapsed against the house, all of my weight becoming too much for me at once. The vinyl siding bounced back against me, weak and loose from old age. A silence so thick followed that I was worried I'd been caught.

Then Matt, in a tone I wasn't sure I was familiar with from anyone—least of all him—spoke up to say, "No. You're nothing to her. You chose that the day you tried to leave her outside a goddamn fire station. Need *I* remind *you* of that?"

I was sitting all the way down on the dead plants and bits of snow by that point. There were thorns on some of the plants, and the snow was seeping all the way through my clothing, but I felt none of it. All over I was numb. Static encompassed me, making me lose a solid chunk of the rest of their argument. By the time the ringing in my ears stopped, all I heard was the final statement.

All I heard was Jin saying, "Maybe *you* should've told her about the baby then, if you're such a good and honest father."

The door flew open and slammed closed. The entire house rattled in response, my body shaking along with it. Somehow Jin didn't notice me as he stormed down the walkway, got in his car, and sped off.

27

I'm not sure how long I stayed frozen in that spot, staring at the place in the driveway where Jin's car had been. I only know that by the time I pulled myself to my feet, using the protruding ledge off the window where there was once a line of potted plants, there was no feeling left in any of my limbs.

How I managed to force them forward, over the pebbled pathway, up the concrete steps, and through the doorway I could then only imagine rattling on its hinges as Jin left through it, was beyond me. There was someone else inside of me, wearing my skin like a suit, making those movements for me, *forcing* those movements for me. I was somewhere else entirely. Floating above, perhaps; being made to watch, but not to act. Being dragged behind, maybe; held onto myself by a tether through the chest—the only thing I could still truly feel, like a thick knife had been lodged there. Buried underground, even; the screams I so desperately wanted to release muffled into nothingness by the weight of everything above me. I was a weightless ghost, a trailing spirit, a body buried alive. I was so consumed with feeling that I felt nothing at all.

Two beads of laser-bright blue. Piercing light popping out of a face that I thought I knew, but truly may not have all along. He stood taller and more far away from me than ever before. I stared back, wondering if my own two eyes were equally as unrecognizable to him as his were to me. The air between us was nothing but a blur of fog; the smoke of our burnt-up trust, the steam of hot, relentless tears.

Eternities passed before either of our mouths opened to form something more than a choked sob or an incomprehensible clump of unfinished words. I was much older by then; much older than the girl who stormed out of Jin and Julie's house after learning about their pregnancy, much older than the girl that Matt held onto on the couch while she cried, much older than the girl who'd left Emmeline staring in shock in her doorway.

Each second for me was a day, each day a lifetime. And what is a lifetime if not a death sentence? A prolonged but inevitable death sentence.

When I finally found the strength to construct words from out of my trembling lips, they were only this: "You knew?"

Matt's signature sign of distress was his hair. If those long brown locks weren't up in perfect buns or ponytails, it was obvious that he was falling apart, too. His hair then, as he stood before me shaking like an animal caught in a trap, was at its worst. It fell in sheets over his shoulders—sweat-dampened, tangled sheets. It made him look like a teenager, like the teenager I had scarce, fuzzy memories of from when I was a toddler.

"They told me they were trying in December," he answered at last, the sound of his voice shredded through his teeth. He'd clearly fought that sentence on its way out, but it was disgustingly lucid to me anyway.

"December," I repeated, mulling it over. I remained detached from myself. The thought of him knowing about this for months, since my birthday, made me want to rip out his hair, and maybe then my own as well, but my body didn't even sway. I simply repeated it again and put the pieces together myself. "So that dinner before my birthday."

"I knew then," Matt verified. "I knew then that they were trying and that's why they wanted to take you out... But Naomi, listen to me, I had no idea that they were already pregnant by then. And I certainly didn't know they were going to put off telling you for so long."

The room swayed around me. The couch where I'd curled into Matt, the place on the floor where we sat with Jin and Julie for presents on Christmas morning, the table where we played *Life* and Julie kept gaining children—me the only one oblivious to the irony of it. All of it was one messy brushstroke of mixed colors. Matt was the only thing in clear focus before me, and even then, I hardly saw him.

"You knew." Words spilled out of me, overflowing like the rattling beneath my ribcage; inexorable. "This whole time, you knew. The phone calls, the arguments... You said they had nothing to do with me. You promised me that, Matt. Why didn't you tell me?"

I received no answer. Only an apology. Only a ceaseless, meaningless apology: "*I'm sorry, I'm sorry, I'm so sorry.*"

The funny thing about betrayal is that it cannot exist without love. I could not admit to feeling betrayed—so deeply betrayed that it was as if my entire life had been tipped upside down, leaving me to fall from within the clouds to the ground below—without also admitting that I loved Matt, that I loved Jin and Julie, even, and that it was love twisting me up inside. If I felt nothing for any of them, then it would bother me none to know that Jin not only gave me up, but wanted to give me up to strangers outside a fire station like some terribly written soap drama. It would bother me none that Julie acted like my mother without any intention of actually being mine, only someone else's. It would bother me none that Matt knew all of this and more, yet kept it quiet. Love is the force behind the whip of betrayal.

"I'm sorry, Naomi," Matt said, taking a step towards me with his palms to the ceiling as if approaching an injured animal.

I slapped his hands away, hoping he'd feel the same lash of the whip as I did.

"Liar," I snarled, feeling myself coming back to life like the controls to my body had finally been handed back to me.

"It just wasn't my place to say," he tried. "That doesn't mean I didn't want you to know. That's why we were fighting so much."

"I don't care!" I shifted backwards, debating running back to the Blackwells where I could retreat into Wren's arms and do the things I kept secret from Matt, the things that would probably devastate him if he knew.

Thinking back to hearing Jin and Matt arguing, to the prickers that poked through my jeans and made blood bead at my skin, I wished only to pass all of these awful feelings from me to someone else. So I let rage simmer inside of me until it was at the boiling point, at the point where I could shove it at Matt in one fatal blow.

Glaring as hard as I could, I asked him, "Whose kid am I, anyway?"

His features cracked like he was a mirror I'd smashed with a brick. My throat was in flames, my eyes submerged under water, my entire body pitching off a cliff I couldn't save myself from. I turned away from him and melted into the floor, having had enough. I couldn't handle seeing him look that way. I couldn't handle being forced to see that it was me who'd made him that way.

I loved Matt so much that his betrayal felt like dying. It bred other feelings apart from betrayal, too; all those other awful feelings that can stem from nothing other than love: fury, vengeance, jealousy, remorse...

Betrayal came from love. But where did love come from?

And once it was fractured, where could love go?

SCENE IV.

"If you drink much from a bottle marked 'poison' it is certain to disagree with you sooner or later."

— Lewis Carroll, *Alice's Adventures in Wonderland*

28

For as long as I've lived, Elizabeth Cohen has been an off-limits topic of conversation. At just the sound of her name—or any words that sound even remotely similar to her name—Jin would clam up and disappear for a while, and Matt would suck in a breath of air so large I felt there was none left for me to breathe. So my sixteen years of life have had nothing more on my birth mother than an old photograph I snuck out of Matt's bedroom as a child.

It's a picture of the three of them: Jin, Matt, and Elizabeth. I've stared at it so many times that I have it nearly memorized. They're standing in what looks like a park; lush green trees and picnicking families scattered around them in the background. Jin's smile is genuine, his arm around Matt's shoulders is steady, and his hand laced through my mother's is tender. His hair is loose and long, nothing like the short, slicked-back mess I know now. The crows feet around his eyes have yet to even take place. The older I get, the more I look like the man in this picture—the man who is my father but doesn't want to be.

Conversely, Matt has changed very little. In the photograph, his hair is a little messier, his eyes a little heavier, and his clothes a little looser, but otherwise age has affected him only minorly. In fact, he looks better now than he does there despite the fact that he's grinning like a maniac beside Jin in the picture and I've only seen him frown in all of the days recently. In the long run, time has treated him well. The thing is, I'm unsure of how that is. The Matt there and the Matt I know down the hall from me are two entirely different people who somehow simultaneously haven't changed at all.

Elizabeth Cohen. My mother. The things I would give to be able to pinpoint the ways in which she was different now from photograph then. The things I would give to have her in the *now* of my life at all...

Not that a picture could truly tell me a thing about her, but for my own peace of mind, I've always allowed it to. She seemed kind. Beside Jin, her smile is small but honest. Her eyes are bright and clear; a deep, ocean blue like my own. Smooth black hair is cropped at her shoulders, flying back with what must have been a gust of wind. Matt and Jin tower at least a head over her each, but her presence remains the strongest. She herself must have been strong, too.

Under the moonlight sneaking past my curtains and into my bedroom, I liked to look at this picture. I liked to examine each piece of it as if it was the very first time I'd ever done so. I liked to assign context to it, breathe life into it, drag the people there right out of it.

The same as I imagined it was a gust of wind that blew my mother's hair back, I imagined Jin fixing it after the picture had been taken. I imagined Matt rubbing the redness away from underneath his eyes, talking of allergies and pollen. I imagined them laughing, staring up at the clear sky, setting out a sheet and eating sandwiches. I imagined they talked about their futures and never once thought that they'd be so wrong about them.

If I could make this one photograph—this one tiny piece of my mother that I'd been given—into a frozen still of a much larger puzzle, a much longer movie, then I could make it enough.

But somehow it never wa. Years upon years of dreaming up scenarios for it, of writing a script to my mother's life as if that would reveal any truth about her to me, did nothing to appease my soul.

I still crinkled the corners of it between my cold fingers and couldn't help but cry. That stupid question still echoed in my head: *Whose kid am I, anyway?*

Days passed since I asked it. Days kept passing. Matt and I didn't talk about it. We hardly talked at all. Avoidance seemed to be our new thing. On top of that, the group chat between George, Emmeline and I had been quiet for just about as many days. That left me with far too many people whose status in my life was unclear. Including my own.

Whose kid am I, anyway?

It felt like the entire world was turning on me at once. Well, *almost* the entire world. One person stood by me unflinchingly. It was only natural that I clung to him like a lifeline.

"Naomi?" Wren's gravelly voice through the phone raised goosebumps across my skin. "It's late, why're you calling?"

"I miss you," I breathed out, dropping the photograph of Matt, Jin and Elizabeth between my crossed legs on the mattress.

"It's hardly been a day," he replied, but he was laughing softly around the words. He told me he missed me too. It felt good.

His side of the call was loud with movement. Crinkling, shifting, rustling. A door shutting, a lock turning, a light switching on.

"Did you just get home?" I asked.

He hummed an affirmative and told me, "Work's been busy."

I was never fully certain what Wren did for work. When I asked, the answer I got only confused me further. As well as I could understand, he worked out of some giant tech company. What he did there, or what they did there in general, never quite made sense to me. There came a point where I just stopped asking. He made decent money, and seemed to like it at least, so that was that. Wren wasn't exactly a big talker when it came to his life anyway. What he shared, and when he shared it, was all on him, and those instances were extremely rare.

I took what he gave and tried to never push for more. I relied on him far too much to lose him over something stupid like that.

"You must be tired," I said after a beat. I was tired, too.

He hummed again. The silence between us made me want to scream. The longer we spent apart, the harder it was for me to get a grip on myself. My emotions went haywire and it felt like he was the only person who could mend them. He knew he was, too. He took pride in it.

"Tell me why you're really calling," he murmured. He knew me so well.

"*I miss you,*" I emphasized, feeling the words in the pit of my stomach. "I need... I need you again."

I hardly knew what I was asking for until he answered, voice lilted but still deep.

"Oh?" The shifting halted completely. I could hear my own breath echoing back at me. "You've been thinking of me?"

"Yes," I replied, because I thought of him all the time, even if it wasn't in the way he was implying. Now that the idea was in my head, though, it wouldn't leave. He'd be able to make me forget everything else for a while.

"Yes," I said again, more urgently.

"Good," he said lowly. "You don't need to think of anyone else. I'm it for you."

"I know," I whispered. Something about his words made the hair stand up on my arms.

"Good," he repeated. Then he quickly demanded I get dressed and sneak outside, for he'd be coming to pick me up.

The call ended abruptly after that. I hadn't even gotten the chance to respond. The time flashed up at me from my phone. Eleven forty seven. No new messages. I turned it off.

I flipped over the photograph of Matt, Jin, and Elizabeth and stuffed it beneath my mattress. Put it out of mind entirely, I told myself, I don't need to think of anyone else but Wren.

Matt was long asleep by then, making it easy for me to slip out the front door. At the end of the driveway, with only the light of the moon and stars, I waited for Wren. It wasn't long before he was there and I was in the passenger seat of his car, laid back flat, allowing him to climb over me.

29

I knew something was irrevocably damaged between us when I failed to return home that night and Matt said nothing about it. Wren and I had fallen asleep in his car so I went to school the following day wearing my dirty jeans and an old t-shirt he had in the trunk.

After Wren sped down every street to the school, I managed to walk through the front doors right as the first bell rang out. Matt's car was visible in the teachers parking lot through the windows so I knew he was here, too. I tried not to imagine how he felt driving in alone, no solid idea where I'd gone, simply trusting I would come back in one piece.

I restarted my phone three times consecutively, waiting for a barrage of messages or voicemails, but none came. At last I resigned myself to being the one to reach out first.

Me
7:28 a.m.
I'm here

The three little dots came up on his end, disappeared, reappeared, disappeared, and reappeared all over again. In the end, his response was only one singular word.

Matt
7:29 a.m.
Good.

Me
7:29 a.m.
I slept over at Emmeline's

Matt
7:30 a.m.
Okay.

I don't know what I expected, nor do I know exactly what it was that I wanted, but neither of his responses were it. A part of me thought that he would instantly lash out, demand proof, and order me to come see him to sort it out. Another part of me knew that was nothing like him and only thought that he'd show a little more relief that I was talking to him at all. And yet another part of me, perhaps the largest part of all, simply wanted him to ask me why.

The white painted walls of the hallways, covered in club flyers, college pamphlets, and lots of loose tape, dragged on for miles in front of me. There was a time when mental patients were locked in padded white rooms in order to keep from harming themselves. This felt like that, only with the opposite effect. The walls around me were hard and endless, my feet hitting the tiles were loud like gunshots, and there were too many objects within my range that

I could use to take myself out. The hallway was my own personal seclusion room.

For a moment, I toyed with the idea of calling Wren back to get me out. He'd understand, as he always did, that I was alone without him. I was absolutely nothing without him. But I held myself back. Him taking me to school in the first place was breaching our deal, our promise, our secret. If someone happened to see, everything could fall apart. I'd have to survive through the day by myself.

Nearly every class I had, I arrived late to. So much as time dragged, I dragged with it. My body was sore. Each step my legs took felt like it would be the last. The muscles had turned to jelly. Wren had not necessarily been gentle with me. Beyond that, sleeping in his car had left a crick in my neck and an awful tight feeling in my right arm.

By the time the final bell rang and I met up with Emmeline and George in our usual spot to walk to the drama club together, black stars had begun to occasionally visit my bleary eyes.

It was awkward between the three of us. They both kept side eyeing me as we walked through the aisle of the auditorium together. George with suspicion and Emmeline with concern. I forced their faces to blur into the background alongside everything else, the same way I'd done to every other bit of surroundings today. I kept myself in a haze. It was okay to disconnect because I didn't need to think of anyone else. Wren was it for me, he said, he was it. This was the right way—the *only* way—to deal with things here.

Because the performance of *Alice in Wonderland* was coming up so quickly, (less than two months off now), rehearsals had gotten longer and more grueling. That meant hours of reciting lines and talking stage directions each rehearsal. That meant hours trapped inside the auditorium with Matt, George, and Emmeline, but no more than a dozen words spoken between any of us. Of those few words, not a single one had relevance outside the drama club.

For the very first time, standing between the blood-red curtains backstage, watching Carla, Emmeline and George practice a scene while Matt called out pointers, I felt truly and helplessly alone. Of course I'd felt lonely countless times before, and I was certain each of those times that I was *alone* because of the feeling, but I knew then that that was never the case. Because before this exact moment, off on the sidelines, hidden in the shadows, I'd never been entirely left behind like this. I'd never felt so completely cutoff before, as if my own body had lost some of its parts.

Tripping over my own feet, I stumbled farther backstage, deeper into the shadows. The backstage area had little to no lighting. All of the light was meant for the stage, for the people who stood center on it and provided a show. So it was easy for me to vanish past the curtains, weave through the haphazard piles of props, and escape entirely.

Behind the stage, there was a thin walkway for performers to run back and forth through. On the far right side of this walkway stood a large steel door, the only one in the entire auditorium that led directly outside. Many art classes and clubs spent time in the courtyard that it led to, where they'd paint and build props we would drag through the steel door when they were deemed ready. Luckily there was no one like that when I cracked the door open and slid my body through it.

The sun was bright, beaming down and sending splotches of white over my eyes while they adjusted. Briefly, I worried that it had given me away, that within those few seconds the door had been open for me to get out, the sunlight had gotten in. But after a solid minute of leaning against the bricks behind me, breath heavy and heart hammering, no one came. Part of me was disappointed by this, and the rest of me hated myself for that.

It was easy from there. The courtyard had a gate, always shut but never locked, leading directly to the sidewalk along the street. Slowly, as not to further upset my trembling legs, I made my way down it. Despite all that sunlight, it was frigid and unpleasant outside. My fingers went numb around my phone where I held it before me with both hands.

Open to my messages, I stared at all the names and the dates accompanying them. At the top was Matt from our stiff exchange this morning, below him was Emmeline from days ago when she sent me a string of random emojis, below her was our *boo shakespeare* chat which had been silent for weeks, and very last was George, who I hadn't spoken to one-on-one in longer than I could recall. Wren wasn't in the line-up at all because I periodically deleted his messages. We agreed it was safest that way. Not that Matt ever went through my phone, or any of my things, really, but better to be safe than sorry. That's what Wren said.

All the messages shifted down a slot as a new message came in. Now the very top of my screen was Jin. It had been a while since I'd spoken to him, too. Cautiously, I tapped open the message.

Jin
5:37 p.m.
she can't wait to meet her godmother!

He'd attached a picture of an ultrasound. There it was. There *she* was. My half sister. My goddaughter. I wasn't even aware they'd learned the baby's sex yet. I suppose this was his way of telling me. It was strange to stare at the black and white blob on the screen and be able to pinpoint her head and her little hands and her developing body. It was even stranger to feel something in my heart swell at it, to feel the hatred I so desperately needed to hold onto slipping through my fingers.

Not knowing what to make of it, and not wanting to admit even that much, I left Jin's message on read.

When I finally got home, I locked myself in my bedroom and stared at that old photograph of my mother, Jin, and Matt again, wondering if the three people there felt anything like this when they saw me in an ultrasound all those years ago.

30

Thomas Blackwell left on business again—indefinitely, as per usual—hardly over a month after he came back. By that point, it was the end of April. He'd been gone for four days before I found out. Wren didn't think to say a thing about it. It was Emmeline who told me, and that was only after her bad moods went on for so long that I forced it out of her.

The effect her father's presence, or lack thereof, had on her life was far more drastic than it was on her brother. Wren preferred to talk about Thomas as little as possible, it seemed. Once I got the truth out of Emmeline, though, it was like a dam had broken. She couldn't *stop* talking about Thomas.

Because our relationship—much like every other relationship in my life—had been so distant and awkward as of recently, hearing so much from her at once was hard to handle. It was like I'd been thrown into a role I was entirely unprepared for; the equivalent of suiting up for one character only to get up on stage and be expected for another.

"Everything was going so well," Emmeline lamented, face buried in between her hands.

We were sitting in her bed in the dark. With Thomas gone, and Wren out doing whatever it was he did when he wasn't home or working, we were the only ones in that giant house of theirs. It made all the more sense to me that Emmeline would feel so empty when her father left town.

"I really thought he'd stick around this time."

If there were words I could have said to ease her suffering, I would have said them. But alas I didn't understand her any more than she understood me. I knew what it was like to have a parent leave, but I never knew what it was like to think they'd come back and stay. At the very least, Jin had made that clear to me. In a twisted sort of way, I was thankful for that. Because then I didn't have to feel like Emmeline clearly did in this moment, crying beside me as if someone had died.

"I know he has to work," Emmeine went on, her voice scratchy. Her little space buns were falling out, hair curling over her hands and down her wrists. Idly, I debated taking some between my fingers. "I know that, but he could choose to work closer to home, couldn't he? No one's forcing him to go away for so long all the time. Most lawyers don't travel like this, right?"

"I don't know," I whispered back, wishing I did.

In the most broken tone I'd ever heard out of her mouth, she lifted her glossy gaze to mine and asked, "Why doesn't he ever stick around?"

I, as a broken record, could only answer, "I don't know."

For a moment, all we could do was look at each other. This was the most substantial conversation we'd shared in a long time. Ever since I let myself slip, since I held onto her with tears in my eyes and declared that I didn't deserve her, something between us had been cracked. We walked on eggshells around one another. Better than with George, at least, whom I could barely get to look me in the eyes these days, but not ideal nonetheless.

In that moment of stillness between us, it was almost like we were meeting for the first time again. I wanted to tell her how much I loved her from the moment I saw her face. I wondered if it would even make a difference anymore.

"I'm sorry, Emmy," I said at last, words hushed in the air separating us.

A small, choked sob fought its way out of her throat. At the same time, she threw herself forward and wrapped her arms around me. Her damp cheeks buried themselves into my shoulder. Her hands gripped at the back of my shirt, right near the nape of my neck, tight but not painfully so.

Tentatively, I slid my hands across her back as well, feeling the pounding of her heart even there. She melted into me, breaths blowing soft and warm against my collarbones. Everything about the hug, aside from the reason we were doing it in the first place, was profoundly tender. I felt then that it had been a very, very long time since anyone had held me this way, even if I was technically the one doing the holding.

It wasn't long before Emmeline began to talk again as if she simply couldn't help herself from it. Her words were quiet and broken, but she unable to stop. It was almost as if she was a leaky faucet, words dripping past her lips in ceaseless, inconsistent patterns. Still, there was nothing I could do.

"It's stupid... I'm being stupid."

"It's not," I told her, straining my eyes to see the room around us, to remind myself that we were truly some place other than eachothers arms. The walls were bathed in darkness but I could still make out the outlines of some posters and picture frames. I knew the faces that sat beneath many of those frames. George, Maya, me. Wren, her mother, *Thomas*.

"You're not," I added belatedly, fiercely.

She shifted backwards the slightest bit, putting enough space between us for our eyes to lock again. I'd never seen her look so miserable. Right then, I remembered one of the only times Wren ever talked to me about Thomas—the only time he'd ever been upfront about how his absence *really* made him feel.

He'd told me this: "I understand why you want Jin to stay gone... Sometimes I wish that asshole would never come back, either."

I'd then asked him why. I knew my own reasons, but I thought perhaps hearing his would help, too; to understand him better, to validate myself, to strengthen the gap I felt in our relationship at times.

His response was simple. He'd only said, "For Emmeline's sake."

At the time, I thought I knew what he meant by that, but honestly I wasn't entirely sure. But now, looking at Emmeline before me with tear-streaked cheeks, I was certain I understood. Perhaps, in some cases, abandonment entirely is preferable to the back and forth the Blackwells had to deal with. I suppose that in many ways, it's easier to accept you've been left behind once and for all than it is to dwell in the fact that you're good enough to visit, but not nearly enough to make someone stay. The worst part of that being that the reasons were, and always will be, unknown.

I remember hearing once that no one gets to choose their parents, they only get to choose how they deal with them. To the thought, out loud I said, "It's not fair."

Emmeline had no idea how much had just run through my head, but she nodded in agreement anyways. Then she dropped her head right back onto my shoulder again.

"Can we all stop fighting now?" she asked, muffled.

Startled, I said, "I didn't know we were."

"Oh... But things have been weird, haven't they?"

"Yeah, they have. Sorry."

"Talk to Prez again, will you?" she pleaded. "Since dad left, I get enough passive aggressive silence from Wren. I don't want that with us."

I sighed. So much as I wanted to deny something was wrong, to declare that George and I spoke all the time and nothing was amiss there, it would be insulting to lie to Emmeline like that. Things had definitely been weird with us. Besides, Wren was very upset these days, and when he was upset, he could be rather harsh. I knew Emmeline couldn't be having an easy time with that. No matter what I'd done to George to earn this tension, I could fix it for her. Or at least do my very best to do so.

"I'll try."

Maybe in the next few days I really would. It wasn't like George was the only person I needed to speak to.

31

I missed Matt so much it hurt. Even though I lived in his house, ate every meal with him, went to the same school he taught at, and exchanged some sort of words with him everyday (even if those words were as scarce as *good morning* and *goodnight* some days), I missed him. Even though I was still wildly upset with him, I felt and regretted the loss of him in my life as if he'd been taken out of it completely.

That doesn't mean I had it in me to forgive and forget, though. I was confident that someday I would, but that day had yet to come.

For a while, Matt seemed okay with that. He gave me plenty of space. He'd allow me out and about without any argument, act natural if I didn't tell him where I was going or where I'd been—the same way he did when I'd snuck out to see Wren that night—and never forced conversation. In that time, I got significantly closer to Wren. Being with him made it easier to stay upset with Matt, like I was allowed to be, encouraged to be, even.

But the days of space didn't last forever. It took a long time, but Matt gave up on that method. He resorted to begging; wanting me to tell him where I kept going, if I was safe, what he could do to fix everything, how many times he could profusely apologize before I believed it.

The worst part of all this was that I'd believed him from the start. Not a second went by where I thought his apology was false. Matt was never a liar. One for theatrics, sure, but not one for lies. As good of an actor as he was, he was a god awful liar. But just because I knew he was sorry didn't mean I was accepting it. Just because he felt bad didn't mean I felt better. At this point, I wasn't sure if I'd *ever* feel better. Some aches don't leave; they simply set into your skin and force you to habituate to them.

Even so, missing him sucked. Missing him when he was right down the hallway from me made the pain flare up in ways I was unaccustomed to. I began to call Wren and slip out the door to be with him just to take that pain away. He hadn't failed me yet.

Late on a Monday night, when I should have been rehearsing lines or studying for my algebra test the following morning, Wren drove us out of town. I left Matt a handwritten note on the kitchen counter in case he wasn't truly asleep. Leaving without asking, or without at least informing him, was less and less satisfying the more I did it.

"Where are we going?" I asked Wren, peering out the window as he sped up the highway ramp.

"It's a surprise."

The ride was long and quiet. Squishing my cheek against the glass of the window, I watched the blur of our surroundings as they went from the limp trees and blinking street lights of home to the wide expanse of deep, starry sky and dark sand a few towns over. The farther Wren drove, the more alone we became.

On the highway, we passed only a handful of tractor trailers and mini buggies with tired-looking people inside of them. Once off the highway, weaving through windy backroads and barely-paved streets without any lights, we passed no one. Nothing. It seemed that no one came through these parts so late at night, much less on a Monday night. Only Wren and me in his fancy car, dressed in pajamas, with no clear purpose.

Wren jerked the wheel to the left suddenly and turned us down a street that I wouldn't have believed was a street had he pointed it out two seconds earlier. His car hardly fit through the passageway of it, fitted between two tall brick buildings with lots of windows—none of which shone any light from the inside. The entire area was unfamiliar to me; and not in that way where it was exciting and there was plenty to look at, but in the way where it was unsettling and alienating. Even with Wren beside me, smiling this small sharp smile, I felt out of place.

Shrugging my shoulders up and curling into myself, I focused on the path ahead where the headlights lit up the space. The gritting sound of the tires made more sense once I could spot the gravel and bits of trash they were rolling over. The space ahead seemed to go on for far longer than it should've given that it was between two buildings and they couldn't possibly be so long. Wren must've been driving under a mile an hour, giving the space the feeling of a tunnel we were trapped inside. If there was enough room for me to even open my door, I would've stepped out and walked the rest of the way.

His smile only made sense, and I only breathed again, when I lifted my gaze up from the gravel and was finally able to see where we were headed. The road, (or the thick alleyway that Wren had claimed as a road for the night), led out to the beach. All at once there was air around us, *space* around us, and a smile broke across my lips unbidden. The sand I'd seen through the windows long ago on the road was right there underneath the car's tires, the ocean I'd yet to visit since moving was right there before us, and Wren's hand was tugging my arm, his warm body right there beside me.

"Come on," he murmured, unbuckling us both and stepping out into the moonlight in one swift movement.

I stumbled out of the car, landing on my hands and knees. Coarse sand instantly dug its way into them. It should've hurt but it didn't. I'd never been happier to feel the earth against me like that. Laughing softly, I sifted some of it through my fingers, cold and rough.

There weren't many stars out, but there were enough for me to see with. Wren stood beside me, offering his hand so I could stand again. I dropped the dark, dry sand and took his hand, allowing him to lead me further down the beach. Our footsteps made no sound, all of our weight being muffled into the ground and overpowered by the crashing of small waves on the shoreline. We stepped out of our shoes and stood against the water, letting it lap up at our feet. Shivers flew up my spine at the first touch.

"How are you feeling?" Wren asked. His eyes were cast across the water, staring somewhere distant and indistinct.

I answered without thinking: "Alone."

He hummed as if approving of the response. Then he took my hand again and led us back up the beach until we were on dry sand. We laid together, arms brushing, hands close but not linked, and said nothing. It didn't take long before I was drifting in and out of light sleep. The soft crash of the waves was relaxing, Wren's breaths were quiet and even, and my own mind was stripped bare. Exhaustion seeped into my skin and I buried myself into the sand, letting it.

A loud, twice-repeated dinging from my phone in my pocket snapped me up. Wren had gotten closer while I was in and out of consciousness, his hand then wrapped around my thigh and his head curled over mine. Drowsily, I tugged my phone out, squinting at the bright screen. My worst fear was that it was Matt, scared and upset I'd left. But it was not. It was worse.

The name on the screen read *President George.* I sat up so quickly that my vision spotted.

"Naomi?" Wren asked, sitting up with me, hand flexing on my inner thigh. "Who is it?"

"George," I whispered, mostly to myself, fumbling to unlock my phone. I should've spoken to him days ago, like I promised Emmeline I would, but I couldn't get my courage up. Something between us had been so wrong for so long I worried he hated me for it. I was eager to see what he'd be messaging me about so late at night.

My finger was finally about to hit the final number to my passcode when Wren's hand over mine stopped me. I looked at him from the corners of my eyes. He was glaring.

"Ignore him," he demanded.

I tried to hit the last number anyway but he pried my hand away. My phone fell to the sand between my legs. After about thirty seconds, the screen went dull. It felt like watching George disappear from me entirely, for him to be gone forever.

Desperately, I said to Wren, "But he's my friend... One of the only ones I have."

"Is he?" Wren slithered his arm between my legs and slapped his hand down over my phone so I couldn't pick it back up again. "You've hardly spoken in days. He abandoned you for no reason."

His brown eyes had always been dark and slitted, but never like this. His gaze on me was razor-sharp like knives, so dark I didn't recognize them at all. His body fit over mine; a head over me, a hand over me, a chest over me. To either side of us, there was nothing but empty, open beach. No one else for miles. For some reason, this made me feel more trapped than the car driving through the alleyway.

"Maybe his messages will explain," I tried cautiously.

I inched my fingers towards my phone but he caught my wrist with a hand to stop me. With his other hand, he finally picked my phone up off the sand. He held it up so that I couldn't see it, to the side so that I couldn't reach it.

"What are you doing?" I asked, feeling like my words were being tugged out in the undertow of the waves, completely away from him.

His fingers slid over the screen in the pattern of my passcode, perfectly in one try unlike me. Then they tapped sharply three times, a serious expression darkening his features.

"There," he answered, flexing his fingers around my wrist. His grip was so tight I was beginning to lose feeling in my fingers. "All gone."

"What? Wren, wait—"

"No." He dropped my phone once again and shoved it away. With both hands, he grabbed me and held me still. "Naomi, listen to me. You're better off with no friends if that's how they treat you. You're better off with no one but me."

"Wren," I whispered, having no idea what to do or say.

Perhaps he was right, but I still cared about George. That had to count for something, right? Besides, I could have texted George as easily as he could've texted me, but I never did. I told Wren this.

"You told me he was acting strange around you all the sudden," Wren pointed out. "That's not your problem to solve. It was his. And he left you in the dark about it. No explanation. No apology. Friends shouldn't do that to each other, right?"

My mouth opened to respond, but no words came. Even if they did, they'd have drowned out in everything else; the ocean, Wren's labored breathing, my pounding heart.

"Right, Naomi?" he urged, laying me back.

Still I couldn't speak. Hovering above me, his nostrils flared. I forced my head to move—chin up and down, up and down, up and down—in the weakest attempt at a nod I'd ever given.

With a hard press of his lips to mine, I knew he'd taken it as my agreement.

I kept my eyes open, staring to the side down the open beach. Watching the stretch of sand around me, blissfully quiet and still, but terrifyingly empty, my chest ached. There was no one, no one at all besides Wren and I, and I was, for the very first time, terrified of that. Tears painted paths down my cheeks.

"*So pretty*," Wren would say, if only he noticed.

32

George didn't try messaging me again. Paralyzed by the inability to decide what the right thing to do was, I didn't message him either.

In school we continued to travel around the halls in a group with Emmeline and make pretend. For her sake, those deleted messages never happened. Hell, whatever made things weird before to make those messages necessary in the first place never happened. George and I still couldn't face each other one-on-one, and our idle chat over lunch was barely convincing, but it was enough for Emmeline to have a smile on her face. That was really all we could ask for.

Wren's words, Wren's tone of voice in speaking those words, Wren's hands on my wrists and grip on my shoulders; they all plagued me. Looking at George, his brown hair stuffed beneath his gray beanie with even less tact than usual, his normally bright eyes dulled out to a muddy shade of green, his posture slouched but bones rigid, I didn't have a clue what to do. It was clear that whatever he needed to say to me was important, and quite possibly dragging him down further and further each day, but how could I explain myself? How could I truly tell him what happened, why it happened, and how I'm now not so sure if our friendship is good for us anymore?

Would it be better to drift away from him and Emmeline both? To force a wedge, tear myself away, make myself obsolete? Or was Wren, who was older than me, smarter than me, stronger than me, somehow wrong? Disobeying his words, his heartfelt advice, felt like breaking the law. So then... *What*?

In the end, the choice was taken from me.

Yet another drama club rehearsal was running late. Much later than any other, in fact, which none of us would've thought possible a week before. It was well past 6:00 PM and the cast and crew were dead on their feet in the auditorium, collectively praying that Matt would take pity and let us out soon. He was in one of his deeply critical moods, nitpicking everything from the inflection Carla spoke one singular word in to the foot TJ first stepped onto the stage with. These moods of his were becoming more and more commonplace, as they tended to be when he was upset.

Matt's feelings, whether they be good or bad, had the strangest ways of manifesting. Sometimes he reminded me of a child who wasn't quite sure what to do with their feelings, and therefore ignored them entirely until they came out in the form of tantrums or sporadic bursts of untameable energy. He'd always been that way; juggling everything quite terribly, dropping one thing after another along the way, but never giving up.

Curled up into a seat in the front row, where I was supposed to be attentively watching those on stage and taking notes (peer-critique was yet another strange quirk of Matt's philosophy as a drama coach), I began to fall asleep. Recently I'd been up into the unholy hours of the night, every single night. If it wasn't to be on the phone with Wren, it was to be between him and the passenger seat of his car. Then there was the beach, of course, where I'd laid underneath him in the sand until the sun was already beginning to peak its way back up in the sky. It was finally taking its toll on me.

Compounding that lack of sleep with how much I missed Matt, how deeply I yearned to talk to George, and how nervous I was constantly thinking about my sister-to-be, I'd become a wreck. Falling asleep in rehearsal, no matter how stupidly late it was running, was a mistake. There was no better way to set off red flags around my head. I couldn't have anyone worrying about it, about *me*. I had Wren for that. He assured me that was enough. I just had to keep believing him.

In true Matt fashion, he called the end of rehearsal in the most roundabout, dismissive way possible. After Emmeline recited the final line in the scene they'd been running, he clapped twice, slapped down his script on the little podium he'd dragged onto the stage, and turned in a dramatic twirl that made the loose ends of his hair fly around. The curtains waved as he waltzed through them out of sight. After about thirty seconds of watching those curtains sway back and forth, back and forth, back and forth, we took it as our cue.

I stayed in my seat, knees tucked to my chest, head resting over them, and watched until the curtains stood still again. Shadows shifted across the stage as people collected their belongings and made to leave. Eventually those stilled as well. Emmeline was last. She hopped down the steps, long hair and thick yellow cardigan both bouncing around with her, and joined me. In the seat to my left, she folded herself into a pose to mirror mine, except her gaze was on me and not the stage.

"Okay?" she asked, knocking her knees into mine.

I hummed noncommittally. The answer to that question was more loaded than we had the time for. And even if we did, my attention was held elsewhere at the moment. Shortly after Matt disappeared through the curtains, George had, too. Though I didn't have the right angle or amount of light to see them, I knew that that side of the stage didn't lead anywhere special. So it was safe to assume that they were still back there together. What I wanted to know was why.

It could be anything—absolutely anything—that they were discussing under the dim lights between those blood red curtains, and I hated that. Knowing George was talking to Matt was different than if it was TJ or Lucy or even Carla. Because if it was TJ or Lucy or Carla, I wouldn't immediately assume the topic of conversation was me.

I shifted into a different position, leaning against Emmeline and using her as support to angle myself just right. I could just barely make them out, standing close together, heads bowed.

"What are you—"

"Shh," I hushed her, as if I'd be able to hear Matt and George from this far away anyway.

I leaned forward another inch, wanting to be that much closer to where they were. Emmeline fell silent and moved with me, eyes tracing my line of vision to watch the same thing. In silence broken only by our soft breathing, we watched Matt and George's conversation together from afar. It appeared as if George was rambling, mouth moving a mile a minute, hands wringing at his waist, eyes on the dusty floor under their feet.

George *never* rambled. This seemed to peak Emmeline's interest as much as it did mine. She sat up a little straighter and cocked her head to the side, deep red lips pursed. I tapped my fingers on her knee, as if to silently communicate that I was confused, too, but we'd talk about it later.

Matt watched George with that look of his that I could call nothing other than the 'parent look'—all his facial muscles were engaged and pulled taut, his eyes were wide but in interest, not shock, and his entire posture was open. His lips weren't in a smile but they weren't in a frown either. He looked so grown up, so mature, so genuinely concerned by whatever it was George divulged to him.

Aside from the hair falling loosely down his face and across his shoulders in knots, he looked entirely too composed. I knew that as his look of seriousness, as if he'd slid off the mask of a goofy teacher, fun guardian, young man, and become nothing but a doting father. I knew it because he did it for me. More than before, desperately, I wanted to know why he was doing it for George.

His hand fell on George's shoulder and he replied, mouth hardly opening around his words, as if he were whispering. I squinted at them both, trying and failing to read their lips. With her head directly beside mine, I could sense Emmeline doing the same. When Matt's eyes flitted through the curtains, looking out towards the auditorium where we sat watching, we both flung backwards. Our heads knocked, the cheap seats beneath us shook, and I tumbled down to the floor.

"Did he see us?" Emmeline asked urgently, rubbing her temples.

In a heap on the floor, I glared up at her. She was the one who could still see them.

Apologetically, she offered me her hand and helped me up. By the time we resettled on the chairs, Matt and George both were gone from view. I flung my head left to right repeatedly, searching for either one of them. Turns out they were already down the steps and into the auditorium with us. They were both casual and relaxed with soft smiles on their faces. Emmeline and I shared a look.

"Everything alright?" she asked the two of them, quite bravely.

"Course," Matt answered smoothly. "Why wouldn't it be?"

Emmeline ducked her head in an attempt to catch George's eyes, which were downcast, and replied, "Because that conversation looked intense."

My heart missed a beat and fell through my chest. My pupils dilated and I stared at Emmeline in utter shock.

"Did it?" George lifted his gaze, his smile going lopsided. His eyes bore holes into me.

I felt pinned to the spot. I couldn't even get my head to nod in agreement.

"Aha, well, the March Hare is quite serious business," Matt added, patting George on the back a couple times.

Him and George laughed together, as if they were in on a joke that Emmeline and I didn't know the punchline to. I'd seen Matt interact with George countless times before, as both a friend of mine and as a member of the drama club, but I'd never seen it like this. Something wasn't quite right. In the space between them, something heavy and invisible to all eyes but their own hovered. They were carrying something between the two of them; a partnership forged over a secret.

When Matt composed himself again, he rounded the three of us up together and asked, "Alright, who's hungry? I was thinking Chinese food. You kids want Chinese food?"

Emmeline seemed to forget all about the strangeness of before and jumped up and down with excitement. George nodded along. Matt chuckled, pulling up a menu on his phone. They input their orders together as a normal, happy family would. I watched it all from the side, struggling to understand what just happened.

George and Emmeline ended up staying over the night, even though Matt had been very adamant about *no boys allowed* only months earlier. All of us, Matt included, made camp in the living room with sleeping bags and one faulty air mattress. We had an impromptu game night with Chinese food and far too much soda. My initial weariness wore off fast and happiness took its place. I'd missed them.

With that, the choice on whether or not to allow George back into my life was made for me. Of course things between us were not nearly what they were before, what with all the things left unsaid, but we were still friends. Just the same as Matt was still my dad, even if we were fighting.

When Wren messaged me late into the night, I decided to keep this all to myself. I told him I was feeling tired and would call in the morning. It was the first time I'd ever told him a lie.

<h1 style="text-align:center">33</h1>

Never did I think I would see the day where I missed talking to Jin through Matt. It may have been tedious, complicated, and excessively annoying, but it was still a million times better than receiving texts directly from Jin.

Finding the words to say back to him all on my own was hard, even in the simplest of conversations with the simplest of answers to choose from. Worse than that, it felt as if we were solidifying a relationship outside of Matt and I didn't want that. We had *no* relationship without Matt.

Jin
8:10 a.m.
going 2 Forks and Spoons for bkfst this AM! Wanna come? Bring a friend!! ^◻^

Forks and Spoons was a small restaurant in the center of town. It wasn't somewhere I'd think of as the typical Jin-and-Julie-type-place since it was casual and cheap and they were stupidly fancy and rich. Matt and I had gone a handful of times before, though, and we loved it. I hadn't been in a while, nor had I seen Jin and Julie in a while, eitherm so I knew I should go. The thought of taking Emmeline along, allowing her to meet them and understand me that much better, was appealing as well. Even still, getting my fingers to type out an affirmative response was like pulling teeth.

After five minutes of typing and deleting, retyping and deleting all over again, I scrambled out from underneath my covers and scurried down the hallway to Matt's bedroom. He always left his door cracked, so I could see him then lounging against his head-board, deeply immersed in a book. I recognized the cover as one I'd gifted him for Christmas.

"Matt," I said softly, nudging the door open wider with my shoulder.

His eyes shot up immediately and he set his book down, current page dog-eared in that way I hated but Matt swore by because he could never keep track of book marks.

"Come in." He motioned with a hand.

I slipped past the doorway and paused. It'd been a while since I'd breached that space, since I'd seen where and how Matt lived when he was entirely alone. His room was smaller than mine. Somehow, amidst everything else, I'd forgotten something so simple as that.

Our house didn't have a master bedroom, only my larger bed-room and his smaller one—which had been advertised as an office space—so there was hardly room for what little he owned. On the farthest wall, beneath the singular window covered by thick red drapes, his bed sat—a full size mattress, despite the fact that he loved space and slept like a starfish. Beside this was his short brown nightstand, covered with all sorts of things: his wallet with loose bills spilling out of it, haphazardly stacked books, a pair of earbuds, a bunch of his rings, an empty mug. The only other thing in the entire room was his dresser, a short, four-drawer overflowing with poorly folded jeans and t-shirts.

Looking around, the white walls stripped bare of any decorations, the space empty of anything more than necessity, I felt my heart stutter. There was no way to describe his room other than sad. Maybe even lonely. And to me, there was no better way to see through someone else's eyes than to take a look at their bedroom; the way they organized, what they kept, how they kept it.

Matt, based on this very reasoning of mine, was a messy, lonely minimalist. I suddenly felt worse than ever for being upset with him, for allowing him to wallow in this sadness for weeks believing that *"whose kid am I, anyway?"* was a question I truly needed the answer to. There was no other person whose kid I could be.

The way I used to do when I was young, I crawled up onto his bed and curled into a ball beside him. He draped his arm over my shoulders lightly.

"What's up, peanut?" he asked quietly.

Pathetically, tears sprung into my eyes. I blinked them away rapidly. I knew I owed him an apology, but I couldn't seem to drag the words out. Not right then. Jin's message sat heavy in my pocket. I pulled my phone out, unlocked it, and dropped it onto the comforter bunched over Matt's legs. The message shone up at us, unanswered. His pupils shifted and shrunk as he read it over. Then the bed frame began creaking as his body shook with laughter.

"What?" I asked, rereading Jin's message to make sure I hadn't missed something apparently so hilarious.

"Sorry, sorry." He continued to laugh, bright blue eyes crinkling at the corners. "It's just that, well, Jin is sort of an idiot, isn't he?"

This pulled a laugh out of me.

"I know," I agreed, unable to stop myself, "but what about that message made *you* realize that?"

"Dunno," Matt admitted, laughter turning a bit manic. "It's been a while since I've gotten any texts from him. Guess I forgot how funny they are."

Half of me felt guilty to hear Jin and Matt hadn't been speaking, and the other half of me was relieved that they weren't, because at least then they couldn't fight. Rereading the text one more time, I began laughing more honestly alongside Matt. Jin's messages were pretty funny now that I thought about it. Abbreviations were entirely unnecessary, as were his emoticons and exclamation points. I laughed until my chest hurt, then listened to Matt snort beside me and laughed some more. For so long, we'd kept each other at arms distance, kept our smiles solely to ourselves, so laughing in the same vicinity was like opening a floodgate.

The feeling was the best one I'd had in a long time.

It took a while for us to compose ourselves. When we did, Matt placed my phone into my open hands. The tiniest bit of seriousness was slipping into his eyes, lighting them up and making his pupils large again.

"God," he breathed, still grinning wildly. "This is what got you so worked up at eight twenty in the morning?"

I huffed some air through my nose as a response.

"Want me to answer for you?" he asked, head tilting, hair falling sideways.

When I was little and crawled into his bed like this after a nightmare, he'd let me braid those loose strands to keep myself distracted. Not that I was ever any good at braiding. It ended up in knots most of the time. Matt never cared.

"I'm sorry," I blurted, heart heavy.

Matt gave up so much for me and I never thanked him for it. Not properly at least. This anger I felt was nothing compared to my gratitude, and yet I'd allowed anger to be the only emotion I let out towards him for over a month.

Matt's expression faltered before softening.

"It's alright," he said, and I hated how easy those words were for him to say and clearly mean. "Just let me know if you want to tag along with Jin or not and I'll answer for you. It might be good to get out a little, hmm?"

He didn't get it. That's not what I was sorry for. That wasn't even close to what I was sorry for. I opened my mouth to push it further, to explain every single little thing I had to apologize to him over, but he cut me off.

"What do you say, Naomi?" His fingers hovered over the keys on my phone in my hands, waiting. "*Forks and Spoons* on Jin and Julie? You could get the loaded pancake stack."

My lips tugged at the corners—whether that be towards a smile or a frown, I couldn't tell.

"It's okay to go," he assured me quietly. "It's okay to *want* to go."

"I... I'll go. I'll invite Emmeline."

"If you're sure."

Matt smiled, soft and genuine, if not a little sad. He typed out a quick, casual affirmative to Jin on my phone and let me hit the button to send it myself. Jin almost instantly sent back a bunch of smiley faces and thumbs up emojis. Matt chuckled. The sound was nothing like his laugh before. It'd gone hollow. I wanted to take back my words and stay home.

"Upsy daisy!" Matt proclaimed, lifting me off the bed and slinging me over his shoulder. I squealed. "Jin'll probably speed his way over here so you've got maybe ten minutes to get changed and call Emmeline along. Hurry, hurry."

He carried me down the hallway and plopped me down on my own bed. It bounced underneath my weight and I nearly fell right back off. As he left—moving a little faster than strictly necessary—he clicked my door shut behind him, but not before turning around to flash me one last smile. I couldn't help but feel like it was empty. Matt was a good actor, that much I'd always know, but I was only then beginning to realize the extent of it. He acted so much that I hadn't noticed the roles becoming a part of him, the masks slipping on and off of his face as easily as gloves on his hands.

"It's alright," his voice repeated, drifting to my ears from the other side of the closed door.

I didn't believe him anymore.

34

An hour later, I found myself sitting in a torn-up booth at Forks and Spoons across from Jin and Julie (whose stomach was finally showing the slightest bump, much to my dismay). Instead of Emmeline at my side, it was George. Apparently Thomas had returned home late last night, so the Blackwells were tied up for a while—at least until he inevitably left again.

Thankfully George and I were talking again. He was more than willing to tag along at the last minute and keep me company. He'd even put some effort into making a good impression on Jin and Julie, though I couldn't have cared less whether he did or not. His trademark beanie was gone, leaving his hair loose and fluffy, tucked behind his ears and curled up at the ends. Instead of a large sweatshirt or graphic t-shirt, he was in a deep blue button down, collar perfectly folded. On top of that, he interacted with them openly. A smile stayed in place across his lips, his normally subdued voice became loud and excited, and his hands gestured around wildly.

Cutting my eyes to him, I watched as he listened attentively to Julie's stories—things that were definitely not pleasant like her swollen feet, constant morning sickness, and new affinity for peanut butter on dill pickles. My disgusted scowl had to be hidden behind my mug of coffee and Jin's amused laugh had to be muffled with a forkful of eggs, but George had nothing to hide, nothing to stifle. He was fully composed. Fully genuine. Julie was enamored with him.

A strange thought hit me as I swallowed a large sip of the bitter coffee: my life would be a hundred times easier if I could love someone like George. He was good, he was patient, he was funny. Most importantly, he was someone I could sit beside in public without worrying about it. Thinking about it made me sad because I didn't love George, not in that way, no matter how much simpler it would make things. I was much closer to loving Emmeline, but I couldn't even let myself think about that.

"Oh, that's right," Julie was saying, cheek smushed up against her palm. "That's so soon now, isn't it?"

George nodded, carefully cutting a square out of his waffle and chewing it in the back of his mouth quickly. "Next weekend."

"What?" I cut in, realizing I hadn't actually heard a word they'd said in a long time, too deep in my own thoughts, too focused on tuning out Julie's pregnancy stories.

"We were discussing your upcoming performance," Jin answered, smiling.

"Alice in Wonderland?" I asked, as if there were any other performances they could be talking about. George furrowed his brows.

"Well of course," Julie exclaimed. "We want to make sure we make it to see you play the Cheshire Cat! That must be such a fun role, dear."

"Sure," I conceded.

I turned to George, wondering how much he'd said while I was tuning out. I never told Jin or Julie about the play at all, never mind what role I'd be playing. Them caring enough to remember and show up was never something I considered. Especially recently with how little we talked, how awkward we were.

"So which is best: opening night or closing night?" Jin asked.

George thought this over sincerely before telling them opening night. Not wanting to say anything more, or to think anything more, I nodded along to his explanation. Jin and Julie putting in the effort towards me—taking me out to breakfast, planning to come to my performances at school, learning about my interests—should have made me happy, but the only thing it did was set a stone in my gut, making everything heavy and sickening.

Underneath the table, George's hand found mine, pressing down against it to hold it still. I hadn't realized I was shaking until he stopped it, not missing a beat in his conversation with Jin and Julie all the while. His hand was cold and smooth. His touch was familiar and comfortable. It was much like Matt's. I swallowed back the feeling that this realization gave me. Somehow, without me noticing, George had become like family to me. Somehow, without starting a fight, I'd have to tell Wren that.

Almost as if Wren had a radar for his name in my mind, my phone began to ring right then. His contact lit up the screen when I tugged it out of my pocket. I scrambled to cover it up, accidentally declining the call in the process.

"Shit," I murmured, fumbling to unlock it and send him a quick text.

My thumbs had barely hit three letters before it rang again.

"Naomi, is everything alright?" George asked, watching my face carefully.

"Yes, sorry, of course. I just—sorry, I gotta take this."

I scrambled up out of the chair and rushed to the bathroom, locking myself in the first open stall I could find. Jin, Julie and George were left behind me in varying levels of shock and confusion. Resting my forehead against the wall, I picked up.

"Naomi."

"Wren, I'm so sorry, I didn't mean to decline." The words rushed out of me in one breath. Ever since our night at the beach, I was terrified of upsetting him. I didn't want to do anything that might make him think I didn't want him, didn't *need* him like he knew I did.

"I'm outside," he said, ignoring my apology. Then, as if it needed clarifying, he added, "*Forks and Spoons.*"

"You're... What?" My heart hammered. "I thought you were with your dad."

"Well I figured you'd need some cheering up after seeing Jin and Julie so I ditched to come to pick you up. I see now that I was wrong."

Trying to calm myself, I traced graffiti on the blue stall. Smiley faces, phone numbers, hearts with initials inside of them. My hands shook, barely able to follow the simplest of lines.

Wren kept talking, "Here I was, going out of my way for you while you were holding hands with another guy. And fucking George, of all people. Since when are you talking to him again? I thought we established he wasn't good for you, Naomi."

Lies come back to bite you. Even little white lies like this one, like neglecting to tell Wren that George and I were friends still. They come back and bite, leaving open wounds that leak and leak and leak until you have nothing left to give. I was draining out in the stall of a cheap breakfast place. A breakfast place I should've thought twice about coming to with George, even just as my friend and moral support. The building was made up of practically all windows. Anyone could see through and notice us. *Wren* could.

When I finally found the words to reply to him with, they weren't the ones I intended to find. I said,"I never told you what restaurant we were going to."

Wren's laughter pierced through the line and into my skull.

"I'm aware of that, baby." His voice was cold, disembodied from his beautiful, warm body. "I wonder why that was."

"It's not like that," I blurted, sounding far too defensive. I knew I was only digging myself deeper into the ground.

"No?"

"No," I asserted. *Spit it out, spit it out, spit it out.* "George is like family to me. Nothing more."

"Family," he repeated, as if tasting the word on his tongue before spitting it back out. "We both know how *uneasy* those can be."

My body shook. Of course I knew. There was no guarantee that anyone would stay, family or not. It only got more complicated once that label was there. No one knew that like me or Wren. That's why I liked him so much; he understood me. Silence filled the line between us for a beat too long before his patience snapped.

"Come on, I want to go. Get out here."

Unlatching the lock of the stall with trembling fingers, I moved to follow his command. The mirror before me was smudged by fingerprints and droplets of water, but even so, I knew I looked awful in the reflection of it. Eyes wide, pupils shaking; hair frizzy, strands falling chaotically over my forehead, red from being pressed against the stall; fingers coated in the residue of ink off those very walls.

I wanted to cry, I wanted to scream, I wanted to pretend the phone call never happened, I wanted to slip out the doors without being noticed and be with Wren for the rest of time. I didn't know what I really wanted, other than someone to tell me that it was okay.

So I left. I said my rushed goodbyes, assured them all that I was fine but needed to leave, and I left. I went to Wren, leaving George high and dry with my birth father and his wife. The second I stepped into the passenger side of Wren's car, he drove away so quickly that, even if I wanted to, I wouldn't have been able to look back.

The entire drive out to yet another abandoned area where only the two of us would exist for miles, he said nothing. In the awkward silence, I stared out at the clouds and hoped and prayed that George hadn't seen a thing. And that even if he had, he would never speak a word of it to anyone.

Wren was angry for the rest of the day and all through the night. No matter how much I apologized, no matter how many times I explained, he remained angry. And yet I stayed there with him, in those fits of anger, and told myself it was what needed to be done. He had a right to be angry, after all. We both knew that. Because while he had been thinking of me and giving up time with his father to come pick me up—so kindly, so selflessly—I had been omitting information, betraying his trust. No matter how sharp his tongue got as we sat alone for hours, I stayed. Even when he pinned me to the ground, fingers digging into my skin and teeth grazing at my neck, I stayed. I put on my best act and kept the tears at bay, pretending that there was no piece of me that was afraid.

At the last second before he finished, he said those special words—the ones that made me go with him in the first place, the ones I desperately wanted to hear. He told me, "It's okay."

I wanted to believe him, I really did, but I couldn't this time.

<h1 style="text-align:center">35</h1>

Final fittings and adjustments for our costumes occurred the day of opening night. The performance was set for 7:00 and our dress rehearsal was only hours before it, directly after school. We hurried through it in order for us to have time for costuming. The poor art and design club in charge of our costumes was forced to rush alterations and add every tiny detail Matt found necessary as we tried things on for the first time. They'd been behind for the entirety of the year and our complex, wacky costume designs were definitely not helping. For the two smallest clubs in the school, we surely worked up a storm.

"Step here, please."

A quiet freshman by the name of Payton was in charge of my costume. They were helping me step inside the legs, pull the cloth over my body, and straighten out the seams. Last minute pins and changes would have to happen between the two of us right then. The costume was a full body unitard, long sleeves and long legs, a bushy tail pinned to the back.

Payton had done a fantastic job; it was perfectly accurate—which was what made it so awful. Bright pink and purple stripes covered the entirety of the skin-tight spandex material, clinging to me like it was soaking wet. The only loose fabric was around my neck, hanging almost as if it were meant to be a hood but it was on backwards. Across this loose fabric was a perfectly stitched cheshire smile to pull over my mouth like a mask.

"Is it okay?" Payton asked, observing me as I shimmied around in the outfit. "Too tight? Too loose?"

They had measuring tape hanging around their shoulders like an oversized necklace and safety pins bunched up at their collar. Placed like a toothpick between their back molars was a sewing needle. The commitment was endearing. I'd never met someone so attentive to their high school club before.

"It's good," I answered, twisting my torso around to stare at the obnoxious tail hanging from my lower back.

Payton stared at me another minute in silence. They had big brown eyes and a splatter of freckles over the bridge of their nose. Part of me suddenly wanted to ask how they knew they were non-binary. I never felt like I was or could be myself, but under the umbrella of queer identities, I always felt... Well, *something*. These days it was bothering me more and more and I didn't know why. I was with Wren. That should have been the end of it. I knew that was what he would say, anyway.

Payton squinted at me and said, "I'll lower the tail before you go on," and I snapped my mouth shut. That tail became my new favorite piece of the costume.

Payton grabbed a pair of ears (also bright pink and stupidly fluffy) from off the table to their left and carefully slid it over the top of my head. They tucked my hair underneath it and shifted it back and forth until it was to their liking. I kept my eyes on the wall behind them, counting stains and trying to keep myself from twitching. Payton was a fine person and all, but they had little sense of personal space and boundaries. It felt unnatural to have a stranger so close to me. At least when they adjusted my costume, there was a clinical distance to their touch, as if they were a doctor wearing sterile gloves. That made it the tiniest bit easier to breathe.

"You really did this all yourself?" I asked.

"Yes," Payton answered, and that was the end of that conversation.

For what felt like hours, I stood there in silence with Payton while they stuck pins into my costume, jotted words down in a tiny notebook, and muttered to themself over the imperfections of their work. All around us, other members of the drama club were enduring the same sorts of things with their costume designers from the art and design club. In between the middle curtains of stage left, George was trying on different colored top hats with bunny ears attached to them while wearing his striped pants and half of his blazer. The girls assisting him were giggling and snapping photos on their phones, but not without finding things to fix in the process.

Past him, standing center stage, was Emmeline. A singular light beamed down directly on her, slowly shifting in colors as the tech people tested them out. She was in her full costume: simple blue dress, white apron and black hair bow. I envied such simplicity.

Matt was right in front of her with a hand on his chin, tilting back and forth as if searching for a complaint. He'd been bouncing around ever since we started, examining everyone one by one. Based on the continual side-eyes of the art and design kids, his opinions were not all that welcome. Not that he cared.

"Too bad your eyes are blue," Payton murmured, face inches from my own.

I snapped my attention back to them and pulled my chin into my chest. "What?"

"The cat's eyes are yellow."

"Oh," I said, "Yeah." As if anyone had naturally yellow eyes.

The conversation ended abruptly there, the same way it had before. Payton was not very good at this. But, then again, neither was I.

Once we finally wrapped up with costume adjustments, there was less than an hour left until showtime. Matt had begun running back and forth by that point, suit jacket off, button-down rolled halfway up his arms. He was frantic and nervous, almost as if he'd be the one taking the stage later. As Emmeline grabbed me by the hand and tugged me backstage to quickly do our makeup, I felt that same swell of anxiety reach me. Acting was fun and I loved to do it, but that didn't stop the pre-show jitters. Especially knowing that Wren, Jin, and Julie would all be somewhere in the crowd, watching me.

Emmeline did my makeup first, and finished it within five minutes. There wasn't much to do for me since I'd have a mask pulled over my face for the most part. She simply coated my eyelids in pink eyeshadow (thankfully a different shade than my bright costume), drew thin black lines over that, brushed some gold highlighter high on my cheekbones, and called it a day. When it came my turn to help her, I held the eyeliner pen between two fingers while she blended foundation into skin, patted blush over her cheeks, swiped light blue eyeshadow over her lids, and painted her lips in their usual red. It didn't take her long to do any of this either.

"Okay, ready," she said, turning towards me. "Eyeliner me."

The rest of the time we had before the show was spent with me doing her eyeliner. I moved painfully slowly, terrified of ruining all her hard work. My hands were never known for being steady, especially then with the stress of the performance and her face so close to mine.

"Knock, knock," came Matt's voice. He stood in the doorway, smiling reassuringly and tapping his knuckles against the doorframe in sync with his words. "Showtime in ten. Let's go, kiddos, let's go."

In a flurry of motion, we finished up and followed Matt to join the rest of the crew backstage. Through a thin crack in the curtains, I could see the auditorium, filled to the brim with people. My eyes scanned up and down the aisles, row by row, across every last chair, until I found the three people I was looking for. Strangely enough, they were all in the same area. Jin and Julie, dressed far too nicely for a high school play, were sitting front and center. No more than three rows back from that was Wren. Surprisingly enough, Thomas was directly beside him.

Emmeline came up on my left side, staring through at the audience with me. For a while, we stood there together and said nothing. Distantly, I could hear Matt's voice over the speakers, welcoming everyone and announcing the show. But it became just another part of the white noise all around me; Emmeline's soft breathing beside my head, our castmates chattering back and forth behind us, my own heartbeat in my ears.

"Come on Naomi," Emmeline murmured, taking my hand and tugging me backwards.

The props had been set on stage for the opening scene and everyone was bustling backstage to prepare for the start. Everyone except for Emmeline, that is, even though she was the only one who really should've been bustling, seeing as she had the lead and would be the first on stage. Instead she was simply standing by my side, holding my hand, saying nothing.

It wasn't until the curtain lifted, the lights came up on the stage, and Matt was nearly having a heart attack from stress, that Emmeline let go. Before taking her place on the stage, she shifted me backwards so that the blood-red curtains were curving around my body, engulfing me within them. Startled, I grabbed at her shoulders for support, feeling like I was drowning in fabric.

She smiled, teeth shining under the low lights, before leaning forward and pressing her lips very lightly to mine.

"Best of luck out there," she told me through a laugh, rushing out and taking her place just in time.

36

"Wh-what?" I stammered, long after Emmeline was gone and I was left alone backstage, tangled in the curtains.

My soul felt like it had been sucked clean out of my body. I brought my cold fingertips up to my chapped lips and tapped, testing the feeling there as if that would suddenly reveal to me that what Emmeline had just done was only a figment of my imagination.

Unfortunately it did not. The truth was: Emmeline kissed me. The harsher truth was: I didn't push her away. Sure, it was hardly a second long, and much more a brief brush of lips than an actual kiss, but still, I had allowed her to do it for that split second. I began to regret not having that *am I queer?* heart-to-heart with Payton earlier.

Blood rushed to my ears. Heart pounding through my skull, I wondered: what would Wren say? What would Wren *do*? If he found out, would he hate her, his baby sister, the same way he hated George? The same way he hated anyone who got a little too close to me? I couldn't take another fight. Not with Wren. I loved him, but sometimes he scared me. Sometimes, when we fought, when he was really and truly upset, it made me feel small. It reminded me how much more experience he had in life, how much more he knew, and, in turn, how young and stupid I actually was. Ever since he picked me up from *Forks and Spoons* and we had that huge fight, I'd been seeing the divide between us more and more.

"Naomi..."

"Naomi..."

"Naomi!"

My head rattled as I shook myself back into focus. Matt was standing before me, eyes wide, hands hovering around my shoulders to push the curtains away from me. More than ever, I wanted to tell him everything. I wanted to start at the first moment I met Wren and end with what happened with Emmeline just now, then let him tell me what I should do about it all. But I couldn't. Matt and I were not in a place for those sorts of conversations right now. There was a devil on one of my shoulders reminding me of that; of how it was Matt's fault that we were having a hard time with each other these days. I held onto that little devil's reminder because if I didn't, then these feelings of mine, the ones with no clear ending in sight, would also have no clear beginning. And then I would feel even more helpless.

"Hey." Matt again. He placed his palms lightly over my shoulders, squashing that little devil. "You're on soon. What's going on?"

Past us, on the stage, Emmeline was absolutely glowing. My breath picked up again. Even admitting her beauty to myself felt like a betrayal, even though I'd always found Emmeline beautiful. Something about that simple fact was not so simple anymore. *Nothing* in my life was simple anymore. I wanted it to stop.

"Dad," I said, stepping forward into his space on shaky legs. I had missed so much of the play already. So much so that I was close to missing my own parts. Even so, I couldn't get myself to move any further, to get out there and perform as I should.

Matt's eyes blew open, that impossibly bright blue boring into me. His jaw fell open with no sound.

"I'm scared."

My voice sounded foreign even to my own ears. It crackled and broke, falling out of me like someone was pulling the words from where they'd been lodged for days within my throat. It should've felt like a weight off my chest to admit that, but it only made the feeling worse.

Matt tugged me into his chest, wrapping me up so tightly that it hurt my rib cage. I held on equally as tight, worried that I would sink through the ground and disappear forever if I let go. My face was getting hot, tears pooling in the corners of my eyes.

"Why?" he asked finally, though something about the tone of his voice sounded a little too hardened for the question to be one of mere curiosity. It almost sounded like he already knew the answer to it and just wanted my confirmation—which was absurd because I didn't even know the answer. There were too many things going on for there to be one answer to that question.

I pulled away, shaking my head like a wet dog. I wiped the skin underneath my eyelids to make sure it was still dry and forced a smile.

"Stage fright." I shrugged, internally begging him to take the excuse.

After a pause so long I thought I would miss my cue to go onto the stage before he answered, Matt smiled. A smile with no teeth, no crinkled eyes, and no dramatic head tilt. A fake smile—just like mine.

"Don't worry about it. You'll be great," he said honestly, crossing his arms tightly as if keeping them to himself. "And if you're still scared after the fact—well, you never have to do it again."

The pink and purple bodysuit all over my body felt more suffocating than ever. I tugged at the fabric around my neck and stomach, trying to get some space, some air. Matt's voice was carefully neutral, but not careful enough. I'd gotten better at reading him, at taking notice of when that mask went up and he slipped away. Right then, he had slipped away entirely.

"Never again," he emphasized, ushering me through the curtains so I could make my entrance.

I stepped onto the stage in a haze. Performing came to me as easily as ever, like it was second nature. Judging by the cheers filling the auditorium at the end, the show must've been good. Not that I properly remember any of it. The world had turned to dark fog around me.

37

Stripping off that bright Cheshire Cat bodysuit was bliss. It was the one and only thing of the entire night that made me feel weightless. Even Payton's look of pure astonishment beside me as I threw the fabric to the ground couldn't take that away. They'd done a great job, truly, and I was thankful for their help in getting into it earlier, but that didn't make it any more bearable to have worn it for hours afterward. And given what had happened *during* those hours, I never wanted to see that outfit again. I hardly wanted to see the color pink ever again.

The lobby outside the auditorium was flooded with people by the time I made my way there. I'd hidden in the dressing room until I was certain no other drama club members were left around the stage. That way I wouldn't run the risk of seeing Emmeline or George as I crept through the aisles. Neither one of them was ready for the whirlwind of emotions I was struggling to hold at bay. *I* wasn't ready for them.

Carla and her family were the first people I recognized as I stumbled through the crowd. She somehow managed to look entirely comfortable and classy amidst her Queen of Hearts makeup and costume, both of which were overly dramatic and objectively unattractive. How she did it, I couldn't say. Jealousy felt sickening in my gut. Not only had I swapped out my costume for sweatpants and a hoodie, but I'd scrubbed off every last bit of makeup on my face. Even then, I felt no better than I had before. Comfortable and classy were the last two words anyone would use to describe me.

Nearby Carla and her family, TJ stood with all his jock friends. They were swarming around him, taking selfies and engaging in complex hand shakes. My feet took me forward in that direction, my body mindlessly shoving through people to get there. As I did, other people I knew began to come into view. The little freshman Lucy and some of her friends to my left, some Jay High English teachers to my right, Maya struggling to get through to TJ just ahead of me, Matt, George and George's parents past her. It was inevitable that Emmeline would find her way to George, and when she did, Wren and Thomas would follow. And then I'd have no choice but to face everyone at once. The plethora of people parted for me as I tripped over my own feet towards the wall, gripping onto it for support as soon as my fingers touched it.

The lights were bright out here, beaming down on everyone like samples on an examination table. It smelled strongly of sweat and flowers. It was rather nauseating. All around me, voices overlapped, different variations of *good job* and *congratulations* on repeat. No one would stop moving. It got to feeling like even the wall I was holding onto was moving. In the thick of all of this, it was hard to hear myself think. Which was the worst possible thing at the moment because there was *a lot* I should've been thinking about.

"Are you alright, dear?" I looked up to see an old woman with jet black hair smiling at me.

I nodded, not yet trusting my voice.

"You look faint," she added, head tilting.

Again, I only nodded. I felt faint, too. Crowds and I didn't mix well on a good day, never mind on a day like this one.

She said something quietly to the gentleman beside her and he nodded vigorously before putting his arm out towards me. I simply stared at it, mapping out the thin gray stripes of his suit jacket.

"Shirley and I could use some air," he said, nodding towards the woman—*Shirley*. "Care to assist some old fellows outside?"

For an excuse to help me, it was pretty sweet. Tentatively, I reached out and wrapped my hand around the crook of the man's elbow. Once I was steadily on my own two feet instead of leaning against the wall, Shirley took my other side, holding my arm like I held his.

We walked together like that along the outskirts of the crowd as best we could, aiming for the big doors on the other side of the lobby. Those doors led straight to a parking lot. Matt's car would be in that parking lot, in the same spot it always was, and I could climb into it to disappear for a while.

Except we hardly made it halfway there. Because before we could move any further than that, I found Wren's dark eyes through the crowd. In the brief seconds that I'd taken my gaze away from Matt, George and his parents, the Blackwells had joined them. The last thing I wanted to do was join that group, but once Wren fixed his focus on me, I knew there was no escaping. So I thanked Shirley and her husband—Jack, as he introduced himself belatedly—and scurried that way. And if my feet moved a little faster once I noticed Jin and Julie walking their way, too—well, no one had to know but me.

"There she is!" Matt exclaimed, pulling me into a side hug.

To him, acting like my outburst earlier had never happened was as easy as breathing. If only it was that way for me. Instead, I felt like I couldn't act, couldn't breathe, because Emmeline, Wren, Matt, Jin and George were all in one small place and I had to find a way to keep every little secret between each of us under wraps.

"Great performance tonight," Thomas Blackwell said, grinning easily between Emmeline, George and me.

George smiled tightly in response and I peeled away from Matt in order to do an awkward curtsy-bow that was entirely unnecessary. At the very least, it made everyone laugh. Everyone except for me, of course. I was too busy trying to suck air into my lungs. This group was a recipe for disaster. Very quickly, I needed to find a way to break it up.

Against my will, my eyes drifted to Emmeline. She was pressed into her father's side, looking elated that he'd shown up. Hugged tightly against her chest was a classic bouquet of flowers: white tissue paper around red roses, daffodils, and all sorts of carnations. She caught me staring and thrust it forward with a wide smile.

"Aren't they pretty?" She shook them around, petals flying loose and floating to the floor by our feet. Her eyes twinkled with mirth.

"Beautiful," I whispered, heart thundering.

"I'm glad you think so," Wren cut in, lifting another bouquet. This one was wrapped in gold paper and overflowing with a much wider variety of flowers. Not only red roses, but black roses, too, red tulips, daisies, peonies, orchids, and even a few buttercups. I couldn't say for certain, but it looked like there was a card pressed deep between some of the stems.

"For you," he added, handing it over.

I tried and failed to control my rapidly beating heart as Wren handed the bouquet to me with one hand and tugged me into an embrace with the other. Normally when we hugged, that was not all we did. Oftentimes his hands would hold my waist or push me against walls and his lips would press against the crown of my head or deep into the crook of my neck.

This time the hug had a distance to it. His arms were wrapped carefully around the middle of my back, absolutely no wandering, and his face was as far from mine as it could get. To top it off, our bodies rocked back and forth together—waddling in that way old friends do when they run across rooms to tackle and hug one another. It felt so unnatural that I knew, even before I pulled back from him, that no one would ever believe that what had just happened was a normal, brother-of-my-bestfriend-type-hug. If this was Wren's way of being inconspicuous, he had failed miserably.

A large part of me wondered if being inconspicuous had ever even crossed his mind, though, as the smirk he sent Matt the second we stopped touching was anything but innocent. Especially because then he finally let his hands skim across parts of me that weren't meant for friends—both hands falling from my back down, skimming over my butt and curving around my hips before going back to his sides. All the while, his eyebrows stayed raised, gaze focused on Matt as if this was a challenge, and he had a burning question that only he could answer.

Matt's eyes were dark, but he began to laugh in response. A sharp, echoing laugh that overrode every single other sound in the lobby full of people.

"You've gotta be fucking kidding me," he muttered, taking a small step forward. Wren took one back. I stayed completely still, stuck in the little space between them.

"Oh god," George mumbled, grabbing both of his parents and tugging them in the opposite direction. They looked lost and terrified, the same exact way that I felt. "I wanted to be wrong so bad."

"Me too." Matt turned to George, his eyes clearing for the split second that they landed on him. His voice was low and even, but I could see his composure waning. "But it seems you weren't. Your heads up about him has helped more than you know, George. Thank you."

There was not enough time between when Matt turned back around to face Wren and when his fist flew forward for anyone to do anything but watch it happen. The crack of Wren's nose was nothing short of bone-shattering. Still, he stayed firmly planted on his feet, smiling through the blood beginning to seep out of his nostrils and over his lips.

Matt grabbed him by the collar and swung again. Someone was shouting, someone else was hysterically crying, and others were simply whispering under their breath. Which one of these people I was, I couldn't say. My feet rooted to the spot, leaving me unable to do anything as Matt kept lunging forward, Wren's blood covering his knuckles.

Gasps went up from every corner of the room, people crowding towards us to get a look at the commotion. It was this that seemed to snap everyone else out of it. Thomas shoved Emmeline towards the Washingtons before grabbing Wren by the middle and dragging him backwards. Matt made to move towards him again immediately.

"Matt, stop it!" Jin yelled, grabbing his arm mid-swing to tug him backwards as well. Matt's entire body jerked as he fought against Jin's hold. "Matt—*Matthew*, stop. That's enough."

Matt went limp in Jin's arms as if those words were a sudden off-switch. Julie stepped forward and took him from Jin, letting Matt lean against her frame like a crutch. Thomas then released

Wren, who sank to the floor in a heap. Emmeline whimpered, but George kept her from going to him with a hand on her shoulder.

Then, for a moment, the entire building went still. The only sound at all was that of Wren's breathing—heavy and labored. So much as I wanted to go to him, to clean his wounds and kiss his bruises, I didn't. Because there was a small part of me, one that had been waiting since the very first day I met Wren, to see him lose something; to see him look as pathetic and vulnerable as he always made me feel. Something about this, as sickening as it was, as nauseous as it made me feel, was strangely validating. So I allowed Jin to take me by the hand and lead me out of the building, leaving everyone and everything else behind us.

The last thing I heard before we were stepping out into the night was Thomas Blackwell's voice.

He asked, "What the hell have you done?" but it was unclear who he was actually asking the question to.

38

When I stepped outside, everything turned to static. It was May and the weather was warm, but nowhere near warm enough for me to have been sweating through my clothes. I was damp everywhere; under my armpits, along my hairline, in the socked feet in my shoes, under my breasts, down the sides of my neck where Wren liked to rub the pads of his fingers. Thinking of him, even unintentionally—distantly—made the sweat worse. This was not the sort of tingly feeling he was supposed to give me.

It must've been nearing eight or nine o'clock, but the sun had barely begun to set. Warm orange washed over the sky, bathing the lush trees planted all around the school in attractive light. Beneath them, flowers were blooming—flowers not all that different from the ones bundled up in the bouquet between my arms. Only those had not been hand-picked for me by Wren, passed over in front of everyone we'd explicitly been hiding from before.

Tearing myself away from them, from Jin, from the bouquet, I crumpled to the ground. My bottom hit the curb and I curled up over it. The entire parking lot stood before me, a wide spread of black pavement and parked cars. It looked eerily like a painting, all blurred lines and blended colors.

This didn't make any sense. Wren and me, we were a secret; a secret *he* wanted to keep. To so blatantly flaunt in front of them was... Stupid, for lack of any better word. Had he even thought at all before pulling me close to him like that? He knew I couldn't control the way my body reacted to his, the way I couldn't contain myself or think straight once his hands were on my skin. It should've been obvious to him that hugging me in front of them was a mistake. He was protective, *possessive*, of me. That back there—it had been careless. It went against everything he'd decided for us, everything I went along with for months in order to keep him by my side.

So what had made him do it?

Jin's hand fell on my shoulder and nearly sent me into cardiac arrest. He hardly flinched when I slapped it away, staring up at him with wide eyes.

"I'm not positive I've grasped the situation correctly," he began slowly, straightening out his slacks before plopping down beside me. The way he folded up his big body in order to fit in the same space as me on the curb was something I normally would have laughed at in any other circumstance. "But if I have, Naomi, there's a lot we need to talk about."

"There's nothing to say," I snapped, instincts kicking in—the instinct to block out Jin, to protect Wren, to hide myself. All of them together worked in overdrive in an attempt for me to escape this any way possible.

Jin took this in stride, folding his hands up in his lap. His wedding band reflected the remaining beams of sunlight the same way it always did, flashing around as if begging to be seen. For once, this didn't make me want to strangle him. It actually made me wish I was a little more like him; a happily married grown-up, able to flaunt my relationship without risking a single thing in return.

"Okay," Jin said, tilting his head towards the sky, letting silence envelope us.

There were bags under his eyes, wrinkles over his brows. His complexion was smooth, though, as if he'd splashed his face with water before coming out. I'd always thought Jin looked older than he really was, but suddenly he didn't. He looked younger, maybe a decade or so younger—like I always thought Matt looked. They'd swapped places seamlessly. For the same exact reason, too: me. Me and all the stress I brought into their lives.

Under stress, Matt turned mature and old, weary and burdened. Apparently Jin did the opposite; shrinking down to a level of vulnerability and humanness he otherwise buried beneath hair gel and suit jackets. He became just a young man, maybe even a kid. The Jin sitting beside me was the one I knew from the photograph buried under my mattress, the one smiling at the mother I never got to know.

Maybe that's why I opened my mouth again, breathing out a question I didn't want the answer to, but couldn't help asking nonetheless. "What do you think happened back there?"

If he was surprised to hear me ask, he didn't let it show. He nodded, as if mulling it over, as if he didn't have an immediate answer, one he'd been biting his tongue on since we left the building. I waited for the words to drop from his lips; the accusations, the anger, the sadness, the disappointment. None came.

"I think Matt allowed his personal emotions to get the better of him," Jin replied.

I startled at that. I'd expected any number of things to come from his mouth, but never that. I knew he was on Matt's side, whatever side that really was, but those words nearly made me believe he wasn't. They lulled me into believing that he'd take mine if only I shared some context.

"Why's that?" I whispered, feigning innocence.

Jin looked at me from the corners of his eyes, light brown like dry dirt. With a wry smile, he answered, so bluntly it felt like the words were slicing open my skin, "Because you're his kid, Naomi, and that man's been taking advantage of you."

"It isn't like that." The words slipped out of me immediately. He almost laughed. I pushed on, grasping at straws, "If it was, wouldn't you be angry, too? But you're out here with me, not throwing punches in there. Besides, I'm not a kid, okay? I knew what I was doing. He let me take the lead."

That was as much of an admission as any. I thought it would feel better to tell someone about Wren and me, but given the situation, it did not. It felt like empty words, contrived words, a-little-too-late words. If I even believed them myself, shouldn't they have been easier to say aloud?

Jin breathed heavily. Hearing the truth outright was clearly worse than assuming it for himself. Regret seeped through my skin down to my bones, making them heavy.

"Trust me." His voice was hard. "I'm angry."

I snapped my mouth closed. Deep within the pocket of my sweatpants, my phone was buzzing incessantly. My fingers itched to retrieve it, to unlock it and respond to him immediately, because I knew it was him. But with Jin right next to me, I couldn't.

"Listen to me."

I angled my body away from him, but I obliged. I listened.

"To Matt, something like this... It runs deep. It's personal." In my peripheral vision, I could still see him, eyebrows raised in waiting as if there was something I knew and could fill in the blanks with.

When I remained silent, he added on quietly, "And not only be-cause you're his daughter."

You're his daughter.

Two months earlier, hearing those words in his voice would've felt like the weight of the world had come off of my shoulders. I'd been searching for that admission from him for so long that I'd forgotten I already had it, that I already knew whose kid I was and I didn't need him to say it to know he did, too. Hearing it then, echoing against the pavement and through the trees around us, it made everything worse.

"Never mind." He shook his head. I turned to him again, dum-founded. "It's not exactly my place to share," he explained, but I could tell his resolve was weak. He wanted me to know whatever this was as badly as I wanted to know it myself.

"He'll understand," I answered, because it was true. Whatever this was, Matt would understand why Jin told me now. Matt un-derstood everything if given the time. Especially when it was to help someone else.

Jin sighed. Briefly, a look passed over his face that I'd never seen on him before. One that held him completely still and silent. I associated Jin with many things—most of which with negative connotations up until recently—but never once did I think he was hesitant or taciturn.

In fact, Jin was quite often the opposite of those things. Whether it be for better or worse, Jin jumped head-first into everything and he never knew when to shut his mouth. No matter what the situation, I'd never known Jin to be one for delicacy. All in all, he certainly wasn't one for holding back. So to see him then, deliber-ating pausing with his jaw clenched shut, I knew something was deeply wrong.

"Tell me," I urged, feeling my pulse race beneath my skin. Jin frowned deeply, lines creasing across his forehead. "Please tell me. What's going on? Why else could this be personal to him? *What happened?*"

The breath that came out of Jin's mouth in response to these questions could be described as nothing other than a muffled sob. The sound of it sent ice down my spine. Jin didn't do this. He didn't hesitate, he didn't hold back, and he most certainly didn't *sob*. I felt like the ground was sinking in and swallowing me whole and he hadn't even given me a proper answer yet.

Without intending for the thought to be verbalized, I murmured, "How bad can it be?"

"Oh, Naomi," he whispered, sounding near-tears, "Nothing worse has ever happened to him in his entire life."

"Please," I emphasized, the skin around my eyes on fire.

If nothing worse had ever happened to Matt, this must've been truly awful. His life wasn't exactly an easy one. Beyond that, I wanted desperately to know why it had anything to do with me, with Wren, with the way our relationship resulted in him losing his composure like that. Never before had I seen Matt fight like that. Stupidly, the idea that he knew how to throw a punch at all had never even crossed my mind.

"Shortly after your mother and I got together," he started, his face going slack with the memory. "Something happened to Matt. He began acting odd."

Everything disappeared around us as he spoke. The parking lot turned to a park, then to old school hallways, then to the locked door of a teacher's office. Jin blurred away into his younger self, side by side with Elizabeth, both chasing after a young, sad Matt.

I melted into the ground, gone, not yet alive as these moments unfolded.

They'd always been a group, the three of them, but Matt had become disconnected at some point. When Jin and Elizabeth became official, Matt retreated far into himself. Something was *off*, something had happened that he wouldn't talk about. He'd begun a relationship of his own. One that he refused to give them any details on. One he asserted he had to keep a secret, just like me with Wren.

Floating outside my body, staring down at memories that were not mine, at moments that had ended years ago, I saw it all. I saw Jin and Elizabeth chasing after the ghost of Matt. I saw them fighting, Matt crying. He kept lashing out, doing his homework under trees at the park only to turn them in and fail the next day, skipping more meals than he ate. His girlfriend pulled some strings, kept him from being kicked out or held back. Because his girlfriend, as Jin and Elizabeth found out on a late night while they held hands and ran through what they assumed to be the dark, empty halls of the high school, was the vice principal.

She was in her late thirties, Jin recalled, and was known to be extremely polite. Students loved her because she listened to them, she understood their references, and she laughed at their jokes. Jin hated her because in her office, on her worn-down couch, fourteen year-old Matt was sitting with her straddling his lap, and that's how he found out that this was the relationship Matt had been hiding.

It went on for over a year, he told me. More than an entire year. Matt refused to talk about it, refused to accept help in getting away, refused to admit anything about it was abnormal, even—though it was obvious he knew it was. He was falling apart at the seams, struggling to stay afloat, clearly unhappy. It was only when Elizabeth got pregnant that he changed his mind about her, about breaking things off. Something about the pregnancy awoke him to reality, made him see that they really were only kids. The vice principal didn't take it well. She didn't want to let him go, didn't want to risk what he might say later down the line.

Jin kept talking, kept filling in more and more blanks, giving me more information than I ever needed, and I felt sick. I couldn't take it anymore. I dry-heaved over the pavement, begging it to stop. Reality crashed back at once like one of the cars before us had rammed straight through my gut. Blinking and blinking, I stared ahead and proved that that had not happened. Nothing had changed, not really, not outwardly, but I knew some things were never going to be the same after this.

"He only successfully broke it off after Elizabeth died," Jin finished, choking up. "He took you in mere months later."

At last, I had one of the biggest questions of my life answered: why Matt's parents were so upset with him for adopting me. He took me at one of the lowest points of his life. Beside the fact that he was still just a teenager, he was a teenager who'd spent over a year in a relationship with his thirty-something vice principal who made him lose weight and push away his friends and cry all alone in the dark. Of course they would be against it, of course they would think it was stupid. It must've seemed like yet another rash decision to cope with everything—with that relationship, with losing Elizabeth, with his disappointment in Jin.

Truthfully, it might have actually been that. And if it was, then what a bad job I'd done. Rather than being useful, I'd only brought him more pain and strife, more struggle he never asked for.

Empathetic pain hurts the worst when it's for a parent. To be forced, through a throbbing heart and a lead-heavy head, to look at the person who raised you and acknowledge that they never 'had it together' the way you assumed they did; it's like jumping out of a plane without a secure parachute. Nothing at all rivals that pain, that panic, that bone-deep ache of coming face to face with the fact no one's unbroken, no one's perfect—not even the people who bury those facts in an attempt to keep you safe from them.

My throat felt raw from dry-heaving and crying.

"I'm sorry. Good God, what was I thinking telling you all that?" Jin mumbled, swiping a hand over his mouth as if he was appalled at the words he'd allowed to slip through it. "I'm sorry. I'm sorry, Naomi, but we won't allow it to happen to you, too. This ends today. My God, I'm so sorry."

With my vision spotted from tears and my throat closed up like barbed wire had wrapped around it, I couldn't argue. I couldn't respond with anything at all.

Wren and I were over. Even if I couldn't wrap my head around him being anything like that vile old vice principal, it was over between us. There was no coming back from this.

SCENE V.

"It's no use going back to yesterday, because I was a different person then."

— Lewis Carroll, *Alice's Adventures in Wonderland*

39

Day after day folded into one another, dragging and passing together as one giant mush of *the after*.

For many nights, Jin slept over. Julie would come, too, but she always left at night with a brief kiss to Jin's lips and a pat on Matt's back. After a while, we ended up leaving an air mattress made up for Jin in the center of the living room, right where the coffee table normally sat, as if it was suddenly his makeshift bedroom instead.

They all hovered around me like the helicopter parents I'd never had, never wanted, always thought were a joke made up to sell sit-coms. Wren's number was deleted and blocked from my phone, but not before any remaining messages between us were forwarded to Matt (not that there were more than about five, as I always periodically deleted them exactly as Wren instructed me to). Emmeline and George were 'talked to' by Jin, whatever that meant, and I hadn't heard from either one of them since. School was skipped, meals were shared in silence at the table beside Matt, Jin, and Julie, and my door was forced wide open at all times.

In their form of after-the-fact, guilt-driven protection, I was always home, always monitored. They asked hundreds of questions and visibly bit their tongues on a thousand others. I left a million of them unanswered. Each night as we sat all together at the table, they pushed for information—softly, cautiously, awkwardly—as if I were a precious vase sitting on the edge of a counter, centimeters from sliding off and exploding to pieces on the ground. It was painful to be seen that way, to be talked to that way.

In the mirror, I didn't see a fragile child who needed to be spoken to in subdued voices and roundabout ways. I saw myself as I'd always been: my face a strange mix of both my biological and adopted fathers, though it never made any sense, with imperfect hair and imperfect eyes and a frown hiding beneath the surface of my lips. I saw Naomi Nakano—tired, confused, and lonely again.

They sheltered me to the point of isolation. Though isolation might have been more favorable because at least in true isolation, I'd have at least a single, solid minute to myself. There was no space for solitude in the house those days. Even the time I spent in the bathroom felt like a group task, as someone always just-so-happened to be loitering outside the door when I came out.

Things that had once been my own stopped being my own: my bedroom, my cell phone, my *feelings*. Jin helped me reorganize, moving my bed from one wall to the other, stripping the sheets to replace with new ones, tossing out the old contents of my desk drawers. Matt eyed my cellphone as if it was a weapon every time I picked it up to scroll through the notifications I didn't have, the photographs of Wren he'd since deleted. Julie suddenly professed herself a therapist, digging for my thoughts every hour, telling me over and over again: *we understand this is hard, we're here for you, just let it out.*

There was nothing I wanted to 'let out' other than myself. I felt trapped in the house like a mouse snapped against a trap. Matt had always been lenient and laid back with me before. This felt like my karma for never fully appreciating it.

After days, something about it all turned me awful. Instead of feeling loved or cared for like they surely intended, I felt coddled and annoyed. I felt insulted by how they whispered about me behind my back when they thought I wasn't listening, infuriated by the sound of Wren's name when it passed through their mouths, and embarrassingly, unbearably lonely without him there to talk me through it. We'd been apart ever since that night after the show and, more than anything, I wanted to see him again. The feeling made my heart drop through my stomach, but I couldn't help it. Cutting him from my life cold turkey was painful.

If I'd known that hug would be our last, I would've put more into it. I would've snaked my arms around his waist tighter and pressed my lips to the base of his throat. I would've been more reluctant to let go. I didn't know what to do with him torn away from me, with everyone else torn away from me with him. It made those words he always repeated, *you only have me, we only have each other*, feel like the only real ones in existence.

At night, after Matt and Jin were long asleep in their respective places—Matt sprawled across the comforter on his bed, the door wide open before him, and Jin burrowed beneath a sheet on the air mattress in the center of the living room—I thought about leaving.

Some nights, when the moon was just dull enough, or the stars weren't quite out, I would slip my arms through a hoodie that still smelled like Wren, my legs through thin leggings, my feet through the moccasins I always wore to meet him, and tiptoe down the stairs. I would stop at Matt's door to peek through and make sure he was sound asleep, then at the bottom of the stairs to make sure

Jin was, too, and then again at the front door, where I never got up the courage to go any further.

They'd tied a bell around the doorknob, one that rang like a colossal church bell with any amount of movement. Even walking by the door too much set it off, as the slightest of winds shook it around. If I had tried hard enough, I could've cut the tie keeping it there and run out the door before they caught me, but I never did. I only stared and stared and stared until Jin's breath would go uneven with a snore and I was sent barrelling back to my room.

There was a cyclical nature to our lives those days. It went on and on in the same fashion day after day, night after night, and nothing changed, nothing improved. No matter how many times Julie told me, *it'll get better, honey I promise*, it did not. No matter how many times they discussed Wren in hushed tones and debated on 'what to do next', he stayed painfully apart from me and no action was taken by anyone. No matter how many times I stood at the front door at one in the morning, I always stayed inside.

It was so exhausting that I felt myself slipping down a dangerous slope. The longer it went on, the stronger my urge to flee, the deeper my desire to see Wren. It got to the point where I began saying cruel things just to spite them, hiding under my covers just to not see them, and skipping meals just to spike their concern for no real reason.

Acknowledging that this behavior was reminiscent of Matt from years ago when he was struggling through his worst, the version of him that I only learned about from Jin, made my skin itch. So I ignored it. I hadn't mentioned to Matt what I'd learned and there was no good time to do so in sight. I assumed he knew, anyway, because he'd become increasingly withdrawn and far more messy. His hair was never done anymore. Sometimes, on the rare occasions when my own childishness became too much for me to keep up the performance of, I would braid it for him. But still, we never spoke of it. I shared nothing of my ended relationship and he spoke nothing of his.

On the twelfth day, my desperation got the better of me. In the middle of the night, rather than creeping down the stairs and stopping at the front door, I tore the screen out of my window and jumped out.

Searing pain shot up my ankle and the yelp it tore from my throat rang like gunshots in the night, but no one came to collect me. I limped around the corner of the house towards the thick bushes separating our house from the neighbors. The ground there was damp when I collapsed into it, but the bushes were thick enough to hide me, and hopefully enough to muffle my voice, as well.

From memory, I dialed the only number I wanted to hear a voice on the other side of—whether that was him or her, I hardly cared.

It rang once, because picking up after one at this hour would be unrealistic. It rang twice, because picking up after two would seem too desperate. It rang three times, because no matter who it was on the other end, picking up after three would be too kind. It rang four times, because *not* picking up at the fourth would make me lose hope, give me a taste of how it felt to be ignored.

At the fifth, the ringing stopped but no voice came through. By the breathing alone, I knew it was him.

"Wren," I exhaled through the line, hands tightening around my phone.

"Naomi," he said back, ever so gently.

Keeping my eyes peeled on the house, which sat meters away from me with all the lights off, I let myself feel. I let myself feel everything I felt at hearing his voice again; from the relaxation that spread across my body, to the confusion and anger pounding in my head, to the burning want in my gut.

"Um, how are you?" I asked, not knowing what else to say. Getting this far was the only plan I had. Half of me had expected to hear Emmeline on the other side of the Blackwell landline, and then I wouldn't have needed a plan. She would have driven the conversation for me with the number of questions she probably had building up. But this was Wren: Wren who'd taken all my firsts, Wren who I wasn't sure what to call anymore, Wren whose fault that was, Wren who got punched until he bled for it.

His breathing stopped for half a second before it came back out in a huff. "I'm brilliant, baby, what do you think?"

Wren's sharp and sudden anger was not new to me, but it was not familiar enough for me to know how to handle it, either. I'd expected him to be relieved that I called, happy to hear from me, and apologetic that he got us into this mess in the first place. To hear none of that was accurate was a slap in the face. He'd caused this, though, hadn't he? So he should know that it was not me who deserved the anger.

I thought of the smallest bit of conversation I'd heard between Matt, Jin, and Julie earlier that evening. They had been discussing Wren and me—not *Wren and me*, but Wren on his own, and me on my own, because we were never a pair in their eyes—when I crept around the corner of the hallway to listen in.

"That asshole is taunting me," Matt had said, chuckling darkly. At the time, my guess that he meant Wren by *'that asshole'* was only that: a guess. "Told me he wouldn't press charges so long as we didn't. I fell right into his trap."

Julie sounded aghast as she replied, "Certainly that can't be a just threat. These aren't equal offenses at all."

"No, but anything's possible with daddy's money and a good lawyer. He's got both in one," Matt said. I knew then that he meant Wren, but couldn't properly process what it all meant. I was focused on keeping myself quiet enough to hear the rest.

"Would Thomas truly do such a thing?" Julie pushed. "He seemed like a fine man."

"Many are until it comes to protecting their children," Matt answered. He lifted his arms, showing off the red across his knuckles, red that stood stark across his pale hands even from the many feet away that I stood. He gestured. "Look at me."

It was at that point in their conversation that the sickness in my stomach became too much and I slipped away again. On shaking legs, I jogged up the stairs and into my room, where I'd buried myself under layers of blankets until nearly two in the morning when I jumped out the window to be where I hid in the bushes on the phone with Wren now.

Finally daring to think about what that conversation had meant, and how awful it had truly made me feel, I wished I'd never called him. But I had. He was there, breathing heavily on the other end of the line, waiting for me to speak again.

"Why'd you do that?" I asked, unable to stop the words from coming out. I hated myself for the pitchy squeak of my voice, as if solidifying to him and the whole rest of the universe that I truly was just a kid.

"I should be the one asking you that," he replied. His voice was nasally. I wondered if that was an effect of having his nose smashed in by Matt, but knew it would be stupid to ask.

My fingers curled tighter around my phone, trying to keep them from shaking. In turn, it pulled his voice closer to me. The deep timber of it shook my bones in a way that wasn't as pleasant as I remembered it being.

"What did I do?" Again, my voice trembled. I was scared. It was silly to admit it because I was the one who wanted to hear him so badly, to *see* him so badly, but I was scared just talking to him over the phone.

His laugh in response sent a spike through my heart. Sharp and bitter, sudden and short-lived. He was so angry with me, and I couldn't—not for the life of me—think of what I possibly could've done to cause any of this.

"You told him," Wren accused plainly. "Your little friend. The one you claimed was *family*. You told him about us."

"George?" I asked, stupidly.

"Ha! *George.* Sure, that's the one. Is that really all you have to say about it?"

No longer caring about if anyone heard, I put my phone on speaker and threw it across the grass, as far from me as I could get it without losing it in the overgrown grass entirely. Matt hated mowing so he always put it off for weeks. It left the yard looking like a mini jungle. The light of the call lit up from between a few long green blades, time ticking away.

"You told him, he told *that man*, and I suddenly became the bad guy. If you'd kept your mouth shut like I told you to, our hugging wouldn't have ended up in assault."

Each of his words felt like another little razor blade being thrown at me, slicing off skin and leaving me fully exposed. *Assault.* Is that what Matt had done to him? Why did that word feel way too harsh to explain what had happened that night? It wasn't that simple to me.

After a pause, I argued weakly, "I didn't tell anyone."

"Sure you didn't. That gangly idiot somehow miraculously figured it out all on his own," Wren grumbled.

"Don't call him that," I said, feeling as if it was pouring rain without a single cloud in the sky above me. "That's my dad, Wren."

"Oh, so now he's your dad?" He laughed again; that same sharp and empty one as before. "You're done having your little crisis about it?"

"Stop it," I murmured, but I must've been too quiet for him to hear me from so far away, because he didn't stop.

He kept rambling, angry and disappointed, offended and betrayed. He said he knew that I told George, that he knew I'd told George at brunch and it ruined everything. Even if *I knew* that none of this was true. He said George must've told Matt, and Matt 'threw a fit' over me having a boyfriend. It was stupid over-protective parental energy, he said, but it was unwarranted. If I'd listened to him and kept our secret better hidden, none of this would have happened. His nose would be unbroken and we would be together still.

Putting my hands over my ears, I drowned it out. I let him lash out, let him call Matt awful things, let him accuse me of lying. I knew how betrayal could hurt. I'd just never been on this side of it.

"I'm sorry," I said in the end, because how could I have said anything else? He was clearly hurting, and I was the one who felt so strongly about allowing other people to feel their hurt without being told not to. "I'm sorry. This is all my fault."

"Remember that," Wren said. Then once more, softer: "Remember that, baby."

He hung up before I could say a word more. I stayed out there in the bushes for nearly an hour before limping to the front door and knocking. The little bell that had been tied to the inner doorknob rattled with the force of my fist banging on the outside. When the door opened, it was Jin's slumped figure, eyes blown out wide, that greeted me. I felt nearly nothing upon seeing his reaction. I simply brushed by him and climbed the staircase on my hands and knees—because my foot hurt too much to walk normally—without answering a single one of his frantic questions.

It was seconds after my head hit my pillows that I knocked out.

<h1 style="text-align:center">40</h1>

As it turned out, jumping out of my bedroom window had not been my brightest decision. Overnight, my ankle swelled to twice its normal size and became red all over. Putting any weight on it was out of the question. It hurt so badly on the first try that I screamed out in pain and woke Matt, who'd apparently camped out in the hallway after I came back inside last night.

I had assumed Jin would go and wake him after my abrupt and speechless entrance at well past three in the morning, but I hadn't expected to deal with the consequences of that so soon. I suppose I should have known better based on how the past week had been around here.

"Naomi," Matt called from the doorway, panting, absolutely terrified. "Are you okay?"

Hobbling on my one good foot, gripping the mattress with both hands to keep myself upright, I looked up at him. I instantly felt awful because he *looked* awful. Long hair all over the place, golden septum ring twisted upside down inside his nostrils, shirt hanging halfway off one of his arms, torn at the collar like he'd tried to rip it off in his sleep. His eyes were crusted at the corners but wide open, wild, searching.

I thought about how I must've looked myself after the night that I had had; having thrown myself from the second floor window, sat for hours in the bushes, then collapsed right back into bed after doing so without bothering to even change my damp clothes. Matt knew none of this yet, and he already looked that bad. Once I told him, would he manage to look worse?

"I think it's broken," I told him quietly, twisting my body to sit back down on my bed. Walking wasn't going to work.

The floor beneath me, where I kept my eyes trained as I heard Matt's uneven breaths and his feet padding closer to me, was coated in a thin, uneven layer of dirt. The slippers I'd worn outside the night before were kicked off inches away, that very same dirt smudged against the soles. A singular brown leaf—dead and crinkled—was attached to the fabric of one, balanced perfectly with the blade pointing out as if posed for a photograph. If I exhaled heavily enough, I could probably destroy the entire thing; set the leaf free and the dirt flying in all directions. But even the thought of that tired me out. I was running on only a few measly hours of sleep, after all. That on top of the searing pain shooting up from my ankle left me feeling like my entire body had been fractured.

I wanted to lay back into my pillows and pretend I'd never gotten up at all. But Matt was already there beside me, rudely awoken but sincerely unbothered. He fixed his gaze on me, concerned, and asked me to repeat myself as if the state of my foot could not speak for itself. I knew that this was his way of asking me what happened without actually having to ask. These days, it seemed he was tired of having to ask me that. He just wanted to know.

Attempting to sink further into the mattress to escape that sad, calculating stare of his, I said what he needed to know—which was, of course, absolutely everything. Well, everything except for what *exactly* was said between Wren and I after I dropped two stories into the night just to call him. That I kept to myself. I was ashamed that Wren was upset with me. I didn't need to give Matt any more reasons to be, too. My failed escape plan was most certainly enough already.

Rather than deeming any of that with the kind of response I'd expected—a heavy sigh, a long lecture, a look of disappointment, an unbridled shout of rage, something else emotional and rash like my own actions—Matt simply pursed his lips together and nodded. He nodded as if I'd provided him with some mundane, everyday information like the weather or a story I'd heard on the morning news. It was far more unnerving than if he'd just gotten upset with me outright.

He kneeled on the ground in front of me, his entire body obstructing the mess of dirt that I'd been examining. His knees dug into the carpet over it and I knew the light gray fabric of his pajama bottoms would be stained by the time he stood again. He didn't seem to mind. It was unclear if he even realized.

Sometimes—most often those days—Matt drifted through the motions of life as if he wasn't aware he was moving at all. He did things with a detached sort of air about him, as if he couldn't be bothered to put all of his attention into it, as if he was someplace else that he couldn't come entirely away from. Though he was there in front of me, and had been so often for so many days, I still felt like he was missing. I felt that if I reached my hand out to touch him, it would sink through him as if he were nothing more than an apparition. Or, even worse, my hand wouldn't go through him; he'd be solid and real, but remain still and without a response to my presence.

It was stupid to only realize it then—as if the story Jin told me about Matt and that old vice principal was the one thing to finally snap me to reality—but it was only then that I realized Matt was never the unbothered jokester of a parent that I made him out to be. He was so much more than that and I could do nothing to change it, nothing to help. I was only a kid—*his kid*— after all, and there was nothing in the entire world a child could do to change their parents. They could only age alongside them, the distance forever remaining, the gap never ending, and hope that someday they would be old enough to actually understand them.

Perhaps I did understand Matt a bit better at that moment, after everything, but it felt inadequate all the same. Part of being someone's child was the feeling of inadequacy—whether that be to them or for them—no matter how good either of you were otherwise.

Matt's voice was quiet and calm as he wrapped a large hand experimentally around my ankle and asked, "Does that hurt?" The touch alone did not hurt, it only felt like a bit more pressure that I would have preferred to feel, so I shook my head no. He then curled his fingers to turn my ankle the slightest bit to the side and I jerked back at once, yelling a slew of profanities that would have otherwise earned me a solid scolding.

He sighed heavily, pulling back at once. The bags under his eyes were heavy and dark, like the skin had swollen from physical attack. Wren had never gotten a solid hit on him, though, so I knew it was a punishment he'd inflicted on himself through lack of sleep and proper self care. I wanted to dig through my things to find the concealer Emmeline had given me at the show and slather it over him to hide that look of bruising. I felt awful in every possible way a person could feel awful.

"We'll have to get you to a doctor," he said evenly, pushing his hands down on the mattress to stand.

He left my room without another word. Jin's voice filtered through the hallways and to my ears, sounding terrified as he asked question after question about me. Whatever it was that Matt responded with, I never heard. He spoke too quietly.

No more than an hour later, after I'd changed into clothes that were not stained by dirt and the grime of the bushes outside, I was on my way to the doctor. It was Julie who came to take me. Jin and Matt were nowhere in sight as she helped me down the stairs like a crutch and buckled me into Jin's car. I never asked why and she never offered up an explanation.

Besides, to be painfully honest, I was glad it was Julie taking me. She showed no signs of being exhausted by me, by everything I'd caused recently. She was glowing, even. *Pregnancy glow*, my mind supplied. Her stomach was small but prominent; a round bump mostly concealed beneath her oversized blouse and maternity leggings. I suppose she wasn't exhausted by me because she wasn't worried in the same way that they were. The child growing in her was the most of her concerns, not me, because that child was her own and I was no more than the estranged child of her husband.

A year ago, thinking that would've sent me down a spiral of poor emotions, but then it only made me feel relieved. I'd come to an acceptance with her, with Jin, with their baby, with the way I would never wholly fit into any of their lives. They were a perfect puzzle and I was the extra piece that could sit alongside them, but never quite click in. That was fine. I was okay with that. Truly, I was. Because if I wasn't, then where would that leave me? There was no other choice but to be fine with it.

Julie and I listened to the radio on volume fifteen—borderline deafening in Jin's fancy car—while she drove so as not to speak to each other. I had my chair back as far as it could go so that I could put my leg up on the dashboard to elevate my swollen ankle. I laid my head back on the headrest and forced my eyes shut until we arrived. If we weren't going to speak, it was easier to not see her, either.

From the drive to sitting in the waiting room, it was another hour before I was actually seen by a doctor. While we waited, Julie read magazines peacefully and I did nothing but glare at the people who were called back before me. Matt had taken my phone. Not shocking, obviously, but still upsetting. And quite an inconvenience at a time like this. The pain in my ankle was getting worse as time wore on. It felt like all the blood in my body was rushing down there and ready to explode out of me at any second.

When the doctor finally called us, I was tempted to collapse on the way back to the room she was leading us to just to make a point of how bad the pain was.

Multiple worthless questionnaires, tests of pain levels, and an X-ray later, my ankle was declared broken. At that point I was so ready to leave that I didn't want the cast at all. All I wanted was to be handed a pair of crutches and go on my merry way. Julie had to talk me down more than once from storming out. The doctor was patient and understanding the whole way through—which, if anything, made it all worse. Doctors were like robots to me. Maybe I wanted the doctor to get upset, to scold me, to lash out. Maybe I needed that. No one else would do it. But she wouldn't. No matter how awful I was the entire time. It was loathsome.

"It will only take a little longer," the doctor said, typing something on her laptop over the counter.

"You said that an hour ago," I told her, scowling.

Julie smiled tightly between the two of us. The doctor stepped out to 'collect her things' or whatever the hell else she had to do before putting the cast on me so I could leave. Julie took this moment to do her usual overly-positive thing.

"Some extra time here could be good," she began slowly, looking between her cellphone and me as if having two conversations at once—which, granted, she probably was. "Doctors can do more than heal your ankle, you know."

"They're hardly doing that," I replied, irritable. She had an ulterior motive, that much was clear, but what it was, I couldn't say. She looked nervous but hopeful in a way I wasn't familiar with. Maybe she was upset? The gleam was gone from her eyes and the rosy red had vanished from her cheeks, leaving her entire face blank and muted.

She cleared her throat quickly and put her phone face-down on the counter where the doctor's laptop had been moments before. I watched as the light dimmed from it.

"Listen, hun, you can confide in them," she said, eyes serious. "About anything, really... About how you're feeling, if you'd like... That would be okay. A lot has happened recently."

I swallowed thickly. "I'm fine."

"Of course," she said, but she was frowning, unconvinced. "I only mean that there are people out there to help you. People who will believe you. People who will stand by you."

"Believe me?"

"Yes. With some help, he can be put away."

"Put away?"

"Certainly."

"Who? What are you talking about?"

My heart was beating rapidly in my chest. My palms were sweating. I knew who she was talking about.

"*Naomi,*" she whispered, sounding sad, so, so sad. It was such a motherly tone that I lost the last bit of my composure.

Tears began pouring down my face before I could stop them, as if a dam had broken within me. My eyes hurt from the force of it, from the heat of them cutting paths down my cheeks. Thankfully Julie didn't ask what was wrong or why I had started crying so suddenly. If she had, there would have been no answer I could give. I knew there was something terribly wrong with me, but pinpointing its exact location, or its place of origin, would be impossible. I could only say for sure that I ached, somewhere deep inside, and I felt in everywhere. Within me there was a deep-seeded pain and I felt it everyday, and I couldn't stop it, I couldn't soothe it, I couldn't handle it for much longer.

The doctor pretended not to notice my state when she came back to the room. I wiped the tears from my face furiously and resumed my act of anger because that was much simpler. Letting people know I was angry was easier than letting them know I was sad, even if those feelings had the same foundation. No one had much to say to combat anger because it was a dangerous emotion. It was a tightrope of an emotion. I could stand out above the trenches alone if I was angry and not many bothered to crawl out after me—not when it was so likely to tip me off balance and send me plummeting down to the darkness below.

I picked the ocean blue color for my cast because it was similar to my eyes and Wren liked my eyes. The doctor noticed this resemblance and told me that it was very nice that they matched so well. At that I grinned—honestly—for the first time in what felt like weeks. I wondered if Wren would notice and say something, as well. I wondered if him noticing would even be possible, if I'd ever get to see him again. Both options felt suffocating. The idea of seeing him again felt like chains wrapped around my heart and never seeing him again felt like pin pricks blooming all over my head.

Getting the cast on was the quickest part of the entire visit. That felt backwards to me, which was irritating, but I was so exhausted that I kept the complaints to myself. Once it was on, Julie helped me get situated on my crutches and sent me outside to start the car while she handled the copay or whatever.

From the passenger seat, through the thin windows of the doctors office, I could see her standing at the front desk for far longer than necessary, talking to my doctor. They seemed to be engaged in a deep, serious conversation, but of course I was too far away to hear anything, and I'd learned from spying on Matt and George in the auditorium that my lip-reading abilities were no good.

Giving up, I propped my head up against my hand, which rested over the center console, and shut my eyes. I fell asleep long before Julie came out.

41

Later that same night, while Matt, Jin, Julie and I were eating one of our usual awkward dinners together at the table—tomato soup and grilled cheese; a lazy speciality of Matt's on days like these when he was tired and in need of comfort food—a sudden knock on the door froze us one by one like a sudden ice storm had swept through the dining room.

First it was Matt, whose spoon clattered from his hand and into his half-empty bowl, tomato soup sloshing up and all over his clean t-shirt, before his body went stock still. Next were Jin and Julie in rapid succession, juggling their napkins and water glasses from hand to hand after the jolt the sound had given them before they, too, froze entirely. Last was me myself, who watched all of this happen with rapt attention before hearing the knocks once more and rooting myself to my chair as if I was a small child being buckled into a tight car seat.

In between the time of the second round of knocking (after I'd gone still) and the third round of knocking (which snapped Matt out of his stupor), the air was so thick between us that it may as well have not been there at all. By freezing our bodies, we'd also frozen our breathing—everything so still both in and around us that we'd probably have passed out if it went on for any longer.

But then it passed and Matt was stumbling out of his chair and across the tiled floor to answer the door. His eyes were wild and his hand that did not reach for the door knob was clenched into a fist by his side. It was the same sort of fist that had flown forward to crack Wren across the nose days before. Though whoever it was on the other side of the door, it was not who Matt had been expecting or fearing. AKA: it was not him, it was not Wren.

"Uhm, hello," the person said, voice so quiet that it was barely audible to me at all. But it was, at least just enough so, and I knew that voice like the back of my hand. I knew that voice *better* than the back of my hand.

I shoved myself away from the table so forcefully that the chair toppled to the ground behind me and the dishes on the table rattled like an earthquake had hit. Disbelief clouded my judgment.

Jin and Julie were not quick enough to stand to pull me back from following Matt. I moved so quickly, so thoughtlessly, that I forgot my injury and therefore my crutches, as well, and pain flared up in my ankle at once. But even that pain was not enough to get me to stop before I was there in the doorway by Matt's side, staring through the open space to where she stood. Long hair in two loose buns, red lipstick smudged in the corners of her mouth, red rims circling her hazel eyes.

"Emmeline," I breathed, her name being both a question and a declaration at once as it fell from my mouth.

Her eyes locked onto me, scanning my body head to toe over and over again. They lingered on the blue cast around my ankle each time, zoned into how I was leaning against Matt in order to stay upright.

"What happened?" she asked at last, very quietly.

If I didn't know any better—if I wasn't painfully aware of how much she loved her brother, of how much he meant to her as the main guardian in her life—I would have thought her tone held a bit of morbid accusation, a deeper fear that this injury was not self-inflicted.

I opened my mouth to respond—with what I did not know—but Matt cut me off before I could utter a single sound. He cut me off to ask Emmeline, quite briskly, what she was doing at our house. Her jaw clicked shut, shock and something else—perhaps offense—settled into her features. Matt had never taken such a harsh, informal tone with her before. As far as I knew, she had only heard him speak this way once before: on the night everything fell apart.

"I... I came to see Naomi," she replied. Her voice lacked all of its usual confidence and bravado. That felt wrong, *so wrong*, as if we were abruptly displaced into a parallel universe where Emmeline Blackwell had something—anything—to feel insecure about; which I could say with certainty that she did not.

"You've seen her," Matt said sharply, fingers flexing around the corner of the door, moments from slamming it shut on her.

Before I'd processed I moved at all, I was wavering on my one good foot in front of Matt, hands braced on either side of the doorway, effectively keeping him from shutting her out.

"Wait," I said, but I wasn't sure who to. "Please wait."

Jin and Julie had come to join us at some point while I was distracted by Emmeline in the flesh before me—Emmeline, who I hadn't seen in nearly weeks, Emmeline, who had kissed me the last time I saw her, Emmeline, whose brother was my... *something.*

The five of us then stood huddled around the same open door-way, in varying distances from it, in complete silence after my plea. Emmeline's eyes darted all over the place, unable to pick something to fixate on: me in the doorway, the blue cast on my foot, Matt behind me with his tired eyes, Jin and Julie on either side of him, pregnant belly and homey pajamas respectively.

I couldn't get my body to move, couldn't get my mouth to say anything more. I wanted, so desperately I felt as if I would actually die, for Emmeline to stay. The ability to articulate that thought just wouldn't come. Jin seemed to know it without my saying, though.

"Matthew," I heard him speak very slowly.

Jin only called him Matthew on rare occasions, I realized; occasions where Matt needed to be tended to like a child himself, as if he needed a parent as badly as any other, as if he was seconds from slipping away to somewhere unreachable, somewhere where there was no Matt or Matthew to be found at all. Jin's next words were whispered—in what I assumed was an attempt to keep them from reaching my ears.

"It's not her fault."

Matt clicked his mouth shut and ground his teeth together so loudly that Emmeline and I both flinched.

But only seconds later, Matt had stepped away, Jin guiding him with a careful hand on his upper arm, and Julie had ushered Emmeline inside. We stood together motionless even as we were left alone, even after Jin, Julie, and Matt were all long gone, giving me my first bit of real privacy in ages.

She was beautiful. Always had been and always would be. Even with a mess of hair, a smudge of lipstick, and clear signs of distress lining the soft skin of her face, she was beautiful as she always had been. And yet I couldn't look at her.

Her cheekbones, her eye shape, her smile—however cautious it was—were all too similar to his. I couldn't find a single feature of hers that didn't draw me back to him, back to those strong Blackwell genes that would forever be tainted in my mind. The differing shades of their irises, of their hair, of their skin tone, even; none of it was enough. No shade was far enough off to stop my chest from heaving with fear, with uncertainty, with that awful feeling of being small. My heart wanted one thing and my subconscious mind, my entire body, another.

"What happened?" she asked again, after a pause so long that her voice had the same exact effect on me then as when I'd heard it after Matt first opened the door. I trembled all over, the urge to throw myself into her becoming at once stronger than the urge to get away. So I did; I threw myself into her.

She hugged me back so cautiously that I felt as if I'd done something I shouldn't have, something wildly inappropriate. Her hands were cold where they touched me, light as a feather over my skin. Light like the kiss she'd sprung on my lips, the one I couldn't—despite all my attempts—forget about entirely. I was more confused than I'd ever been before. If I loved Wren, couldn't I love her in that same way? They were so similar after all. And Emmeline was kinder, softer, simpler. What if it was her I had wanted the whole time? Or what if it was always him and she'd just thrown a wrench in my feelings at a bad time? I didn't know. I just knew that hugging her, feeling her there in front of me, was the best thing I'd felt in ages. I'd been so lonely.

"I'm sorry," she said, pulling away.

Judging by the look in her eyes, the one I glimpsed for a split second before needing to lower my gaze back to the floor at our feet, heart rate spiking, she was sorry for more than just letting go of our hug. I wanted to hear none of it.

Footsteps passed over our heads, the sound of someone pacing across the floor of Matt's bedroom above. By straining my ears and halting my breathing, I could hear all three of their voices talking up there. I could hear urgency, anger, sadness, all sorts of things they'd been wrestling with for days. Emmeline listened, too, looking green in the face the longer it went on.

"I'm fine," I told her belatedly, trudging to the dining room for my crutches which were propped up against the table.

Our half-eaten bowls of tomato soup and plates of grilled cheese remained over it. The smell of the tomato soup gone cold, like old marinara sauce, made me nauseous. With great difficulty, I stacked them all and tossed them into the sink under hot running water. Emmeline drifted after me, hands up as if a safety bar for if I fell.

There were thousands of words unsaid between the two of us, thousands of words that needed to be said, and yet we remained silent still. I couldn't say for certain what reason that was for her, but I knew what it was for me: it was fear. It was the fear of saying too much or too little, of revealing more than I should've or withholding too much for her to understand. It was the fear that no matter what I did, my speaking would be equivalent to ruin. A ruin that there would be no coming back from, a ruin that I was truthfully already in the midst of, but refused to acknowledge. I refused to acknowledge it as much as I refused to look Emmeline in the eyes.

Instead, she followed me around in silence as I finished clearing the table, rinsing the dishes, and pushing in our chairs. She followed me as I threw my crutches down at the bottom of the staircase and used the railing to drag myself up each stair. She followed me as I landed not in my own bedroom, but in the hallway outside of Matt's, where even through the firmly closed door and what appeared to be a blanket shoved against the space at the bottom of it, their voices were clear as the water from the faucet downstairs.

"...no good after seventy-two hours," Julie was saying, that tone of devastation in her voice that I'd come to recognize all too well.

Matt swore. The pacing feet got louder and more rapid. Even without being able to see through, I knew where he was: right in the center of his room, in the only open space there was, making circles. Emmeline stood so close to me that I could smell her warm breath as it hit my shoulder; a strong cool mint from the toothpaste she always used too much of in the mornings. Normally this would relax me, but then it only made me overtly aware of how near she was, of how nearer she could be if only I didn't have to keep her far.

"I tried," Julie added hastily, "I truly did, but it's no use now. We should have gone the second we figured it out."

"Without that proof, this will be impossible!" Matt snapped.

In tandem, Emmeline and I lurched back, his voice so loud we feared he would throw open the door and find us eavesdropping. After a moment's quiet, we realized that was not the case. He was simply so upset he'd begun yelling.

"Even with a rape kit," Jin said, and I felt the world swirl into darkness before me.

I missed the rest of his sentence, the whole rest of that line of their conversation, because my ears were ringing too much—that word piercing in my skull on repeat. So that was what Julie spent so long discussing with my doctor. I could hardly believe it. That wasn't something they should've been saying. It made no sense.

No, I forbid it from making any sense. It couldn't be that way. I didn't *want* it to be that way.

"Naomi," Emmeline whispered, so shakily that I didn't dare to open my eyes in fear I would open them to tears. "Come on, let's not listen to this anymore."

I allowed her to tug me to my feet again. When I'd slipped to the floor, I'm not sure. Everything was heavy. It was no wonder I couldn't stand it any longer.

Emmeline led me to my bedroom and sat with me on my bed. The mattress felt stiff and foreign. Her hand on mine felt even worse. Remembering what Wren and I had done there, over those same sheets, bile rose in my throat.

"I'm sorry," Emmeline murmured again after a while.

I shook my head. If she said it even once more, that would be all it took to tear me apart. After we sat there together, saying nothing, for what felt like hours but was apparently only ten minutes based on the clock blinking red numbers at me on the nightstand, she found another way to do that. She'd been watching our hands—which were clasped together on the mattress in the space between us—and seemed to be getting more restless with each circle of her thumb over mine. Finally, she slapped her thumb still with her other hand and turned entirely towards me, her face so close I could once again smell that strong mint toothpaste.

"Naomi, I love you," she said suddenly, words torn out of her like vomit. "That's why I kissed you before the show. I shouldn't have done that to you, but I love you, okay? I love you in the way you think you love my brother. And I'm so sorry for what he did to you. I'm so sorry I couldn't help it."

A silence so thick it felt physical fell over the room. It reminded me of that acting exercise in drama club, the one where Matt would yell out *now the room's peanut butter!* and we'd all make-pretend our limbs were struggling through the air, our voices muffled through invisible mush. Only there was nothing besides the weight of her confession making it hard to breathe, harder to speak.

For the first time since she showed up, I forced myself to look at her and stare. I forced myself to look and truly see her. It hurt so badly I thought my heart would burst out from my chest and leave me empty. She looked earnest but terribly sad, the bags under her eyes as bad as purple bruises. Her bottom lip was quivering. Despite how much I wished to make it stop, there was nothing I could do. She had to have known this.

"I can't..." I trailed off, not recognizing my own voice.

I had no clue what to say to her, no clue what to think of her. I was offended, vaguely, in some way, that she had said *how you think you love my brother*, as if I wasn't capable of understanding my own feelings. I was relieved, somehow, deeply within me, that she loved me, that someone like her found me good enough to love. I was miserable, intensely, outright, that she was apologizing again. I knew that if she wasn't on Wren's side, not a single person in the world was. It was startling to realize that because I was a person in the world, after all, and I still knew he was all alone now. I knew he was alone because I wasn't on his side either.

With an awful clarity, I accepted that. I loved Wren, in a lot of ways that I couldn't fully comprehend, but I also hated him.

With Emmeline crying beside me, admitting feelings I was incapable of reciprocating, I hated him so much it lit my blood on fire.

42

By the time I returned to school, it had been so many days since *Alice in Wonderland's* opening night, since Matt had gotten into it with Wren in the middle of a lobby jam-packed with his very own students and their families, that I thought I might be okay to handle it.

With optimism bordering on naivety, I had hoped no one would bat an eye when I stepped through the doors. Part of me had even expected it to have blown over completely while I was stuck at home under constant watch by Matt and Jin; replaced by some new novelty moment for the everyday highschooler to obsess over—something like Carla getting a boyfriend (which, apparently, she did), or TJ supposedly planning to quit the baseball team (very quickly and easily debunked).

Of course, as my luck would have it, none of this was the case. My return to Jay High was highly anticipated, if the bated breath of the building upon my entrance was anything to go off of. It was not so much a 'no one batted an eye moment' and much more of a 'no one dared to blink an eye' moment. Once the first person noticed me, it was a domino effect of bodies turning, eyes widening, and whispers spreading until every last person had taken notice of me.

Dumbfounded, and embarrassed on a level I wasn't aware I could feel embarrassed on, I froze. I let them stare, I let them whisper. It felt like a moment tugged straight out of a movie script; one of those cliche and overly dramatic teen rom-coms where the girl has it horribly rough until all of the sudden her dream guy swoops in to solve it all—only, I didn't have that.

Conversely, Wren—who I once thought was my dream guy—was the very reason I had it rough; standing there in front of a bunch of people I didn't know like a deer in headlights, listening to the horrible insults they threw around, wishing I could crawl into a cave and die, all before eight in the morning.

It helped none that Matt was on a leave of absence. A *mandated* leave of absence. The school had launched a full-blown investigation into his altercation with Wren since it happened on school grounds, and, in turn, his position as a teacher at Jay High was as uncertain as ever. More than once over recent days, he'd gone in for meetings with the principal (something that always made my stomach turn over on itself as if a heavy door was shutting behind them and a scarred, fifteen year old version of him would be the one to come out afterwards), but the outcome seemed to fall more into the hands of the Blackwell family than the school boards.

Without any confirmation or denial that Wren would press charges, Matt was to stay on leave. Which made it so that I entered the building that morning entirely alone, drawing more attention to both myself and the lack of beloved *Mr. Molina* around the halls.

I scanned the crowd with shaking eyes, feeling as if I was staring through a kaleidoscope of shattered glass—all their faces disjointed and unclear but somehow everywhere at once all the same. Though the year was nearing its end, meaning I'd had plenty of time over the months to learn a few names, I couldn't identify a single one of them. Every face was a person I didn't know, a name I couldn't place, a stranger I was being judged by.

My heart pounded in my ears, blood pulsing throughout my body like it was rushing to get out, to be rid of me. I felt on the brink of collapse and yet I stood stock still. My life over the past year—or maybe it was simply my entire life, ever since I was born and stole Elizabeth's future from her—had felt like an onslaught of moments that stunned me so badly it hurt, so much so that it trapped me. Each day felt like another push further away from everyone else, as if some force stronger than me or anyone else was dragging me by the hair, singling me out and leaving me alone to rot.

Right then, while I could not find the ability to do anything other than stare back at those staring at me in the lobby of Jay High, I was quite possibly as lonely as a person could get.

The bell for first period rang out above us, piercing and obnoxious; music to my very ears. The noise snapped the crowd out of their glaring and gossiping and sent them instead racing down the halls to their respective classes. With much effort, I dragged myself forward to do the same. In my periphery, faces swirled in and out of focus, passing by like storm clouds.

My crutches hit the floor like blocks of lead as I walked. Without truly looking, I could sense that it drew eyes back towards me, that people had overlooked this injury in the heat of the moment when I'd first walked in, but now they saw I was broken both in and out. No one offered me their hand to help. I walked on.

Even as the halls began to clear out, I could not escape their words. I heard every last whisper like it was sent through a megaphone directly into my ears.

"Wait, she was with Emmeline Blackwell's brother?" one asked. "But, like, I thought he was old."

"He is," the other answered steadfastly. "Gross, right?"

Then onto the next pair, also saying something equally as awful; something like, "I can't believe Mr. Molina hit him, though. That's insane."

And, "Well I don't blame him. That guy's a creep for dating Naomi."

It went on and on and on, and the more I heard, the less I understood. I didn't know whether or not these people were making fun of me or pitying me, whether they were believing me or scoffing at the very thought, whether they would *stand by me* like Julie promised people would, or if they would leave me in the dust the second any of this got too real. Which it most definitely was; what with Matt's job on the rocks and me entirely alone, entirely considering that the fault for this might not lay solely in my own hands.

Everyone was already settled into their stations when I arrived at Chemistry. Due to how slow I'd been moving, I was late. Mrs. Dion stopped her sentence short when she saw me, once again bringing all eyes my way. Yet again, I froze. Apparently I was incapable of continuing on if more than one person was looking.

Clearing her throat and plastering a smile onto her face—in an attempt to act normal for my sake rather than her own, I realized—Mrs. Dion said, "You're late, Naomi. Please take a seat."

For the first time ever, I wished my seat was not in the back corner, as far from the door as possible. To get there, to where Emmeline's usual seat was empty and our station was barren, I had to hobble helplessly past all the watching eyes. First and foremost, Carla.

Her backpack was a bit further into the aisle than others, so when I tried to go past her—quite quickly—one of my crutches caught the straps and I stumbled. To keep myself upright, I released the crutch and grabbed hold of her countertop. It clattered to the ground with all the grace and quietness of a mini explosion. Her partner, a rather quiet boy who played some sport or other that got him roped into the popular kids group, shot out of his stool to help me. He pushed Carla's backpack under the table and handed me my crutch, helping me to resituate myself over it. He even offered to walk me to my table, but I turned him down, unable to handle that much more embarrassment.

Once he was back in his seat and I was back to attempting to walk like a normal human being, Carla scoffed, "Attention whore."

It was loud enough for surrounding students to hear, but not enough for Mrs. Dion. Some chuckled, some rolled their eyes, and some did nothing at all. I looked towards where Emmeline should have been, but the seat remained empty. Never before had I felt the absence of a person so strongly. It was as if a piece of myself had been taken out with her, as if I could not function the same way without her beside me. I thought of her hand over mine, of her lips over mine, and I nearly fell over again.

"Well," Carla's voice followed me to the back of the room as I picked up the pace to my stool. "I guess I could just say *whore*."

I knocked my forehead down against the top of the table, halfway hoping it would be hard enough to knock me out cold. Though I'd agreed to come back to school, (as if there were another option), Matt and Jin agreed that I couldn't be trusted with my phone. So no matter how badly I wished to text Emmeline for some much needed moral support, or to call Matt and demand he come bring me home, neither were even an option.

The entire rest of Chemistry class, and the entire rest of the school day on a whole, I listened to people talk about me like Carla did. And worse. I was *stupid*, I was *a slut*, I was *manipulative*. I was *not pretty enough for that*, I was *not mature enough for Wren*, but I most certainly *was troubled enough to go for him.*

With each new passing insult, I had to bite down harder on my tongue to keep myself from screaming, from sobbing until my lungs gave out. It was a confusing battle because although I didn't agree with any of them, I didn't exactly disagree, either.

Once safely in Matt's car at the end of the day, there was blood in my mouth and so, so many tears in my eyes. Neither one of us said a thing about it for the entire drive back home to where Jin and Julie were already waiting.

43

Though we had made an attempt to return some aspects of our lives to normal by that point—as in I was forced to return to school and the bell around our front door knob came down—Jin and Julie continued to come by every night and whisper conspiratorially with Matt whenever they thought I wasn't around.

But I was always around; I couldn't go anywhere else. And if they were talking about Wren or me, I wanted to know. I kept my footsteps near-silent and crept around corners, hid in closets, ducked under tables and counters and whatever else around. I did anything and everything in my power to conceal my presence so I could listen in on the words they were keeping from me.

Unfortunately I learned very little. Days after I returned to school again, the words I'd heard over the past nights had amounted to just about nothing. It seemed to me that the three of them simply repeated the same conversation over and over and over again each night; leaving Matt more irritable, Julie more depressed, and Jin more weary. They repeatedly discussed how helpless the situation was, how angry they were about it, and how unsure the entire future was in response. Listening to the same reiterations of those morbid sentiments day after day made me wish I hadn't bothered to eavesdrop in the first place. All three of them were miserable recently—and truthfully so was I—so there wasn't a single thing I could say or do to change any of it.

It all came to head the night I vowed to myself that I would stop listening. Because of course it did.

Matt, Jin, and Julie were in the living room then, all in an entirely separate space as if they couldn't be any closer than five feet each. Matt was curled into his usual spot on the couch, a baby blue decorative pillow (gifted to us by Julie) hugged against his chest, Jin was sitting straight as a board in the arm-chair, fingers interlaced over his knees, and Julie was stand-ing with her back against the wall beside the television, both hands underneath her baby bump as if she was holding it up.

They were all in their own forms of pajamas, too—Julie head-to-toe in pink silk, Jin in a matching plaid set, and Matt in a white t-shirt and torn-up sweatpants three-sizes-too-big for him. Somehow, despite these stark differences, each one of them looked to me as unguarded as they'd ever been. Almost like I was glimpsing much younger versions of them that had long since passed.

I was crouched behind the kitchen counter. The living room and kitchen were attached in such a way that if you stood in a very specific space in the kitchen, you could see the living room but a wall blocked anyone in the living room from seeing you. It worked a bit like a one-way mirror. By crouching in that specific space, I had an even better view with even less risk of being spotted. Plus, I could hear them as if they were right next to me. That was—at least at that very moment—one upside of living in a cheap house with thin walls and poor acoustics from all the hard floors and surfaces: sound traveled.

"Thomas hasn't answered a single one of your calls?" Julie was asking Matt. She thumped her head back against the wall when he shook his head no. Her hair spread around it like a halo, all static and frizz.

"It was a long shot to ask for his help," Matt told her, hugging the pillow even tighter. By the time he let go, the cotton inside it would most definitely be destroyed and the pillow would lose its shape entirely. "Can't say I expected any less."

"So we don't stand a chance?" Julie asked, sadness palpable in her tone. The closer she got to her due date, the more her sadness leaked out like water from a faulty faucet. She was losing control over it. Hormones, probably. "Wren gets to walk away free from all this?"

Matt hummed, one shoulder coming up in a shrug. "Wouldn't be the first time."

Julie's lips tugged down into a frown that brought out the wrinkles on her cheeks. Jin sat forward a little, hands tightening around one another. I pressed my palms into the cold floor as hard as I could.

"It's not too late," he began cautiously, "for us to change this. We can still fight. For Naomi... Or for you."

Matt's harsh intake of breath was louder than their voices had been the entire conversation thus far.

"No," Matt said with finality. "No, that's not necessary. That's long over. I don't need to fight that. I'm entirely over it." He forced out a dry chuckle that was quite possibly his worst performance ever.

"Matt," Jin began.

"No, really, I'm fine. Besides, this isn't about me anyway," Matt insisted.

"Matthew," Jin said, more urgently.

"Goddammit, Jin, *I said no*," Matt snapped, voice rough.

Julie's head thumped against the wall again as she jumped at his voice. Jin jerked backwards, hands coming unclasped and gripping the armrests of the chair instead. For a long time, Matt's heavy breathing was the only sound. I, on the other hand, held my breath. It felt like I had been watching Matt unravel for days and at last the final string had come loose, leaving him an empty spool. I felt that way, too: *empty*.

Jin stood and walked over to Matt, his feet padding against the floor like bricks dropped off a ten-story building. He crouched beside him and I shifted backwards jerkily. Once someone became on the same level as me, those high chances of staying hidden were exponentially lowered.

My view was then a bit obscured as I watched the rest unfold; as Jin brought his hand to Matt's arms and gently tugged them away from the pillow, as Matt threw himself forward into Jin's chest like a child. Jin held him as his body shook violently.

I begged myself not to believe what I was seeing, that Matt couldn't possibly be crying in Jin's arms, but that was exactly what was happening. Julie looked as astounded as I myself felt from the other room.

His voice may have been muffled against Jin's plaid button-down, but I heard his words loud and clear all the same. Over and over, like a broken—no, a *shattered*—record, Matt kept saying, "It's my fault, I should have known, this is all my fault, I should have known."

Jin did well to keep himself composed. He rubbed Matt's back and denied his words even as they came out through sobs, telling him *it's not your fault* twice as many times as Matt said *it's all my fault.* I folded my lips into my mouth, feeling nauseous. It wasn't his fault, It was mine. Matt had dealt with this all himself before and I'd forced him to think of it again.

At last, Matt forced his tears back and pulled away from Jin. Wiping at his eyes and straightening his back, he smiled and said, "Wow, sorry about that, not sure what came over me."

Jin tried to tell him not to be sorry, but Matt simply said it again, forcing another pained laugh through his lips. Then he stood, wobbling on his feet, and said, "Please go home now. We'll be alright without you. Go home and we can talk more tomorrow."

Jin looked hesitant, but Julie took his hand and neither one of them said anything more as they heeded Matt's words. Together they slipped out the door and left, silhouettes passing over the lawn before disappearing into the night.

44

"Matt."

At the sound of my voice, he startled so much that his knees knocked the edge of the coffee table and he tumbled to the floor. Once he was down, he didn't bother standing again; just stayed there in a heap against the carpet, unmoving.

Hobbling without my crutches—which I'd abandoned long ago to keep my presence hidden as I overheard the earlier conversation—I crossed the living room to him. He hardly lifted his head as I entered. Mere feet from his body, I folded my legs underneath myself and sat back against the armchair where Jin was no more than fifteen minutes earlier.

"Matt," I said again, more desperately, upset that he was upset.

"What did you hear, Naomi?" he asked, rolling his head around his shoulders before squaring them to look at me head on.

His eyes were red-rimmed and heavy, the blue of them even more bright and unnatural than normal. His tears brought out the color tenfold. I could hear Wren's voice in my head saying, *it really brings out the blue. It's pretty.*

But it wasn't pretty. Not really. It was just sad. It made him look unreal, as if something had snapped and he was completely different now; like his eyes were holding something before and they'd lost whatever it was now. It didn't look like him.

"What did you hear?" he repeated, squinting at me.

Words failed me. He said my name once more and they failed again. He asked me that same question—a little louder, but not any stronger—and they just kept on failing. My thoughts were rampant but still at the same time. It was like running for my life on a treadmill; moving but never truly getting anywhere. It was like being pulled so tight that I'd snapped, run so dry that I was barren entirely. The air grew thick around me. It was all I could do to pull it into my lungs and just breathe.

Matt was never someone other than this. He was never the carefree, untroubled guardian I'd made him out to be; the one I'd convinced myself he was for so much of my life. I'd come to this conclusion before, but I hadn't let it truly sink in until now. He was never truly that person. He was the one here with me now; walls down, splotchy skin over the sharp bones of his cheeks. Matt was just like me. He was young, he was sensitive, he was anxious. He was tired, he was scared, he was way too good at keeping secrets.

Deep inside, more than anything else, Matt was sad. The word felt far too small for this—and for him—but it's the only word that even comes close. He was sad. He'd always been. Even with a personality like fireworks and strength like absolutely no one else I'd ever met in my entire life, he'd always been sad.

"Everything," I answered him at last, throat raw and eyes burning.

He nodded as if this answer was a confirmation rather than an admission. It probably was. Matt wasn't stupid. His lips pursed into a tight frown, and his throat bobbed with a thick swallow, and then a few lone tears began to fall from the corners of his eyes. They fell slowly and almost calmly, if crying could ever be considered *calm*. There was no heaving for air, no loud sniffling, no puffy cheeks. Just two tracks of tears steadily dampening curved pathways down his face. It tipped the last remaining piece of my composure—of my sanity—right over the edge, careening down into the black abyss I'd felt trapped in for weeks.

"I don't know how I possibly could've forgotten," I said to him, hysterical, "how sad you were... And for so long. So long, Matt, it never really stopped."

Matt's eyebrows raised halfway up his forehead in shock, color draining from his cheeks. The tears became clear water over a white canvas.

"Sometimes, when I'd crawl into your bed after a nightmare, I'd wake again hours later to another one. But those second ones were never mine," I recalled, dizzy.

Memories flooded back into me at once, constricting my chest one after the other. *How could I forget? How dare I forget?* Matt had struggled for my whole life, and he'd suffered for nearly all of *his*. I'd shoved it so far away that it disappeared: this truth that was as much a part of him as this misery right now was a part of me.

"Why'd you never care about yourself the way you care about this? How come you bottled that all up this whole time—that *involvement* you had with Alexis?"

Her name burns on my tongue, lashing out and burning Matt, too. He jolts back and hits his head on the arm of the couch at the sound of it. Jin had let her name slip once during one of their many conversations I wasn't meant to overhear, and I'd filed it away immediately, assigning terrible thoughts to that name, to the former vice principal *Alexis* who ruined Matt's teenage years. I wanted to push it so deep inside of my mind that it disappeared entirely—just like the harsh truth that Matt was a human being, too, capable of despair and lacking all the answers—but I'd failed. Her name stuck like a leech.

"Involvement," he repeated, an out-of-place lilt in his voice that was most likely meant to be humor, but fell short by miles. "What an undeservingly kind way of phrasing what she did to me... What *he* did to you."

"They aren't the same," I argued instantly, reflectively. It wasn't. I wasn't fourteen, Wren wasn't nearly forty, I wasn't his student, he wasn't my teacher. Wren thought I was special, he told me I was pretty, he... He loved me. I loved him. If I couldn't keep telling myself that, convincing myself of that, then an entire year of my life would fall out from beneath me. It was already cracking at the edges. I was terrified for any of myself to slip through.

"No," he agreed, almost dismissively, "but they're no different either."

You're wrong, I wanted to tell him, but I simply nodded instead. My body reacted in the way that felt right, and the way that felt right was agreeing with Matt's words. With all these contradictions, I hardly knew what to make of myself anymore.

"It's not your fault," I began awkwardly. He needed to know that, but getting past those words to convince him was nearly impossible.

Having heart-to-hearts like this was never really our thing; as I always assumed they were never really anyone's *thing* with their parents. It's not easy to say what you truly mean, or to express how you actually feel, if it's to the person who raised you, the person whose job it was to protect and nurture those very feelings in the first place. Even if none of the bad ones were their fault. It felt like trying to speak around a giant ball of cotton in my mouth to say anything more. My incoherent mumbling may as well have been nothing at all.

"Every last bit of it is my fault," he said sternly. If his words were anything else he would have sounded exactly like a scolding father, but because those were the words he'd said, he only sounded sullen. *Sad.*

"It's not," I argued. "I chose this. Every last bit of it. You didn't know anything."

"That's the problem, Naomi! You weren't in a place to *choose* with him—you're a kid! And I should have known; I should have known *everything*. That's my job! I would do anything for you. What kind of father—"

He stopped himself at once, clamping his mouth down so hard that his teeth made a loud *clack*. I felt a splinter go through my chest. In all my sixteen years, had Matt had never once referred to himself as my father, and that hurt sometimes, but it had never hurt like hearing him choke it back after the word was already past his lips—almost as if he wanted to shove it back and pretend he'd never said it, as if he hated it, as if he didn't *want* to be my father.

"Listen, kiddo," he began again, lowering his voice, "I get it. You know I know what you're going through."

Again, I wanted to argue, but I said nothing. He ran a hand through his hair, shaking.

"It took me a long time to believe it, too, but this—all of it—it's not your fault. There's no fault in being hurt. And we can deal with that hurt however you want, okay? We can press charges and fight it out, or we can flee the country, or we can drop it entirely. You can hate me for the rest of your life if that'll help. Protecting you from this hurt was my job—and I know I'm not your real father, Naomi—but I've always tried to do everything I can to raise you how you deserved to be regardless and I... I failed this time. I failed terribly and I'm sorry. If you need someone to blame..."

His open palms came up in a gesture towards himself before falling back to his lap again. His eyes were on the ground. I swallowed thickly.

For a split second I did want to blame him. I hated Wren for causing this mess but I also missed how he held my hand, how he listened to me talk, how he stayed by my side. I wanted him back in a way that felt like a different part of me fighting to be released. But I couldn't blame Matt, either. It was no more his fault than it was mine. And no one gave me options like he did. Wren told me I chose everything, that I was in charge, but was I ever really? Julie told me things would be fine, that people would help, but did she ever ask me how I wanted to receive that help? Jin told me this would stop, that we would fight back until *justice was served*, but was he aware that I'd tired of fighting? And Emmeline... She apologized and apologized but that was the last thing I wanted from her.

Even if the thought of fleeing from the country was ridiculous, Matt was the only one who gave me that choice for myself.

A wet laugh forced its way out of my mouth. My emotions were going haywire, tugging in every possible direction at once and leaving me a mess. I laughed through sobs and held my chest through the red-hot pain there and I told him, "I don't know how you can say all of that and still think you aren't my dad."

In the most genuine voice I'd ever heard come from his mouth, he looked at me with wide eyes and asked, "Well am I allowed to think that?"

I laughed again, the sound choked. "You're an idiot, *dad*."

A tiny smile curved his lips. His eyes were suddenly so soft it was like they'd been swapped out for new ones. I smiled back.

There was so much more that we needed to say, but it didn't matter then. I hugged Matt—*my dad*—and decided to deal with it later. I already knew I wasn't going to blame or hate him, or flee the country, or drop it entirely, but I didn't want to battle it out either. I needed to find a safe space in the in-between.

Right then, my safe space was there with him, like it was always meant to be.

45

In the end, no charges were pressed. Not against Wren for being with me, nor Matt for punching him. When I made my decision not to fight it—a decision I labored over for days, feeling tired and guilty even as I came to the conclusion that I had no interest in taking things to a level I wasn't certain I could win—Wren made his decision as well. He let it go.

With those choices, Matt was free to return to work and Wren was simply free. In stark contrast, many things were taken from me. Or at least that's how it felt. At the beginning of the year, I had what now feels like everything: two best friends who loved me as I was, a blood father *and* an adoptive father who both trusted me undoubtedly, and a boy who thought I was beautiful. In one way or another, all of those relationships had been burnt to ashes with my one slip-up.

Although everyone kept telling me it was for the best that the slip-up happened, I found that hard to wholeheartedly believe. My life had flipped upside down since and it was becoming harder and harder not to throw myself out of another second-story window over it.

I finished the year out at Jay High with plans to never return. Walking through the hallways, I glared at anyone who whispered about me, telling myself it was fine despite the thundering in my chest because I'd never have to see them again. Passing by Carla, I kept my chin tilted up and refused to frown, because I'd be damned if she got the last laugh. Sitting in classes, I zoned out staring at white boards and posters on the walls, trying to take snapshot pictures in my memories to revisit if someday later on I ended up missing this place.

The decision to switch out was one I didn't take lightly, but it was one I took entirely by myself. It was my own choice whether or not I decided to stay after everything, just like Matt promised. And by the last day of school, an excessively hot day mid-June, the decision was *not*. I couldn't walk by Emmeline and keep up the facade that I was okay, that I didn't miss her, that I didn't miss *him*. If I left, then maybe someday I could not only walk by her again, but walk *beside* her, too.

"Naomi, wait up."

Ice raced up my spine in trepidation at the sound of his voice. I stopped at once in the threshold of the doorway I'd been racing to get out of. When the final bell had rung, my legs carried me down the hallways faster than ever before, itching to pass through the entrance of Jay High and leave it behind forever. This wasn't supposed to happen here. My plan didn't include this conversation.

George deserved both an apology *and* a thank you, but I wasn't prepared to give them. Not when we hadn't spoken since that night, not when I missed our old friendship so much that it left an aching hole in my gut every time I looked into those surprisingly green eyes of his. None of that stopped me from turning to face him head-on anyway.

"Can we talk?"

"Now's not really a good time," I mumbled hopelessly.

George sighed. It wasn't a tired or annoyed sound, but a resigned one. His face screamed that he deeply understood everything I wasn't saying, but couldn't accept it all the same. That was one thing about him that I feared would never change: he caught onto just about everything through his natural observation skills, but that only ever made him push further. He may have appeared innocent, but he was ruthless.

"So you were just going to walk through that door and never come back?" he asked, voice strained. Pain was not a sound I was accustomed to hearing from his mouth. But it was there then, and it was overpowering.

My gaze flickered behind me and through the glass. Lush trees, blooming flowers, parked cars. All vivid, blurred colors. Students passing down sidewalks and across the street. All animated and consistently in motion. The sun burned bright and the heat was so high I could see waves in the air. Objectively, it was a rather perfect day for school to let out. It was the sort of day that should've ensured a good mood. And yet I stood there feeling like all of the storm clouds in the world were hovering above my very head, obstructing the sunlight and killing every last beautiful tree.

"Yes," I answered him finally, deciding that if I could do nothing more, I could at least tell him the truth.

"You truly have nothing left to say to me? To *Emmeline*?"

I flinched. His throat bobbed with a swallow.

"I know I went behind your back to talk to Matt," he began, jaw clenched so tightly it changed the sound of his voice, "but that doesn't mean you have any right to ditch us without a word about it. I care about you. I'd never have done it if I didn't care so much."

Embarrassment burned up my cheeks. I felt eyes on us as people swept by to leave through the doors we were partially blocking. In one jerky movement, I leapt forward to grab George by the wrist and tugged him outside with me. Keeping a hold on him and my crutches both was as hard as learning to walk all over again. Luckily he came along without any resistance. Under the canopy of a large tree around the corner—where the administrator's offices sat on the other side of the building—I faced him again and forced myself to talk.

"I know that. I'm not mad at you."

"Oh." His eyes fell to where my hand was still around his wrist, fingers clenched so tightly that his circulation was beginning to cut out. In a poorly hidden wince, his nose scrunched up. I dropped his wrist at once.

"I don't know what to do," I admitted, feeling hot all over with shame. His gaze jerked back up to me, pupils large.

"You.. You did the right thing, I think, but I don't *feel* like thanking you for it. And I don't want to lose you either, but I already lost— I lost... Listen, everything is falling apart right now and it's easier for me to deal with if I don't think about it, alright? I thought if I left without dealing with whatever this is with us then I" —my hands moved around erratically but made no real motion— "I don't know. I just don't know."

After the words were out, I panted heavily as if out of breath, as well. George stared at me like he had no idea who I was. Then my crutches were falling out from underneath my armpits to the dirt beneath our feet and George's arms were holding me up instead. My body felt stiff and awkward. Though we'd been friends for nearly a year—friends so close that I allowed myself to entertain the thought of him being more like family—we had never hugged.

Sure, we had that strange group hug that Emmeline initiated during one of our first drama club meetings, but that was hardly comparable to this. His arms were strong and steady, much more so than I ever would have thought given how scrawny he was, and his embrace didn't make me feel small. It took a moment for me to find my bearings, but once I did, my hands were gripping into the fabric at his shoulders so aggressively it was a wonder nothing tore.

"What am I supposed to do?" I asked him quietly, hoping he'd understand all the intricacies of that question that I left unsaid, like he always did.

"What do you want to do?"

I wanted to reverse time and stop any of this from ever happening. I wanted to tell him I was sorry and that he was the greatest friend I'd ever had. I wanted to hug Emmeline like he was hugging me then and not worry about how it would inevitably make me think about Wren. I wanted to stop crying so much.

"I have no clue," I settled on.

"Then it doesn't really matter." He pulled back and held me by the shoulders, catching my eyes. Normally he had a beanie on, pushing his messy hair down to cover his eyes. It was rare that they were fully exposed like this, that our eyes could meet with nothing in the way. "Don't think about what you do from here. Just keep going. Keep moving forward and don't stop. Someday it'll lead you somewhere. It has to. No matter what else you decide to do, Naomi, please keep going."

Swallowing around the barbed-wire ball stuck in my throat, I told him, "Okay."

He released me, picked my crutches up and helped me back onto them, and then he was leaving. Without another word, without proper closure, he began to walk away. He wasn't angry, but he was upset. It was clear by his short strides, the long swing of his arms, the overall pattern of his gait. My heart rate picked up as his body shrunk with distance. He was becoming mixed in with the crowd of other students, blurring away from me. It felt too much like goodbye. And while I wanted to get away, and I had been planning to leave without so much as a word to him about it, I didn't really want this to be the end.

"George!" My crutches left thick indents in the dirt as I pushed them down to propel myself forward. "George!"

He was one of a dozen faces that turned to face me. I stood on the cement of the sidewalk near the building and he was already down by the road, waiting for cars to stop at the crosswalk alongside a group of others. He took a step back towards me, eyebrows pinched together, creases forming between his eyes and across the bridge of his nose. Even from afar, that much I could tell.

"Someday," I exclaimed. His head cocked to the side. "Not now, not yet, but... Someday, okay? Someday, George..." I trailed off, but what I thought was, *someday it'll be okay, someday we can come back together again; all three of us. I promise this isn't the end.*

He smiled, absolutely blinding, and nodded once. He knew what I meant. Of course he did. Then he crossed the street away from me and didn't look back.

Someday, I told myself, trying not to let it hurt that he was soon gone from my sight and I had no idea how long it would be before he returned to it again.

46

Summer had never felt so cold before.

Nearly every day I spent at home without the people who I'd originally planned to be with. George and Emmeline both respected my distance and had only reached out to me once since school let out. George's message was short and to the point, expressing that he would give me time with this, but not forever. Emmeline's was a much longer, and sappier, version of the same idea. Alongside numerous apologies for numerous different things; all of which she had no responsibility to apologize for. I reread each of their messages so often that I had them memorized by the first day in July. Even still, I couldn't recite those words without feeling like throwing up. It had been my choice to cut them out for a while, I knew that, but it hurt all the same. Terribly. But still not enough to be worse than reuniting with them prematurely.

So each morning I woke alone and I slept alone. In between, Matt and I worked on rebuilding our trust, on flattening out the many bumps we'd caused in our paths. Jin and Julie often became a part of this as well, stopping by for dinner or game nights, but they'd lessened up on visits overall. The need to excessively coddle me slowly died out in each of them.

When they *were* there, though, things were better. Strained, but better. Matt and Jin had a long, long talk one of those first nights and ever since, the arguments had stopped entirely. With every secret laid out bare, there wasn't much left to argue over. At many times, it was certainly awkward while we sat around the table and grappled for words to say to one another, but it was no longer nerve-racking. I wasn't afraid that the slightest wrong step would end in disaster. I was only afraid that the energy would never fully settle. Nonetheless, time passed. And it kept on passing, and I did everything I could to keep my promise to George and keep going with it.

Before I knew it, summer was more than halfway over. My transfer out of Jay High and into another school had yet to be solidified. My mind was made up—*mostly*—but we hadn't gotten around to filling the proper forms for it yet. Without any clue where I would attend if not Jay High, it was hard for Matt to sign his name in good conscience. One night he jokingly suggested homeschooling, but when I didn't laugh—thinking it actually sounded quite nice to never leave our house again—he clamped his mouth shut and never brought it up again.

It's unclear whether or not that had anything to do with his decision to quit Jay High himself. But he did. He resigned as the drama teacher in early August, only days before he was set to return. The two of us hadn't talked much about that in particular, but he did warn me of it right before he left the house to officially drop off his letter. From what I gathered, he was leaving for much the same reason I wanted to. Our reputations had been tarnished, our wills cracked, our comfortability worn down to nothing. Seeing Emmeline would hurt, seeing George would spur guilt. Walking the halls, sitting in the auditorium, crossing the parking lot; it would all breed too many bad memories. As cowardly as it may seem, it was much easier to run away.

Matt—yes, still Matt, because though we'd established I saw him as my dad and I'd begun to address him as such more often than not, it was hard to change sixteen years worth of a habit—assured me I had no responsibility to bear in his decision to quit. No matter how many times he said it, though, I didn't believe him. Of course I had some responsibility to bear, if not all of it.

Hence why I spent many nights berating myself. It was hard not to. All across my bedroom walls were pictures I didn't have the heart to take down, despite how hard they punched me in the gut to see: Matt smiling while he taught, George curled up in my fluffy pink chair, Emmeline pressing her cheek against mine and grinning. My room was like a shrine to the people I'd lost (Emmeline and George), or to the people who'd lost pieces of themselves because of me (Matt). It was my fault that Matt had to give up doing what he loved, it was my fault that George was only a picture in the chair and not truly there, it was my fault Emmeline could no longer hold me and grin. I felt the fault lying with me like dead bodies.

Perhaps the worst part of all was even all of this was not enough to wipe Wren from my mind completely. I still thought about him so often that it was as if he never left, as if we were never caught. The only difference then was that my feelings swung back and forth like a pendulum; one second I'd be near tears missing him and the next I'd be throwing my phone across the room, angry we had met in the first place.

Nothing felt worse than that; than not knowing how I truly felt because my opinion changed so often, and so rapidly. Sometimes I thought of Wren as the jerk who destroyed my life and other times as the love of it. It was only when I honed in on Emmeline's grinning face, features far too much like his, that I could reel myself in and acknowledge that it was somehow a little bit of both.

Removing the tack from the wall holding her picture, I let it flutter to the floor by my feet. Heaving in breaths, I watched it fall. To my dismay, it landed face up, her grin mocking me as it morphed back and forth in my vision from her face to his. I knew they were different, they couldn't be *more* different, and yet their faces blurred together. There were similarities in them that I couldn't pinpoint, couldn't decipher, and therefore couldn't put out of my mind. They were both Blackwells through and through and as much as my feelings for Wren confused me, those for Emmeline did, too.

Hands trembling, I removed the next tack, a different version of Emmeline falling away. Then the next, George drifting out of view. And the next, that time Matt. And the next, and the next, and the next, until the carpet was littered with photographs and tacks dropped into it. Some landed face-up, some face-down, some sideways up against the wall, some underneath the crack at the bottom of the closet door. My hands moved on autopilot until the walls were barren and I couldn't move without risk of piercing my bare feet on one of many tacks. The box fan in my window blew slowly, pictures rustling on the ground. My hair shifted back and forth over my eyes and I eagerly let it obscure my view of them.

How long I stood there, I couldn't say. Only that it felt like forever before I was jolted from my thoughts to the sound of knuckles rapping on the door frame. Turning my head in one harsh tick like the hand of a clock, I faced Matt. His lips were downturned at the state of my room, but otherwise he looked better. His hair had recently been trimmed so the ends were all soft where they fell over his shoulders in sleek piles. The blue in his eyes was brighter and the deep purple bags that had become so commonplace I worried they'd never leave were dulled out to a light brown. He offered me a weak smile.

"Alright, kiddo?"

I swallowed thickly. That simple question was loaded. At the current moment, I supposed I was alright. Overall, though, who could say? The answer changed from a weary yes to hard no in seconds every passing day. I just kept dragging myself through it in hopes that one day the answer yes would stick.

No matter what else you decide to do, Naomi, please keep going, George's voice rang in my ears. I sucked in a breath and looked back to the piles of pictures littering the floor. I vowed to myself that one day they'd return to the wall. *Someday.*

"Getting there," I settled on, a smile tugging at the corners of my lips.

47

Hana Elizabeth Nakano was born August 20th that summer. 18.3 inches and 7.9 pounds. It amazed me how tiny she was, how at one point in time all of us were that tiny. The hospital room was brimming with nothing but love when she came out crying.

I thought I'd feel a little worse about it, maybe confused at the very least, but I didn't. At the sight of her, my chest warmed up with the realization that I was a big sister, a godmother, and this little wrinkly person would be looking up to me. I'd never felt like someone worth being looked up to before, but I wanted to be. I really wanted to be. I knew that it would be hard, and that at some points in time I would definitely revert to being upset, or maybe even jealous, of Hana, but right then I was nothing but hopeful. Happy.

Jin hugged Julie first, tears in his eyes, then Matt next, tears over his cheeks, and me last, tears falling onto the top of my head. He thanked me over and over, voice thick, and I could do nothing but hug him back. I couldn't remember the last time I'd hugged him, if ever at all. It was a stupid thing to fixate on, but I did. This was my birth father and I felt like this was the first and only time I'd ever seen him with enough love to give that I received some of it.

If he realized the heat burning my cheeks and the tears stinging at the corners of my eyes because of it, he didn't mention it. Nor did Julie or Matt. For once, we were simply a family. All five of us. Not a perfect one, but one nonetheless. Was there really any perfect family?

When Jin released me to return to Julie, Matt tugged me into his side. He was smiling honestly in a way I hadn't seen him smile in ages. When Jin and Julie first announced her name, *Hana Elizabeth Nakano*, (because they refused to share even their ideas for names before she was born), Matt's breath had stuttered to a stop. It took me a while to understand why, but once I did, I found it best not to mention. Elizabeth Cohen. My mother. Jin's first love and Matt's best friend. I felt more connected to this child, and to Jin and Julie, than ever before. Whether that feeling would wear off or not, I didn't quite care at the moment. Hope clung on for dear life.

"Okay?" Matt whispered to me.

"Okay," I confirmed, dropping my head against him.

Possibly more than okay. I was getting better every day. We were all getting better every day. That was all anyone could ever really do, wasn't it; just get better each day? No matter what happened before, it was in the past. It should stay there. That was where it belonged.

Because I can never go back to who I was before all of this. I can never be who I was before meeting Wren, or who I was six months earlier, or who I was yesterday, even. I can never go back; I can only keep going forward. And maybe that's okay, because maybe someday I'll be able to look back at the person I am right now and gladly think, *I'm not her anymore.* Maybe that someday will come when I can call George and Emmeline and they'll take me back with open arms. Then being unable to return to yesterday won't seem so bad anymore. I'll be able to look ahead towards the person I can become tomorrow instead and that'll be good enough. Maybe that's all there is to it.

With time, everything settles. With effort, anything can be resolved. Even this much. Even me.

Unlike Wren Blackwell, I don't like it when I cry. With a bit more time, I'm sure I can stop doing it over him.

No matter what else I do from here on out, I'll keep going. I will move forward with the passage of time and be glad that what's gone has gone. That's enough.

ACKNOWLEDGEMENTS

First I would like to express my deepest gratitude to the Oprelle Publications team for taking a chance on me to make this publication possible. To both Karen Croftcheck and Brooke Meachum, thank you for your support and dedication. From the very start Karen has been nothing short of lovely and it's been a welcome journey to do this all the first time with her at my side. Brooke, my ever-so-patient editor: I know combing my manuscript for overused commas and em-dashes was a full-time job on its own, so, seriously: *thank you.*

I would also like to thank my partner, Paxton Lippert. In everything I do, you're the first one there to hype me up. From outlines, to rough drafts, to queries, (and subsequent rejections up until this point), you've kept me sane (and in touch with the sunlight outside). I couldn't have done this without you. I love you always.

Jae Wells. Thank you for being my best friend, and for never giving up on me. You are the only person aside from the publishing team who can say they read this before it came out so rub it in someone's face for me or pat yourself on the back or something. Let's celebrate with a kitchen floor sit sometime, okay?

To all of my family who have always inspired, encouraged, and believed in me, and never once doubted that I could get to this place someday, even if I did myself. Specifically: Kerra Hogan, Brandon Hogan, Amber Jackson, Lisa Lippert, John Lippert, Melinda Jackson, David Jackson, and Alex Little.

Lastly, I must give huge thanks to Lewis Carroll and his numerous works that inspired me. Not only is *Alice in Wonderland* the main play the drama club puts on within this novel, but *Alice Through the Looking Glass* gave me my title, (if you hadn't already noticed). I used the theme and arc of his stories as an allegory for my own, from the title right down to the final lines. Carroll says, "I can't go back to yesterday, because I was a different person then." I took these words as a starting point to writing the final passage.

AUTHOR'S NOTE

There are as many journeys of coming-of-age, family, and relationships as there are individuals on this earth. Naomi's personal journey—both in how she begins, thinks throughout, and comes around at the end—is in no way intended to be representative of all of them. All her story is here to do, and the only story I am trying to tell, is one of a million out there in hopes that someone reads it and finds something valuable inside. So many forms of media represent relationships such as hers with Wren in a damaging way for young people, making them believe it's acceptable. It is not.

I like to say that I write the heavy stuff with a dash of hope. The heavy stuff is very real, and I know we all know that, but do we all know that hope is too? If you get nothing else out of this story, please remember that.

If you need assistance—in any way—know that help is out there. You are *never* alone.

Rape Abuse & Incest National Network (R.A.I.N.N.) — r ainn.org | National Sexual Assault Hotline: 800-656-5O5-HOPE (4673) *available 24/7*

National Teen Dating Abuse Helpline — loveisrespect.org | CALL: 866-331-9474 TEXT: loveis to 22522 *available 24/7*

Darkness to Light — d2l.org | Helpline: 866-FOR-LIGHT (367-5444)

Stop It Now — stopitnow.org | Hotline: 888-PREVENT (773-8368)

Crisis Text Line — crisistextline.org

Break the Cycle — breakthecycle.org | *Inspires and supports young people 12-24 to build healthy relationships and create a culture without abuse.*

Gay, Lesbian & Straight Education Network (GLSEN) — glsen.org

Teen Mental Health Organization —mentalhealthliteracy.org

About the Author

Dakota Jackson is an author and editor native to Connecticut. She is a proud genre-hopper of fiction (though typically within the young adult range) that will always feature queer characters, complex families, and a whole lot of angst before the hopeful ending. Her mission is to shine light upon queer identities like her own and show readers that fear, confronted head-on, can give way to hope.

Dakota has an MFA in Creative Writing from Southern New Hampshire University and a Bachelor of Arts in English with a minor in Film Studies from the University of Connecticut.

When she isn't reading or writing (or pretending to do one of the two), Dakota loves Zumba, kickboxing, rearranging her bookshelf, and binging a good anime.

The Other Side of the Looking-Glass is her debut novel. For more information, visit her online: https://dakotajacksonbooks.wordpress.com/